ANDREW G.
NELSON

Brooklyn Bounce
An Alex Taylor Novel

ANDREW G. NELSON

Brooklyn Bounce

Copyright © 2017 by Andrew G. Nelson

Cover Design Copyright © 2017 by Huntzman Enterprises

Published by

First Edition: December 2017

ISBN-10: 0-9987562-3-7
ISBN-13: 978-0-9987562-3-3

Printed in the United States of America
1 3 5 7 9 10 8 6 4 2

Other Titles by Andrew G. Nelson

DEDICATION

Those of you familiar with my books know that over the years my dedications have focused on recognizing the impact of both God and my wife, Nancy, without whom none of these books would have ever reached fruition. As I sit here writing this today it remains truer than ever.

The good Lord provided me the ability to write, but he also gave me a wife who would encourage it. Nothing you read would have been possible without them and I will never cease crediting them or singing their praises.

Today I would also like to thank you, the reader, for being with me on this incredible journey. Any artist, be they an actor, painter, or author, longs to connect with their audience. Over the years I have had the opportunity to speak with many of you and I cherish each and every one of those moments; especially when you discuss the characters with such passion. It is that feedback that allows me to know I have created something special. I sincerely thank you for your continued support. God bless you all.

Romans 8:28

No one can appreciate just how tough life can be in Brooklyn unless you have worked those streets. When crime occurs in other parts of the city, folks gather around to gawk at the scene, but when it happens in Brooklyn North, folks look at what they can pick up. It's not uncommon for a cop to chase a perp only to have them toss their shit along the way so that they don't get caught with contraband or a weapon. If you're not quick enough it takes a 'Brooklyn Bounce,' meaning it never hits the ground twice.

Out here, someone is always nearby looking to scoop that shit up.
— Brooklyn North Cop

CHAPTER ONE

Alex took a drag on her cigarette, as she stared out into the blackness of the ocean. Off in the distance she could hear the thunderous roar of the surf crashing violently against the shoreline. As bizarre as it might sound, there was actually something very calming about it.

A bone-chilling breeze was blowing in off the water, this late December night, but the alcohol had numbed her mind, if not her body, to its effect. Inside her head, a million thoughts swirled around, as she struggled with the question that had just been posed to her. In theory, it was any easy question to answer, but the reality was that it was not so easy to admit.

Even in her inebriated state she could still hear a faint voice that kept admonishing her, *Actions, and words, have consequences.*

It was a statement she had heard repeated countless times by her police academy, social sciences instructor, Police Officer Angela Cartwright. In fact, right before they had graduated, her class had tee shirts made up with the saying along with a caricature of Cartwright. At the time they had all had a good laugh, but tonight she was beginning to fully understand what her instructor had meant.

In the darkness of her bedroom, when no one else was around, it was easy to say the words, but she wasn't alone now and the choice was not so cut and dry.

How long have I kept the secret locked away? she wondered.

In truth, she couldn't recall a time when she hadn't felt this way about him, but the fear of rejection was strong enough to suppress any desire to make her feelings known.

And where exactly has that gotten you?

It was a legitimate question and one she had continuously struggled with. But the feelings she had for him were so strong, that the idea of being rejected was simply terrifying. At least they were up until now.

Now she simply had nothing left to lose.

"You, James," Alex finally blurted out. "I want you."

"What?" Maguire replied, a mix of shock and confusion on his face.

Alex walked over, coming to a stop in front of him, then reached up, taking his face in her hands, and kissed him. Then she stepped back and looked at him.

"You wanted the truth," she said. "Now you have it."

"I don't understand, Alex," he replied.

"What's there not to understand, James, I love you," she said.

"Alex?"

Finally letting go of the secret, which she had kept buried deep inside her for so many years, was cathartic.

"Alex?"

Suddenly, the images quickly faded from her memory, like the shifting sands of the beach she had been standing on, as she was pulled away from her memories and thrust back into the present moment.

Alex looked up at Dr. Peter Bates, her on-again / off-again boyfriend, who was sitting across from her in one of the booths that filled the interior of Linda Mae's Dinner. He had a genuinely concerned look on his face.

"Huh?" she replied, trying to quickly snap out of the memory.

"Are you okay?" he asked.

"Yeah, sorry, I'm fine, Peter. I've just got a lot on my mind."

"What's going on?"

"You really want to know?" Alex asked.

"I do."

"Well, let's see, the board is on my ass because we have been experiencing a surge in petty crime recently. They seem to be incapable of accepting the fact that, with Joe Anderson's retirement, we need to fill the vacancy on the evening shift as a deterrent."

"What do they want you to do?"

"Move someone from day shift to cover the slot. They're looking at it as a way to save money so that they can fund more of their bone-headed community enrichment programs. Yet they'll be all over my ass when we don't have enough cars available during the day tour."

"That's just asinine."

"No argument here," Alex replied. "They don't want to believe that being down a man has had an overall effect on the crime, yet somehow it's my fault that the fine young citizens of this community don't seem to respect other people's property. So now I have to figure out how to come up with a plan to fund an officer without it coming out of my already stretched-to-thin budget."

"Can you?" Peter asked, as he stabbed the pie in front of him with his fork.

"Realistically, no," she replied. "On top of that, I was also notified by the state that they are having a major fishing tournament down in Lake Winnipesaukee the same week as the annual regatta, so they won't be able to provide any extra coverage on the lake. I tried to float the idea of a summer auxiliary program to the board, but they shot that down because of supposed insurance concerns."

"So what are you going to do?" Peter asked.

Alex frowned and shrugged her shoulders.

"I don't know," she replied, as she picked up her cup of coffee and took a sip, "and that's what I have been thinking about. Happy you asked?"

Technically, it wasn't a lie. She had been thinking about it before, but just neglected to include the rest of her thoughts.

"I can't imagine what it must be like dealing with that kind of bureaucracy."

"There's a part of me that would like to think I'm just being paranoid and that there is some nefarious plot underway to get rid of me; but another part of me thinks they really are just as dumb as a box of rocks and I think that scares me even more."

"Surely you must have some friends on the board that can help you?" Peter asked. "I mean, I know Sheldon Abbott wields a lot of power, but he doesn't have *everyone* in his pocket; or does he?"

"No," Alex replied, "not everyone. Rebecca Norwood and Troy Wilson are pretty solid, but they are the minority board members. The rest just go along with whatever Sheldon wants them to do."

"What if you could change the make-up of the board?"

"I'm not sure if I could ever make that happen," she replied. "I don't care how long I live here the fact is I will always be viewed as an *outsider;* besides which, I'm not really into playing the whole political game. I think it's just a bullshit power trip some folks get off on."

"I don't know about that," Peter replied. "You may not realize it, but not everyone is happy with the way things are run around here. Even some of the *insiders* think that maybe it's time for some new blood in City Hall."

"And how exactly do you propose making those kinds of changes?" Alex asked. "My understanding is that Norwood and Wilson are only there because Sheldon allowed them to run unopposed. It was his concession to the other party to at least *appear* to be a representative board."

"That's true enough," Peter replied, "but Sheldon might have misplayed his hand this time."

"How so?"

"The way the Penobscot charter works is that the board is divided into two groups of three; each of which is elected for three year terms. For continuity of government, one group appears on the election rolls in odd numbered years and the other in the proceeding even numbered year. Norwood and Wilson were just elected last year, meaning this year all three members who are up for re-election are from Sheldon's party."

"So?"

"So what if one or even two of them could be knocked off?"

"Never happen," Alex replied, taking a sip of coffee. "In order to get their two people onto the board, the party bosses had to promise not to run anyone in this election."

"What happens if they aren't the ones running them?"

Alex eyed Peter suspiciously. Something untoward was afoot and it didn't fit him; which actually intrigued her. "Explain yourself."

"Folks are angry at the way things get done or don't get done around here," he replied. "Everyone is talking about national politics, but it starts locally. I hear it every day at my practice; even among the staff and patients over at the hospital. They think that their voice doesn't matter any longer. That only the party's get to decide who does or doesn't get elected."

"But the reality is that they do," Alex replied.

"Yes and people are fed up with this political nepotism."

"Whether they like it or not, the folks with the money get to make the rules."

"But what if....."

"What if? *What if* is a rhetorical question asked by people when their hearts are in the right place, but they don't have a realistic plan to change anything."

"Suppose someone had a plan? Not a thought, not an idea, but an actual plan to change things."

"Then I would love to hear it."

"What if someone else were to run against them this election cycle?" he asked. "It could change the political make-up of the board.

"What? Like a third party candidate?" Alex said with a laugh.

"Why do you laugh?"

"Because we all know how well that works out. Peter, third party candidates usually mean well, but they generally get pummeled in elections. They just don't have the money the other parties have to get their message across."

"Ah, but maybe you're wrong about that," he said with a smirk. "What if there was someone willing to financially back a candidate?"

"Are you telling me that you're getting into the *king-maker* business?"

"Me?" Peter asked with a quizzical look. "Heavens, no, maybe if I was a doctor in Manhattan or Los Angeles I would have the money for that, but not up here in Penobscot."

"So who is it?"

Peter glanced around the diner conspiratorial. Most of the dinner crowd had already left and the stragglers who remained seemed to be engaged in their own conversations.

When he was sure no one was eavesdropping on their conversation he leaned forward and, in a hushed tone, asked, "Have you ever heard of Conrad Kreutzmann?"

Alex's eyes went wide with surprise, "Sheldon's father-in-law?"

"I see you have," Peter replied.

"I thought he was the money man behind Sheldon's party."

"He is, but his loyalties are divided. He still holds a grudge over what happened with the industrial park deal."

"You're telling me that he's willing to change his allegiance now?" Alex asked.

"No, at least not outwardly, but he doesn't have to. I think he saw the handwriting on the wall years ago, when most of us were still clueless, and he set-up up a political action committee through some associates. Then he just waited for the right timing."

"And what pour schmuck did they talk into putting their head on the chopping block?" Alex asked.

Peter reached down and silently picked up his coffee mug; letting the question hang in the air unanswered. It only took a moment before a huge grin began to appear on Alex's face.

"Are you shitting me? You're running for office?"

"Why not?" Peter said defensively. "I'm not an outsider. People here know me and they trust me. I've never been politically active with one party or the other, so being an independent won't seem strange."

"Yeah, yeah, fine, whatever," Alex said, waving her hand dismissively. "If you somehow managed to get elected, you'd still be a minority voice. Even if you sided with Norwood and Wilson, that would still only be three to three and Sheldon would be the tie breaker."

"I didn't say I was the only one running."

"One person running as an independent wouldn't phase Sheldon, but two people would cause him to take notice that something was awry. He'd bring down the full weight and fury of the party to crush that type of political rebellion."

"What if only one person ran as an independent and the other ran with the parties blessing."

"They already agreed to not run a candidate...."

"Not that party," he replied.

Alex leaned back in the booth, eying him curiously.

Now it was Peter's turn to return the grin.

"Who?" Alex finally asked.

"Mildred Parker."

"Oh for the love of God...."

"No, wait, hear me out," he pleaded. "There is no one more beloved in this town then Mildred. If she runs she's pretty much a shoo-in. Sheldon might not like it, but even he won't oppose the wife of his late friend and former police Chief. By the time Sheldon figures out what happened it's a four-to-two ballgame and he'll be shit out of luck."

Alex's eyes narrowed darkly and a frown formed on her face, as she stared at Peter.

"You know the two of you are playing a very dangerous game," she cautioned. "Conrad Kreutzmann is wealthy and he can withstand any potential blowback, but you and Mildred won't. Sheldon doesn't play nice with folks who cross him."

"So because he's ruthless we shouldn't try to change things? Just accept that this is all just business-as-usual and meekly submit to it?"

"No, that's not what I meant," Alex replied, "but you need to be realistic and understand the risks, especially if you don't win."

"I imagine that was what the Founding Fathers meant when they said, 'We mutually pledge to each other our lives, our fortunes, and our sacred honor.'"

"You do realize that at some point he will put two and two together, knowing how close I am to both of you. He'll assume that I am either directly involved or at least complicit in your schemes."

"Does that worry you?" Peter asked with genuine concern.

He had to admit that he hadn't considered how his relationship with Alex would be affected by his decision to run for office.

"Oh please," Alex said dismissively. "The day folks like Sheldon Abbot start worrying me is the day I hang up my gun belt and take up cross-stitching inspirational verses."

"Oh really? I'm almost afraid to ask, but what would be your first message?" Peter asked, as he picked up his coffee cup.

Alex thought about the question for a moment.

"Probably something along the lines of, *'Dear life, could you at least try using lubricant?'*"

The impromptu reply caught Peter in mid swallow and he began choking on the liquid.

Alex waited patiently, as he struggled to regain his composure.

"You really should be more careful," she said dryly, as the coughing fit subsided. "I never got the hang of that whole Heimlich maneuver thingy."

"Is there ever a time when you aren't irreverent?"

"Church?" she replied. "Which is probably why I avoid going there."

"Maybe you should consider starting."

"My hypocrisy only goes so far," Alex replied, in her best Doc Holliday impersonation.

"On a more serious note, is this going to cause problems for you?"

"Only if you get elected," she replied. "Sheldon's smart and he has his people securely positioned on the public safety and finance committees. At best you'd only succeed in removing one of them, so he could always screw with me if he wanted to prove a point or just to try and keep you in line. On the flipside you could screw him over in other areas, so he'll probably just play nice till he can hatch a plan."

"If you don't want me to do, just say so."

"Don't be silly, Peter," Alex scoffed. "I'd love to watch Sheldon get his comeuppance. I just don't want you to take it lightly. If you run, you had better win."

"I will," he said with a wink.

"So when do you have to put your name in?"

"Open filing runs through the end of the month."

"Nothing like waiting until the last moment, huh?"

"Well, my fear was that it would give Sheldon a chance to find someone to run against me. I thought I could lessen that chance by waiting till the very last moment to file."

"That's actually pretty smart."

"How'd you like to be my campaign manager?"

"I thought you said you wanted to win?"

"That's true, how about just an office staffer?"

"Why, do you want to sexually harass me?"

"Maybe," Peter said with a smile.

"Take me home and I can give you a sample of my *dictation* skills."

"I'd love to, but I have a meeting scheduled with Conrad tonight."

"Wow, I never thought I'd fall so far in my life that my sexual advances would be rejected for an older *man*," she replied.

"Sorry," Peter said with a laugh. "I've made the choice to enter the political arena so it's all about the Benjamin's right now."

"Yeah, well remember that the next time you come knocking on my door," she said. "You'd better have something larger than a stack of singles in your wallet to throw at me."

"Hey, how about I pick you up in the morning and take you to church. Then we can head over to my place and you can impress me with those dictation skills."

"Sorry, I have plans tomorrow," Alex said with a feigned pouty expression.

"All day?"

"I'm afraid so," she replied. "Too bad, so sad. Lesson number one: Politics is all about making *hard* choices, dear."

CHAPTER TWO

Alex extended her hand out, grabbing hold of a small oak tree and pulled herself up the rocky incline. She'd hit the crest of the small ridgeline and was now looking down into the valley below; the swollen waters of the Birney River cutting a path through the countryside.

She paused for a moment, taking in a deep breath, as she enjoyed the unspoiled scenery displayed in front of her.

"They don't have views like this in Brooklyn North," she said in almost a whisper, as if in some way her spoken words would disrupt the tranquility of the forest.

It was springtime in northern New Hampshire and the forest around her seemed to be alive with the sound of birds chirping, wind rustling through the countless trees and the rushing water below. It all combined to fill the air with a cacophony of nature which rivaled the urban bedlam that she had long grown immune to.

Alex dropped her backpack onto the ground next to her and leaned back against a tree, surveying the land in front of her as she plotted her next course. She carefully noted the best areas that would allow her to descend into the valley below.

She had lost track of just how long she had been walking, but it had been several hours. She glanced up at the sky, trying to judge the approximate time by the position of the sun.

You should have spent more time paying attention in school, she thought, as she estimated that it was just about *half-past-fuck-if-she-knew*.

She decided that she probably needed to head lower, toward the river, a bit quicker, so that she could find a nice flat area to camp for the evening. The last thing she wanted to do was get down there and it be too dark to set up her tent. She picked up the pack, slinging it back over her shoulders, and began to make the journey down the mountainside.

This section of the forest was particularly rocky and made for a rather slow decent. With each footfall she felt the loose stones shift and give way, causing her to tread lightly, as she weaved in and out of nearby trees. Even on the most brutal days in the gym, when Abby Simpson rode her ass like the trainer from hell, nothing made her thighs and calves burn worse than traversing these hills. By the time she had made her way to the river's edge she was physically exhausted.

The sound of the rushing water was particularly intense now. Heavy rains, caused by the melting snows, had caused the Birney to swell beyond the outer edges of its banks. She watched as the racing water broke in places, causing white caps to appear. It was a kayaker's dream, but she also knew that one false move would likely mean certain death for anyone unlucky enough to be caught up in the cold, swift moving currents.

She found a grassy section, not too far from the water's edge, and sat down to rest. She removed the backpack and began rummaging inside for one of the protein bars she had packed away. After that trek she needed a quick boost before she began setting up her camp for the night and gathering the wood she would need for her fire. The crunchy mix of granola, nuts and dried berries was just the thing she needed.

As she ate the bar, she took a moment to reflect upon how she had gotten here. This coming July would mark her two year anniversary since taking over as police chief. It was a far cry from being a sergeant on the mean streets of New York City, but she was finally acclimating herself to her new home. It was her shot at redemption, a place where she could overcome the demons of her past that had plagued her career in the city. Maybe one day she would get her chance to return back there, like a triumphant Roman general, decked out in a *toga picata*, celebrating his victories abroad.

Yeah, that would go over like a lead balloon with some, she mused.

Of course, that didn't necessarily mean that all of the residents of the picture-postcard town of Penobscot, located in the northern region of New Hampshire, were as smitten with her.

In terms of crime, Penobscot was light years away from NYC, but since her arrival they had experienced what she dutifully described as a slight *uptick* in crime. Which of course was a quaint way of saying the murder rate had skyrocketed under her stewardship; not that it was her fault. Well, except for one, but Alex was quick to point out that the folks behind those heinous acts had been lifelong residents who predated her arrival.

Still, the jury was out on the often brash, fiery-tempered cop who didn't play by the rules.

That wasn't completely true, she corrected herself, as she took another bite of the bar. Her cops liked her and in the end that was all that really mattered to her.

She suddenly began to feel very tired and realized that sitting down had been a stupid move. She should have just gotten the camp ready instead of taking a break. She reached into the backpack and removed the plastic water bottle from inside.

"Fuck me," she said, as she stared at the empty container.

Grudgingly, she got to her feet and made her way over toward the water's edge. She knelt down and cautiously dipped the water bottle into the fast moving waters; watching as it filled up rapidly. She made a mental note to remember to refill it before it got too dark. The last thing she wanted to do was stumble around in pitch blackness to get a drink.

As she capped the bottle, she noticed something fluttering just beneath the surface. She squinted, as she tried to figure out what it was. It was difficult to make out, but it looked to be bright red, with black striping. At first glance it looked like one of those tropical fish you see in aquariums, the brightly colored ones, but the water was too cold for that.

Was it a fishing lure? she wondered.

Alex set the bottle on the grass behind her and leaned forward to retrieve whatever it was. She gasped, a chill coursing through her body, as her hand pierced the surface. Despite appearing close, the item seemed just out of reach as her fingers wiggled, trying to draw it closer. Suddenly, she felt something lock onto her wrist.

"Jesus Christ," she exclaimed, as her body suddenly lurched forward

She dug her free hand into the muddy bank for support, feeling her fingers slip into the dark brown ooze, as she struggled and fought to keep from being sucked into the water. She felt her hand hit something hard in the mud, which gave her some momentary leverage.

Alex tried tugging free, but it was useless. It was as if her hand was locked in a vice. She thought about screaming, but there was no point. This particular section of the river was about as remote as you could get. Even if someone just happened to be nearby, the roar of the rushing water would be too loud for anyone to hear.

Her immediate thought was that a catfish had grabbed her hand and she actually laughed at the idea. The thought that the badass ghetto cop known as *La Diabla Rubia*, the blond devil, survivor of multiple gun battles, was going to be done in by a fucking fish struck her as wholly absurd.

She tugged backward, struggling valiantly, and finally felt some give.

"Not today bitch," she exclaimed, as she continued to draw her hand free.

Then, without warning, Alex felt her body unexpectedly lunge forward, as if she had been pushed from behind. In an instant she was plunged into the icy clutches of the Birney, her body completely submerged. She thrashed about, as she felt herself being pulled down into the freezing waters. Her eyes went wide with terror, as she scanned the dark abyss for the source of the attack. The suddenness of being dragged beneath the water was like being hit with a bat and she couldn't help but gasp, releasing precious air from her lungs.

She was aware that consciousness was slowly slipping from her grasp. As her vision began to darken, she saw a faint image approaching, like a specter emerging from the depths.

Alex blinked and when her eyes opened again she saw the ashen face of Cory Childers in front of her wearing the familiar bright red and black striped flannel shirt.

Then the young boy smiled at her and pulled her into the darkness.

Alex let out a scream and bolted upright in her bed. Her body was drenched in sweat and she could feel her heart beating in her chest like a jack hammer. It took a moment for her to acclimate herself to the fact that she was in her bedroom and that it had only been another bad dream.

"*Sonofafuckingbitch*," she exclaimed, as she rubbed at her face.

She rolled her legs over the side of the bed and sat on the edge, as her heart rate began to subside. She reached over and turned on the lamp, then grabbed the pack of cigarettes off the nightstand. She tapped one out of the pack and lit it, taking a long drag, as she began to calm down. It was always the same ritual.

The nightmare had been a reoccurring visitor since she had first discovered Cory's body in the river six months ago. She had tried everything from alcohol to over-the-counter sleeping pills, but nothing could dislodge the images from her head. She'd even flirted briefly with the idea of asking Peter to prescribe something stronger for her, but she didn't want to open that can of worms with him. She knew what he would say, that she needed to see a professional, and she knew that he was probably right, but that didn't mean it was ever going to happen anytime soon. Civilians just couldn't seem to grasp the mental shit that went along with this job and the last thing she needed was some witchdoctor claiming she was unfit for duty.

Alex gazed out her bedroom window, watching as the blackness of the night sky began to lighten in the east. Soon she would see the first rays of light break over the horizon.

She laid back in bed and stared up at the ceiling, blowing smoke rings up toward the white-washed wood rafters.

Something's got to give, she thought.

After a few minutes, she glanced over at the alarm clock and then crushed the cigarette out in the ashtray. There was no point in trying to go back to sleep and she didn't want to run the risk of the dream repeating itself. The only thing she knew was that she needed to find a way to make it go away before it drove her crazy

She got out of bed and headed out to the kitchen, to turn the coffee maker on, before grudgingly heading off to the shower.

CHAPTER THREE

"Morning, boss," Abby said, looking up from her computer keyboard, as Alex walked into the police station. "You're in early."

"Mmmm," Alex replied, tossing a Dunkin' Donut's bag onto the woman's desk, before heading into her office.

"I hate you," Abby said, as she peered inside the bag at the frosted chocolate donut inside. "Why did you bring me this?"

"Because you're mean to me at the gym," Alex said, removing her jacket and hanging it up on the coat rack. "Besides, you're a big girl and no one's twisting your arm."

"But its chocolate," Abby replied sadly, reaching into the bag and withdrawing the donut. "It's my kryptonite and you know it."

"What can I say, I'm a bitch."

"Ooh, did someone have a rough night?"

"Rough night, rough morning," Alex replied.

"Again?"

"Right now it's about the only consistent thing in my life."

"Oh, boo-hoo," Abby said, before stuffing the donut in her mouth.

She got up from her desk, grabbing her coffee cup in one hand and a stack of reports with the other, then she made her way into Alex's office. She deposited the reports onto the desk and then took a seat.

"Love letters?" Alex asked, as she sat down behind her desk and removed the plastic lid off her own coffee cup.

"More like hate mail," Abby said. "One of our aspiring young talents got ahold of a spray paint can and went all *gangsta* over on the north end of town. They tagged the high school and a couple of garages. Needless to say some of the residents aren't their usual little rays of sunshine this morning"

"Awesome, that should make the next town council meeting a glorious event," Alex replied sarcastically, as she opened a pack of cigarettes and removed one. "Perhaps this time they'll ask for my head on a pike at the city limits."

"At least they didn't tag any houses or cars, Abby replied.

"Yet," Alex said, as she lit the cigarette and took a drag. "Reach out to the shops that carry spray paint and give them a warning as to what is going on. Ask them to let us know if any of the local hooligans try to buy spray paint."

"Will do."

"So do you have any good news hiding in that stack of papers?"

"Nope, just the usual statistical heartache and misery for your early morning reading enjoyment."

"*Outfuckingstanding*," Alex replied.

"So what are you planning to do about your nightmares?"

"I'm considering becoming an insomniac," Alex said. "I'll be exhausted, but I'll be able to get a lot more done."

"I don't recommend it," Abby replied, reaching over and grabbing the pack of cigarettes off the desk. "I went through a bad

22

time a few years back, right before a big meet. I over-analyzed everything, training, eating, you name it. Bottom line was that I would lay in bed for hours every night, unable to turn off my brain. By the time the competition came around, I was a walking basket case. I ended up placing twenty-fourth out of twenty-five. The only reason I didn't come in last was because that other woman suffered an injury three weeks prior and couldn't work out."

Alex leaned back in the chair and rubbed at her weary eyes. She knew Abby was right. Police work was a hard enough job to stomach at times without adding any other shit onto the plate.

"So what did you do?"

"I went to this holistic hippie chick, outside Franconia, that a girlfriend recommended" Abby replied. "Actually, I think she was a mental health counselor, but she was that really *earthy* type. You know the beads, sandals and patchouli oil crap."

"Did it help?" Alex asked.

"I guess. She gave me this CD that I was supposed to meditate to. Allegedly it would be put me in a relaxed state and allow me to work through my issues, but I never actually made it through because I kept falling asleep. I think by that time I was just so physically exhausted I could have slept standing up."

"Falling asleep isn't my problem," Alex said, taking a sip of coffee. "It's what comes after."

"I think you're going to need to see a real doctor for that."

"Like I don't have enough shit to do," Alex replied. "By the way, when did doctors stop making house calls?"

"Doesn't *Dr. Hunk* still make house calls to your place?" Abby said with a mischievous grin.

"Peter is the last person I'm going to talk to about this," Alex replied. "He means well, but the next thing I know I'll be a test subject hooked up to machines trying to read my mind and that would be a very scary thing. I'd end up being committed within the first twenty-four hours."

"No argument here," Abby said. "I'll see if I can dig out that hippie chick's number for you. Speaking of men, have you heard from your old partner?"

"Yeah,...."

"And?"

"And what?"

"Don't give me that, you know what I mean, have you guys talked about what happened?"

"No," Alex replied. "There's no point. We're like two ships in the night, heading in opposite directions, on different oceans."

"That's bullshit and you know it," Abby replied. "Turn your ship around and go after him."

"He has a fiancée for crying out loud."

"So? You were there first; you have a dog in the fight."

"I just don't how much fight this old dog has left in her."

"That's just a lame excuse and you know it," Abby replied.

"Yeah, yeah, yeah..... whatever"

"Now I know, that you know, I am right."

"I hope that donut goes right to your thighs," Alex said, crushing out her cigarette.

"Such hate," Abby said with a laugh, as she got up and headed out of the office. "Oh, don't forget, you wanted to have a chat with Sheldon Abbott about that denial letter the board sent regarding the new computer system."

"My day is already ruined," Alex replied, "I might as well share the joy."

She reached over, picking up one of the reports and began reading it. All in all there were eight reported cases of graffiti, the worst being the high school where they tagged a fifty foot section of the building. There was going to be hand wringing and gnashing of teeth from the board members, but she didn't care. She would just make sure to remind them of the reason they needed to hire a replacement for Anderson and that all the little shits, who were ultimately responsible for the damage, were all members of *their* community. It always amazed her how the cops were perennially blamed for everyone else's bad behavior.

"If you wanted to be a hero, you should have become a firefighter," she said dryly, signing off on the reports.

When she was done, she lit another cigarette and picked up her cell phone, selecting the first number in the contacts list.

"You're up early," Maguire said, when he answered the call.

"I don't have the luxury of a driver, Mr. Hotshot Police Commissioner," she replied, "or a staff to fetch my coffee for me."

"Bitch, bitch, bitch,........." Maguire said with a laugh, "Don't you have anyone local whose balls you can break?"

"Oh I have a long list, but you're the only one who truly appreciates my talents."

"So what do I owe the pleasure?"

"What? Now I need a *reason* to call up and harass my old partner?"

"It's never stopped you before," Maguire said.

"I was just wondering how you're holding up," Alex replied. "Becoming P.C. is a tough enough job, under the best of circumstances, let alone the way you inherited it."

"Some days are easier than others," Maguire replied. "It's still hard walking into this office. I keep waiting for Rich to come in and tell me to get the hell out of his chair; something I would gladly do in a heartbeat."

"I bet," she replied. "I liked Rich. He seemed like a really stand-up guy. Not many of them left in the world, especially within our profession."

"Truer words where never spoken," Maguire said.

"Any progress on the killer?"

Maguire paused, choosing his words carefully.

He already knew the outcome of the manhunt, but it wasn't for public consumption and that even included his own former partner. It wasn't that he didn't want to tell her that Rich Stargold's killer had been brought to justice; it was just that he couldn't. The elimination of Gerald Spangler had been deemed a matter of *national security* and had come at the direction of someone else; someone much higher than Maguire's paygrade. Eventually Spangler's body would turn up in the desert and the case would be officially closed, but that would take a little while longer to happen.

"James, are you still there?"

"Yeah, sorry, just had someone come in for a signature," Maguire lied. "No, we've sort of hit a road block with the investigation. We're still chasing leads, but for now he has vanished. It seems he had a lot of resources at his disposal."

"That sucks, any thoughts on where he might have headed?"

"West most likely," Maguire said. "He has the survival training and, with all the heat on him, he would probably seek out the most remote area he could. For all we know he could be living in a cave in New Mexico or the mountains in Montana."

"That makes sense," Alex replied, taking a drag on her cigarette. "Find a place to hide out where you can see anyone coming for miles. I wish there was more that I could do to help you."

"No need to feel that way, but I understand the sentiment. I have a cadre of detectives working on it, along with a bunch of feds, and I have to force myself to not get in their way."

"It's tough, isn't it?" Alex asked. "Being the boss, watching everyone else do what you feel you should be doing?"

"Yeah, it is," Maguire replied. "I remember right before Christmas Rich and I went out for lunch and ended up responding to a 10-85 in Midtown. Not sure whether the cop was happy to see the police commissioner and first dep backing him up or scared shitless."

"I'm betting a little bit of both," Alex said with a laugh. "Talk about pressure not to screw up. Hell, I got nervous when just the sergeant would show up on our jobs."

"Remember that time we chased old *Lazy Eye* Wilson over on Belmont?"

"Remember? I thought I was going to lose my job because of that Forest Whitaker looking motherfucker."

Maguire shook his head as he recalled the particulars of that little event.

Jamal 'Lazy Eye' Wilson was one of the Seven-Three Precinct's most well-known street dealers. Back in the day, Wilson had cut his teeth in the drug business working for one of Hip-Hop's most prolific stars, back when running drugs was the up and coming singer's primary source of income. Wilson didn't really have a lazy eye in the traditional medical sense. His was the result of a gunshot wound to head, that he had suffered at the hands of some *business associates,* which caused his right eye to turn inward. The shooting also resulted in his middle-of-the-night relocation from the Marcy House's to his cousin's place in Brownsville. Lazy Eye didn't think he needed to give them a second chance to improve their aim.

One afternoon, Alex and Maguire had spotted Wilson over on Belmont Avenue, doing some hand-to-hand deals from atop his *construction cone orange* colored Schwinn bicycle. As they pulled up a startled Wilson fell off the bike and took off on foot, with Alex giving chase. Despite the initial surprise, Wilson quickly kicked it into high gear, jumping fences like a gazelle being chased by a lion, as he made his way back to the safety of the projects. By the time Alex made it to Sutter Ave the fleet-footed felon was long gone.

Furious, Alex returned back to the scene, grabbing the abandoned bike and tossed it into the trunk of the radio car. Upon arrival back at the station house she proceeded to dump the bike onto the ground and then ran it over, twice, leaving it a mangled mess. As she stood there admiring her handiwork, a shit eating grin on her face, the precinct commanding officer, who'd just arrived for his evening shift, walked up and asked her what was going on.

Alex turned to look at the man, the grin fading from her face just as quickly as Wilson had disappeared, and fought to come up with an explanation for actions.

"Found property?" she stammered.

"From where?" the captain asked, a scowl clearly visible on his face.

"Lazy Eye Wilson," she said, "over on Belmont."

The man paused, considering what she had just told him, and then nodded his head approvingly.

"Voucher it," he replied gruffly, before turning to walk toward the door.

Alex rested her hand on the fender of the car and exhaled softly, as she contemplated the career killing bullet she had just dodged.

"Oh and Officer Taylor," the captain said, standing in the doorway. "Let's work on those parking skills, shall we?"

"10-4, Sir," Alex replied.

Maguire chuckled, as he recalled the image of his partner, sitting in the car ashen faced, as clear as if it had happened yesterday.

"You're just lucky the old man had a major hard-on for Wilson," Maguire said. "Otherwise you'd have been looking at charges and specs, along with a major case of *highway therapy* to contemplate your poor life decisions."

Highway therapy was what you got when the NYPD wanted to screw you as much as they could. Basically, they found the shittiest precinct furthest from where you lived, preferably one with tolls, and transferred you there. Depending on the shift you worked, some officers spent nearly as much time diving to and from work as they did actually doing their job.

"Ain't that the truth," she replied. "I swear when I turned around and saw him standing there you couldn't have driven a straight pin up my ass with a sledge hammer."

"God, those were good times," Maguire reminisced. "Do you ever miss it?"

"Only on the days that end in Y," Alex replied, crushing her cigarette out in the ash tray.

"So tell me, how are things up in Shangri-La?"

"The usual," Alex said. "It's that awesome time of the year when you open the windows, to enjoy the spring breezes, and find out that even the birds are assholes at 5 a.m. I mean really, what they hell do they have to be so chipper about?"

"At least pigeons only coo."

"God, I can't remember the last time I saw one of those *rats with wings*," Alex said nostalgically, "but I certainly don't miss them shitting on my car."

"They do seem to have good aim, especially after you just washed it."

"Hey, James, while I have you on the line, can I ask you a personal question?"

Immediately his mind went back to the conversation they'd share at the Christmas party. He was still trying to come to terms with Alex's revelation about her feelings for him, as well as his own feelings for her.

"Sure," he replied, with a slight bit of hesitation. "Is everything okay?"

"Yeah, no, I'm fine. I was just curious. With all the cases you worked, did you ever have any nightmares?"

"What, like the ones that got away?" he asked, with just a bit of relief.

"Yeah," Alex said, trying to sound as nonchalant as possible. "The ones that got away, the ones you couldn't get to in time."

"Everyone does," he replied. "They are an occupational hazard in law enforcement. It's like that one where you're in a shootout and you can't pull the trigger."

"I'd be happy if it was just that simple."

"Why, what kind of dreams are you having?"

Alex paused, tapping out another cigarette from the pack and twirling it around in her fingers, as she argued internally about what to say.

"I just keep having this dream about Cory Childers," she said, lighting the cigarette up.

"The boy you lost a few months back?"

"Yeah, that's the one."

"Don't beat yourself up too bad; there was nothing you could have done. I don't want to say those dreams are normal, but after a case like that it is to be expected.

"Yeah, you're probably right," she replied.

"Alex, let's be honest for a moment, you swear like a drunken sailor and you wear that tough-girl persona like armor, but deep down inside you actually do care. So is it any wonder that when you're asleep that you have dreams like this?"

"Shut up about my feelings, rookie," she said with a laugh. "Besides, I just wanted to make sure I wasn't boarding the train to looneyville."

"God no, you made that trip years ago," Maguire responded.

"That's because they gave me you to train," Alex replied sarcastically. "I'm surprised I didn't go prematurely grey."

"That'd be a look," he said. "Get yourself one of those black latex uniforms and you could be a comic book superhero, *Ghetto Girl*."

"I only wear black latex to social events."

"Speaking of social events, how you doing with the drinking?"

"Been dry as Granny Gulch's Gash," Alex replied, "but thanks for asking."

"Now that's an image I'm gonna need a therapist to overcome."

"How do you think I feel," she asked. "Hey maybe if we go together we can get a discount."

"We would need an entire mental health practice to address our issues, partner."

"What's life without a little crazy?"

"Boring," he replied, "and speaking of which, I have to go over to City Hall for some bullshit, *diversity in city government*, meeting."

"Better you than me," she replied.

"I'll catch up with you in a few days."

"Sounds good, go do that *ass-kissy* thing you do so well."

"Be safe," Maguire said, ignoring the barb.

"You too, James," Alex replied and hung up the phone.

CHAPTER FOUR

"Good morning, Candi, is Sheldon in?"

"Hold on, Chief Taylor, let me check," the woman replied, before putting the call on hold.

Check? The fucker sits in the office next to you, what's there to check?

It was a mind game that Sheldon played with everyone; in an effort to make himself seem more important than he actually was. No one ever got through right away and if you went to his office the door was always closed because he was *in a meeting.*

Alex had a mental image of him sitting there, with a big blow-up doll of himself, talking about his favorite topic: *Sheldon Abbott.*

Nah, that's not the blow-up doll he probably has, she thought.

She waited impatiently, drumming her fingers on the desktop, as her overall mood just continued to deteriorate.

For Christ's sake, Juggs, did you get lost? she wondered, as she watched the second hand slowly tick away.

It was a well-accepted, if little talked about, fact that Candice 'Juggs' Montgomery hadn't gotten her job as Abbott's secretary because of her stellar skills behind the desk, as much as she had for her stellar skills *under the desk*. Alex didn't actually have a problem with the woman because of that, she was a firm believer in to-each-his-own, but she was reasonably sure that the woman could get lost inside of a closest.

She reached over, snagging another cigarette and lit it, as she waited for Abbott to pick up. A full minute passed before she heard him come on the line.

"Good morning, Alex," Sheldon said in his typical cheery *politician* voice. "How are you this fine day?"

"Angry, cranky and armed, so cut the bullshit, Sheldon and explain to me why you denied me my new computer system."

"I didn't deny you, Alex," the man corrected, "the board denied you."

"Jesus Christ, Sheldon, you *are* the board," Alex said angrily. "The village idiots sit in their chairs, but they wouldn't know when to take a piss unless you told them."

"You give me way too much credit, my dear."

"Oh please, cut the crap," Alex replied. "I'm not in the mood for it today. I don't even want to know why it was denied, I just want to know when it is going to be approved."

"The board can't seem to understand why you need a new computer system," he replied, "when you already have a perfectly good one."

"Sheldon, the current operating system for the rest of the world is like Window's *gajillion*, our computers are running *Wooden Shutters* 2.0," Alex replied. "We can't even connect with most of the state police programs because our system is so damn old."

"It's just that money is so tight right now," Abbott replied. "There's sewer and road repair work that has to be done up on the north end of town. Then there are improvements on the marina that have to be completed before the summer boating season gets under way. Maybe next year we can do some incremental upgrades for your office."

It was always the same story. The folks up on the north end of town, the *rich end*, bitched and the board members tripped over themselves to do their bidding. She acknowledged that it made sense. After all, the folks up in the north end had the money and the votes, so they held all the power.

"Sheldon, I don't give a rat's ass what direction the shit flows up in the north end of town," Alex said. "What matters to me is that my guys have the tools they need to do their jobs safely. So if the board wants to play *who has the biggest balls on the playground* then game-on."

"What are you going to do, Alex?"

She didn't understand why they had to do this tango every time she wanted to make improvements. It was like the whole rifle debacle. She eventually got her way, but not without first threatening to make it her mission to find new employment for his beloved secretary. Now it seems she would have to up the ante and hit him where it would really hurt: his wallet.

Maybe he just likes being verbally abused, she thought.

"Oh, don't worry, Sheldon," she said. "After this next season you won't have to worry about making any more improvements on the marina, because after my enforcement blitz, everyone will be heading to Lake Francis."

"Alex, you don't mean that," Abbott said in an exasperated tone.

"I do and I will, so help me God," she replied. "One or two asset forfeitures of boats, being driven by some pill-pushing spoiled college brat, and I'm pretty sure that I will be able to pay for my own computer system. Hell, looking at some of those boats, that those *north-enders* love so much, I might even be able to hire my own IT guy."

"You wouldn't dare," Abbott replied.

"I might even be able to get the state boys to come up and play with me," she lied. "There's this really cute looking sergeant in the marine division, down in Gilford, I bet he'd love to spend the summer with me on the lake showing off maritime enforcement abilities."

"Let me talk to the board," Abbott said. "Maybe I can convince them to reallocate some money from the discretionary fund."

"You're so good to me, Sheldon," Alex said, in an overly sweet tone. "What would I ever do without you?"

"You really need to learn to play well with others, Alex," he cautioned. "One day I might not be around to make things run smoothly."

"Sheldon, this town will burn to the ground before you ever surrender power."

"You know me, Alex; I serve at the pleasure of the people."

More like to service the people, she thought.

Just then Abby knocked on the door. "I need you, boss."

"You're the man, Sheldon, but now I got to get back to work."

"Goodbye, Alex."

She hung up the phone and turned her attention to Abby.

"What do you need, Abs?"

"I just got a call from a monitoring company for a commercial burglary alarm over on Renlow," Abby said, as she walked into the room and handed her a slip of paper with an address written on it. "Hutch is out handling another vandalism call across town, seems like the graffiti artists are expanding their turf."

Alex looked down at her watch. It was just about that time of the morning that most commercial locations were opening.

"No problem, it's probably just an accidental trip," Alex said, as she got up from the desk. "Besides, I need to get some fresh air. Arguing with him drains me."

"I hear that," Abby replied. "I think he secretly has a crush on you."

"I don't think even I could drink that much," Alex said, as grabbed her jacket and headed out of the office.

"Be careful."

"Oh, Abby," Alex said, pausing in the entrance doorway. "How many people do we have working the four-by shift?"

"Just Steve Harper, why?"

"Call Paul Murphy and ask him if he wants some overtime," she said. "See if he can do a modified shift, like a six to two, and have him give special attention to the area hit with the graffiti. I don't want the board bitching that we aren't being proactive about it."

"Sure thing, boss."

Alex headed out of City Hall and got in her car. Renlow was on the southwestern side of town and was specifically zoned for commercial business. It was also one of the few places that she rarely responded to. Burglaries, commercial or residential, were just not that big of an issue in Penobscot. In fact, it had been almost a year since they'd had one and that had involved a keg of beer being taken from a storage shed behind the Lion's Head bar.

The problem with commercial burglary alarms was that most times they were accidental trips, meaning that the most likely culprit was a careless employee who had forgotten to enter their code when they arrived or had inadvertently hit a panic button. The problem for law enforcement occurred when it wasn't.

Alex slowed down as she entered the general area, watching the street signs, as she searched for the address. It was one of the last buildings before the train tracks, a non-descript white stone structure that featured a single door next to a closed loading bay. A small sign above the doorway identified the business name as *Internal Affairs*.

You've got to be shitting me, she thought.

Nothing good had ever come out of a trip to Internal Affairs for Alex.

She drove around the location, making sure there were no other entrances or exits that she could make out, before returning to the front. She parked the car on an angle, away from the door, to give herself maximum amount of coverage in case things went south quickly. She got out, unholstering her gun, and held it down at her side, as she approached the front entrance.

Alex stood off to the side and peeked through the door, scanning the interior to see if she could identify any potential threats. The door opened into a long, narrow hallway that ended about thirty feet ahead. She could make out an unoccupied desk, which sat near the back of the room, along with two closed doors positioned on either side of the hallway.

Well that's not ugly, she thought.

It was a cluster-fuck scenario for a cop, especially one going in alone. Alex would be going in blind until she cleared out the doors on either side of the hallway. If she chose the wrong door to clear first, well, it was basically *goodnight, Alex*. She would be entering a funnel of death if someone happened to be behind the other door.

"Fuck me," she said softly, as she weighed her options of which there weren't many.

Sucks to be you, she thought, as she reached for the door handle.

"Hello?" Alex called out, as she stepped inside the location. "It's the Police, is anyone here?"

She listened intently, for either an answer or to hear any type of movement.

"Guess it's time to dance."

She raised her gun up, scanning for threats, as she made her way down the narrow hallway. The door on the left came up first and she reached over and opened it, immediately moving to her right, as she *cut-the-pie* and scanned the interior.

Alex breathed a sigh of relief when she found it to be a small, unoccupied bathroom.

"One down, one to go," she said.

She continued down the hallway, taking everything in, her senses working overtime; she reached down to grab the door handle when it abruptly swung open.

For a moment time stood still. She felt herself retreat, moving backward until she hit the wall behind her, even as her finger began wrapping itself around the trigger. The twenty-something young man, who'd been wearing a pair of earphones and carrying a large cardboard box, dropped the package and let out a high-pitched squealed like a teenage girl at a boy band concert.

"Don't shoot!"

"*Sonofabitch*," Alex exclaimed, as she lowered the gun and grabbed the kid.

She yanked him out into the corridor and pushed him against the wall, quickly patting him down for weapons. "Are you alone?"

"Yes, ma'am," he replied, his voice breaking with fear.

"Do you work here?"

"Yes, I do."

Alex stepped back. "Okay, junior, let me see some ID, slowly."

The young man reached into his back pocket, withdrawing his wallet, and slowly handed his license to Alex.

"Jacob Adams," she said, as she read the license, noting that he was a resident of Penobscot.

"Yes, ma'am, that's me."

"I know it's you, hotshot, I see your photo here," she replied.

"Sorry, ma'am," the man replied nervously.

"Do you have an alarm here, Jacob?"

For a moment, the kid stared at her with a blank expression and then his eyes went wide, as he came to terms with the extent of his screw-up.

"Oh shit, I forgot to turn it off again, didn't I?"

"Winner, winner, chicken dinner," she said, handing him back his ID. "Now how about you and I go correct that little error?"

"Yes, ma'am," he replied, as he turned and began walking down the hall toward the desk.

Alex watched as he keyed the code into the pad and the light changed from red to green. The young man turned back to look at her, the color only now returning to his face.

"You're not going to tell my boss are you?" he asked.

"Well, that depends, Jacob," Alex said, making a show of replacing her gun into the holster and locking the safety in place. "We're not going to have this problem again, are we?"

"Oh, God, no," he replied. "I swear."

"That's good, because I'm really not a morning person and I'd hate to shoot you before my first cup of coffee. So why don't you take me on a tour, Jacob, just to make sure everything is buttoned up tight."

The young man led her back through the doorway he had come from and into a large warehouse. The cavernous room was filled with row upon row of large, industrial grade, steel shelving units. After a few minutes it was clear that the place was secure and that there were no other persons present.

"So what the heck kind of place is this, anyway."

"Mail order," he replied. "We ship online orders out from here."

"What? Like those fancy foam pillows and rubber sealants?" Alex asked.

"Uhm, no," the man said sheepishly, "its other stuff, ma'am."

"Other stuff?" Alex asked curiously. "Like what, funky colored cookware?"

"Mostly adult stuff," he said. "You know; DVD's and things like that."

"Ah, gotcha," Alex replied. "Got anything good? Any recommendations?"

The young man stared at Alex, a look of fear and apprehension gripping is face, as he tried to formulate a reply.

Alex let out a laugh, "Don't worry, kid, I'm just messing with."

Relief washed over the man's face.

"Don't forget to turn off your alarm from now on," she replied, as she headed out the door.

"I won't, I promise."

Alex got back in the radio car and picked up the radio mic.

"M-11-1 to base."

"Base, go with message, M-11-1," said Abby.

"Mark it as an accidental trip, worker on scene and properly identified."

"10-4."

"You need anything before I return to the office?"

"We're low on coffee, boss," Abby replied. "If you don't mind swinging by the store on your way back here, that would be great."

"Copy, I'll pick some up before I come back in," Alex said and hung the mic back up on the holder.

Who the hell buys movies anymore? she thought, as she put the car in drive and headed back into town.

CHAPTER FIVE

Alex slowed her patrol car and rolled down the passenger window, as she approached the parked vehicle.

"Hey, you want to do my shopping for me too?" she asked, directing the question toward the woman loading groceries into her trunk.

Mildred Parker, the wife of the former police chief, turned to look over at Alex.

"I already do, sweetheart," the woman said with a laugh, as she walked over toward the car. "With the amount of time you spend eating dinner at my house I'm going to claim you as a dependent on next year's taxes."

"You can come over to my place for dinner anytime," Alex replied.

"Alex, you overcook minute rice."

"I said you could come over for dinner; I never said say it was going to be edible."

"I think we will just keep things the way they are," Mildred replied.

"I can't help it if you're a great cook," Alex replied.

"Flattery will get you everywhere, my dear."

"I'd settle for an apple pie," Alex said.

"God, I know you so well," the woman replied, reaching into the trunk and removing a large bag of apples.

"Have I ever told you that you're my favorite?"

"Kiss ass," Parker replied, placing the apples back in the trunk.

"Hey, from what I hear you're going to have to start pandering for my vote pretty soon."

"Oh really," Mildred replied, eyeing her suspiciously. "And who is this vile wretch that is spreading such slanderous rumors about me."

"Oh, you know me," Alex said coyly. "I never kiss and tell, Peter Bates."

"Mmmm, remind me never to do a crime with the good doctor or with you, for that matter."

"Well, I think he was just trying to give me fair-warning for when Sheldon explodes."

"Good Lord, that's a scary mental image."

"So are you serious about running as well?"

"Actually, I was waiting to talk to you about," Mildred replied.

"Me? Why?"

"Why to get your opinion, my dear. I do value your judgment on things."

"Momma, not to seem snooty, but I'm a big-city cop who's been banished to working out in the sticks, I wouldn't rate my *judgment* as being all that very high."

"Okay, well then you're a scrappy little shit who, despite all her messing up, still manages to land on all fours."

"Well, since you put it that way....."

"We'll discuss this matter later, in private."

"Yes, ma'am."

"Don't forget, Friday at five. If you're late, the bunco ladies will have everything devoured before you get there."

"I won't be," Alex said, craning her neck in an attempt to peek into the trunk of Parker's car. "Hey, you don't happen to have coffee in there, do you?"

"Sorry, you're on your own with that."

"Is it crowded in there?" Alex asked, hooking her thumb in the direction of the grocery store.

"It's Monday morning and that pathetic excuse for a store manager has only one bubblegum chomping cashier working, what do you think?"

"Not worth it for a container of coffee," Alex said. "I'll just head over to the quick mart"

"Smart girl."

"I have my moments," Alex replied. "Love ya, I'll see you Friday."

"Love you too, Alex, be safe."

"I will," Alex said, closing the window.

She put the car in drive and made a left onto Main Street. A few blocks later she pulled into the parking lot of the Penobscot Quick Mart.

Alex sat in the car for a moment, as her mind went back to the burglary alarm call. She had come so close to shooting that dumb kid. She tried never to second guess things, but she couldn't help question if the lack of sleep wasn't going to end up causing her to make a stupid mistake one day.

If he had reacted any other way would it have ended differently? she wondered.

It wasn't like he would have been the first person killed for being dumb. In fact, she had a mental list of dumb asses that she would like to shoot and that list grew daily.

She took a final drag on her cigarette then dropped it to the ground, stepping on it as she got out of the car and headed toward the front entrance.

"Like Sheldon," she muttered to herself, as she reached out to open the door, "or at the very least, Juggs."

That last part made her smile, as she removed her sunglasses and allowed her eyes to acclimate to the dark interior. She had been in the store enough to know where the coffee was kept and she headed to the left without even thinking.

The store wasn't crowded, which was normal for this time of the day. Just up ahead a young, blonde-haired girl quickly turned the corner and she noticed a woman was squatting down, holding onto the bread rack for support. Another step forward and she realized that there were several others on the ground as well. The woman looked up at Alex; her face ashen and eyes wide in terror.

The sudden clarity of the moment hit her like a ton of bricks; she had blithely walked headlong into a shit-storm.

Asshole, she chided herself, as her hand instinctively moved toward her sidearm, drawing it out of holster, and she began scanning the area for threats.

She knew better than to walk into a store without first looking through the door.

Alex motioned with her hand for the group of terrified shoppers to stay put, as she began methodically checking out the store. The Quick Mart had four main aisles, each of which was roughly forty feet long, with a small produce area up front and a frozen food / dairy section along the left wall. Up front, along the far right wall, was a small, elevated cashier area, behind which the store kept a small quantity of hard alcohol and cigarettes.

Alex heard a shuffling noise that came from the direction of the cash register area.

"Police, let me see your hands," she called out, as she began to advance forward.

The police response to incidents like this is generally counterintuitive to what the average human mind wants to do. Take a look at any major incident, like a mass shooting, and you will see folks fleeing the scene or hunkering down behind shelter. Even when their numbers vastly outweigh those of their attackers, they will do anything they can to put as much distance as possible between them and the perceived threat. Inevitably, the police respond to the scene and, going against all human logic, they run *toward* the threat; often putting themselves between the victims and the perpetrator.

For the responding police officer things are much more different. As they move forward, things begin to slow down immensely, as the mind tries to process all of the incoming data. Split second decisions must be made as to who is a potential friend or foe. Eyes continually scan the scene for threats and weapons; as they continue to move forward. As if this wasn't enough, they must also fight to stave off a condition that is known as *tunnel vision*, which can occur during high stress and elevated production of adrenaline. When this happens, the individual suffers an extreme loss of peripheral sight resulting in a constricted, circular *tunnel-like* field of view.

Alex felt it begin; the slowing down of movement, the muffling of sounds, the narrowing of her vision. She had been here before and she fought back against it. She was just about at the cash register when she caught movement at the far left end and swung around in that direction, focusing on the Smith & Wesson's front sight.

"Police, don't move," she screamed.

As Alex watched, a figure clad in dark clothing emerged from behind the counter and began running. She knew she was screaming orders, but they were too muffled for her to hear. She could feel the rush of blood in her ears, as she moved toward the potential threat. Then she saw the figure turn slightly, their arm rising up, and she caught the glint of polished steel.

Time stopped.

She watched as the front site came to rest on her target, felt her finger begin to constrict on the trigger and then in an instant the interior of the store was filled with a thunderous roar as her weapon fired.

The .9mm round struck the dark figure, slamming him backward into a shelving unit that held an assortment of wine bottles.

The figure collapsed to the ground, followed a split-second later by a number of bottles whose shattering glass added their own noise to the chaotic scene.

Alex continued moving ahead, scanning as she went, until she reached the crumbled body lying on the floor. She extended her foot forward, stepping on the gun, and slid it back on the floor, away from the body. Then she reached down, pulling the mask from the perpetrators head.

"Jesus Christ," she muttered, as she stared down into the lifeless eyes of a young kid.

Blood was already beginning to pool beneath the body, mixing with the alcohol. She reached down, feeling for a pulse, but she already knew that it was too late.

"Fuck," she exclaimed.

Alex's head suddenly snapped around, as she heard a noise coming from the back of the location. She brought the gun back up and began moving forward, as the huddled group of shoppers took the opportunity and fled, knocking over two end displays, as they ran out the front door to safety.

She cautiously made her way back toward the rear of the store, as she reached her left hand up to her shoulder and retrieved the mic for the portable radio.

"M-11-1, shots fired at the Quick Mart."

"M-11-1, did you say shots fired?" she heard Abby ask.

"Affirmative, shots fired."

"M-11-3, clear from assignment and respond to the Quick Mart, forthwith. Confirmed shots fired."

"M-11-3, 10-4," Hutch replied.

As Alex made her way into the backroom she found the owner, Sanjay, laying on the floor unconscious and bleeding from a laceration to the back of his head. She scanned the stock room, ensuring that it was empty, before opening the door which led out into the back parking lot.

Alex paused for a moment, standing off to the side, as she allowed her eyes time to adjust to the brightness. When she could see clearly, she made her way out, sweeping the lot for any potential threats. Once she had cleared the area, she made her way back inside to check on Sanjay.

Off in the distance she heard the sound of a siren wailing, as Hutch responded to the scene.

CHAPTER SIX

The problem with being up in God's country was that the music selection was really limited. It was either some twangy, angst ridden, country song involving some love-sick farmer lamenting about being rejected by the milk maid, or a lecture about the evils of alcohol and fornication from some down station preacher. Neither of which were particularly appealing to her at the moment.

Tatiana reached over and hit the selector button, watching as the radio scanned frequencies.

"C'mon, give me something good for a change," she muttered.

After what seemed like forever, she finally found a song with a heavy metal beat and raised the volume up.

She reached over and grabbed the pack of cigarettes from the cup holder. She lit one up, as she glanced back over her shoulder.

How long does it take to get beer? she wondered.

She reclined back in her seat and was enjoying the music when she saw the unmarked police car pull into the parking lot.

"Oh shit," she said, as she slinked down lower in the seat, trying to make herself as invisible as she could.

Tatiana kept a watchful eye on the car. Then she saw the door open and the blonde haired cop get out.

"Well hello, beautiful," she said.

She immediately felt an immense feeling of relief come over her, because she had originally wanted to go into the

ANDREW G. NELSON

store herself, but Susan had insisted that she would go. Susan seemed to enjoy the game of being out and about in public, here in Penobscot, as if daring anyone to identify her, but the reality was that she had *grown-up* and changed her looks over the last two years. Tatiana doubted anyone would ever be able to recognize her. Even if she did look *familiar* they probably wouldn't recall where they had seen her until it was too late.

She continued to watch as the cop walked across the parking lot and then entered the store. Her mind was immediately drawn back to that day up in the cabin, when she had first encountered her. Almost immediately she could feel the raw emotions begin to well up inside her. It drove her crazy to think just how much desire that woman seemed to evoke in her.

She closed her eyes, thinking about the way she had come on to her in the cabin. How seductive she was and how easily Tatiana had fallen for her. Then she remembered the first kiss, the warmth of the woman's lips, and she felt her body shudder, as if a bolt of electricity had coursed through her.

Suddenly a gunshot rang out; shattering the intimate moment that had been replaying in her mind.

"Jesus Christ," she exclaimed, as she twisted around in her seat.

As she looked around, she was struck by how normal everything appeared.

Had it just been a car that backfired?

A second later she got her answer when the first person burst through the door of the store, followed a moment later by about a half dozen more.

"Fucking hell," Tatiana exclaimed, as she prepared to drop the car into drive and put some distance between her and the cop.

Then she saw Susan emerge from the store and begin running toward the car.

"What the heck was that all about?" Tatiana asked, as Susan climbed into the car and slammed the door shut.

"Shut up and drive!"

Tatiana was about to say something when she saw the look of sheer panic on Susan's face.

"Drive!"

She pulled away from the curb, tires squealing, and headed down the street.

"Turn left," Susan ordered, followed a moment later by a command to turn right.

Tatiana dutifully followed her directions, whipping the car in the announced direction, as Susan led them out of town. Once they were clear, she began to slow down.

"Fuck," Susan said, as they saw a marked police car coming toward them with its lights and sirens activated.

She slid down in the seat, waiting for it to pass, and then sat back up.

Both women looked back, waiting for the car to turn around and come after them, but it continued heading in the direction of the store.

"What the hell happened back there?" Tatiana asked.

"I don't know," Susan replied. "It all happened so fast."

"What do you remember?"

"I got the beer and I was walking toward the front when I saw one of my old teachers. I got nervous, so I ducked into another aisle and started walking toward the front. Next thing I knew I heard this screaming and people started crouching down on the floor, like some serious shit was going down up front, so I got down too."

"Did you see anything?"

"Not at first, I tried to get a better look, but then I saw that female cop come in so I tried to put some distance between us. Next thing I know I heard a gunshot. I thought we were all fucked, but then I saw everyone begin to run out of the store and so I made my way to the front."

"Did anyone see you?"

"No," Susan replied. "Everything happened way too fast for that."

"Well you dodged a helluva bullet on that one," Tatiana said.

"I did, but I'm pretty sure that cop is screwed."

"Why? What makes you say that?"

Tatiana watched as Susan reached into her jacket and removed a small, stainless steel snub-nosed revolver.

"Where the fuck did you get that from?"

"I saw it slide across the floor and it went underneath a display. So, in all the confusion, I just reached down and grabbed it as I went out the door."

"Let me see that," Tatiana said.

Susan handed the gun over to her.

Tatiana examined it, alternating her gaze from the roadway in front of her to the gun in her lap. She opened the cylinder and examined it, noting that none of the rounds appeared to have been fired.

"It looks like the gun shot you heard was from our lady cop friend," Tatiana said. "This gun hasn't been fired."

"Well, then it looks like someone might have a bit of explaining to do," Susan replied.

As they pulled out of town Tatiana felt a wave of relief wash over her. She tucked the revolver into her waistband and pulled her shirt over the top of it.

"It certainly does indeed," she said with a smile.

CHAPTER SEVEN

Alex sat in the Penobscot Police Department's small interview room. Across the table were Captain Thomas Blackshear of the New Hampshire State Police, Major Crimes Unit and the Scott Nichols, the county's state's attorney.

"Okay, let's go over this one more time, Alex," Nichols said.

"This is bullshit, Scott, and you know it."

"Alex, I'm not that bad guy here."

"Fine, fine," Alex said with a tone of annoyance, as she reached into her jacket and withdrew the pack of cigarettes.

"You can't smoke in here," Nichols said.

"Arrest me," she said, as she lit up the cigarette. "Let's not forget that you're in *my* house, Scott, not yours."

Blackshear began shuffling through some papers, as he fought to stifle a laugh.

Nichols sighed, "We don't have to make this adversarial, Alex. I just need to know what happened."

"Whatever. Just ask your questions, *again*."

"Okay, so what happened when you first walked into the store?"

"Jesus, Scott, did you write any of this down? I told you, it was dark so I couldn't see clearly at first. Once my eyes adjusted I realized something wasn't right."

"What about the scene didn't seem right to you?"

"Well, for starters most folks don't crawl on the ground to do their shopping."

"Well, were they crawling, kneeling, bent over?" Nichols asked. "I mean what were they doing that made you suspicious?"

"Are you serious, Scott?" Alex asked, taking a drag on her cigarette. "When was the last time you walked into a grocery store and saw a bunch of folks cowering on the floor and thought to yourself, 'hmmm, I wonder what kind of sale they are having on that shit down on the bottom shelf?'"

Blackshear laughed, dropping his head into his hands, as Nichols shot him a dirty look.

"Really, Tom?" he asked. "That's not helping."

"Look," Blackshear said, "I get it, you have to ask the questions, Scott, but you and I both know that you don't walk into a store wearing a mask to get a gallon of milk."

"What I know and what I can explain to a grand jury are not always the same," Nichols said, "and under the circumstances I have a lot of explaining to do."

He turned to look back at Alex. "So please, for the love of God, humor me."

"Based on my experience, I could see that the shoppers were clearly in distress and hiding from someone."

"Okay, then what did you do?"

"I drew my sidearm and began scanning the interior of the store for threats."

"So at what point did you encounter the deceased," Nichols said, skimming through his papers. "Mr. Chase Akins?"

"When the deceased pointed his gun at me which ultimately lead to his *deceasededness*."

Nichols removed his glasses, setting them on the table-top and rubbed his eyes.

"Alex, how did you know it was a gun?" Nichols asked.

"For Christ's sake, Scott, you think this is my first rodeo? That I never saw a gun before?"

"No, Alex, I don't," Nichols replied angrily. "In fact it's the second shooting I have handled with you. You know how many shootings the chief's in Penobscot have had prior to your arrival? Zero,...... Combined. That's how many."

"Okay folks, I think it's time we took a little break here," Blackshear interrupted. "Maybe get a bit of fresh air."

"Sounds good, I need a breather," Nichols announced, as he got up and headed for the door.

Alex crushed the cigarette out on the floor, as she took a sip of the now cold coffee.

"This is bullshit, Tom," Alex said, when Scott had left the room. "Do you think I shot that kid for shits and giggles? I saw the damn gun."

"I'm not saying you didn't, Alex, but we don't have that gun and that's a big fucking problem."

"You think I don't know that. Is there any chance the crime scene folks might have missed it?"

"They've been over the place twice already and I have them going over it a third time," Blackshear replied. "They look any harder the place won't have a floor or walls left."

"I appreciate that, Tom," Alex replied. "I'm not trying to be an asshole here, but I didn't shoot that kid because I was bored."

"I know you didn't, but what I think, or what Scott thinks for that matter, isn't going to mean much to a grand jury."

"Then I'm royally screwed."

"Let's stay positive," Blackshear replied. "I made sure they bagged the kid's hands. At least they can check and see if he had any residue on them when they do the autopsy."

Just then Nichols returned, carrying a cup of hot coffee.

"Truce?" he asked, handing the container to Alex.

"Truce," Alex replied, accepting the proffered cup. "Any luck with witnesses?"

"Two of them stayed at the scene and were interviewed," Scott said, "One was an old woman who has vision issues and didn't see anything. The other one said she heard a man yelling and waving something around, but that she got scared and didn't get a good look at what it was."

"Well that has to at least corroborate what I said."

"Waving a gun around and waving *something* are going to be seen as two entirely different things, I'm afraid."

"What about the owner, Sanjay?" Alex asked.

"He said he had just come in from dropping off some boxes in the recycling bin and the next thing he knew it was lights out," Blackshear replied. "He couldn't tell us anything more."

"What about video?"

"It's Penobscot, Alex, no one has video," Nichols said.

She took out another cigarette and lit it up. "You know, I keep hearing that shit, but every time I turn around this little gem of a city is looking a lot less like Paradise and more like Peyton Place."

"We have to play the cards we are dealt, even when it's a shitty hand," Nichols replied.

"There had to be at least a half dozen people in the store when I got there," Alex said. "Someone had to have seen what went down before I arrived. Those folks weren't hiding for the fun of it."

"I've requested additional investigators," Blackshear said. "We'll do our best to try and come up with the missing witnesses."

"Okay, so getting back to after you fired the shot, what did you do?" Nichols asked.

"I approached the suspect, I kicked the gun away and then I checked for a pulse."

"Why didn't you secure the gun?" Nichols asked.

"I didn't have a chance," Alex replied. "I had no backup and I had no idea if there was anyone else around. I didn't want to lean down and try to pick-up a gun when I didn't know the condition of the perp. So I just stepped on it and slid it back away from him with my foot. I guess I slid it harder than I thought."

"Did you check the condition of the suspect?"

"I did. I didn't find a pulse."

"Did you administer aid?"

"No."

"Why not?"

"Before I could do anything I heard a noise from the back of the store and feared that there was a second perpetrator."

"Did you investigate the sound?" Nichols asked.

"Yes, that's where I found Sanjay," she replied. "I then made my way out to the back parking lot, but didn't see anyone else."

Nichols looked over at Blackshear. "You have anything Tom?"

"No, I think we've covered as much as we can."

Nichols looked back over at Alex.

"Listen, I hate to be the bearer of bad news, but this shit has already hit the airwaves, Alex."

"What's that supposed to mean to me?"

"It means that the usual suspects down in Concord are beating the drum that this was another police murder of an innocent child."

"Innocent child? Are you friggin' kidding me, Scott? You saw the arrest printout. That little shit had a record longer than your dick, including, I might add, a charge for armed robbery. So cut the crap, he was far from innocent."

"And those charges were all juvenile and you're not supposed to know that because his record is sealed," Nichols said. "More importantly the grand jury won't know it either."

"That's such bullshit," Alex said angrily. "Next it'll be the 6th grade graduation photo and how he couldn't wait to go to college nonsense. They'll make a martyr of a career criminal while they try and fuck me dry for doing my job."

Silence gripped the room. Both men knew she was right, but their opinion didn't matter.

The local television satellite trucks were already arriving and it wouldn't be long before the cable ones showed up as well. What might have been a little blip on the media radar had the unfortunate bad luck of coming on the heels of a questionable police shooting in Chicago that was caught on video and immediately uploaded to social media. As a result, the media was looking to cash in on anything they could tie-in for a bump in their ratings.

"There's no easy way to say this," the man said. "So I'm just going to. Alex, you're not being suspended, but your being suspended. Call it an unplanned vacation."

"What?" Blackshear said.

"You can't be serious, Scott."

"I am and before you ask this wasn't my call to make, I'm just the deliveryman."

"Who?" Alex asked angrily.

"The board," he replied. "Don't ask me which member, because I can't tell you, but I need you're shield."

Alex sat there seething, but knowing there wasn't a damn thing she could do. Finally she stood up. She reached over and unpinned the shield from her jacket.

"Tell *them* they can kiss my ass," she said, "but, if I'm only on *vacation,* then I pick who fills in while I'm gone."

"Well, that went well," Blackshear said, as Alex stormed out of the room.

She made her way out to the squad room where Abby, Hutch and several other officers were standing.

"What's going on, boss?" Abby asked.

"Oh, it looks like I just hit the lottery, Abs, and I won an all-expense paid vacation at home."

"Are you serious?" Hutch asked.

"Oh, yeah, I'm as serious as a heart attack, Hutch," Alex replied, "but guess what."

"What?" Hutch asked.

Alex reached out and took his hand in her and placed her shield in it. "Tag, you're it, junior."

Hutch looked down at the badge in his hand, a mix of fear and confusion on his face.

"But, chief, you're the chief," he stammered.

"Apparently not right now," Alex replied. "Right now I'm gonna go home and get hammered while the rest of you wonderful *sonofabitches* do your damndest to keep my pretty little ass out of jail, *capiche*?"

"Yes, ma'am," Hutch replied.

"Good, send someone over tonight to pick-up the car. The keys will be inside, don't bother ringing the doorbell, I'll be passed out by then."

"Boss,...."

"Don't say anything, just do your job."

"Yes, ma'am."

They watched as Alex turned and walked out of the office, then Hutch looked over at Abby who seemed in a state of shock.

"I don't believe this," she whispered.

"You?" Hutch asked. "What about me? I don't know the first thing about being the chief of police."

"Then I suggest we do everything we can to get her back to work."

"But what if there was no gun?" Hutch asked.

Abby looked around the room and then nodded toward Alex's office. Hutch followed her inside and she closed the door behind her.

"What's wrong?" he asked.

"This can't leave this room, Hutch. Do you understand that?"

"Yeah, Abs, what are you talking about?"

"I swear, chief or no chief, I will kick your ass."

"Abby, you know me better than that," Hutch said. "Just tell me what you know."

"I'm worried about her," Abby said. "She's been having a rough time with the Childers' case."

"Well, I don't think any of us have had an easy time with that one."

"No, I mean she has been having a really *rough* time, like nightmares and not being able to sleep, that kind of rough time."

"You think it might be affecting her?" Hutch asked.

"I don't know, I don't want to think so, but I just don't know," Abby said. "What if she only *thought* she saw a gun?"

"You think it's that serious?"

"She's been exhausted lately," Abby said.

"Look, this might be something we should tell Nichols," Hutch said.

"No, not yet," Abby replied. "If they think she's losing it, they might not investigate as hard as they should and right now we need to do what we can to find those other witnesses. If we can't, well then we can go to Nichols, but if we do it now they might stop looking."

"We don't have much time," he said. "If we wait too long it will look like we are covering for her."

"Then we'd better make sure we find someone to corroborate her story quickly."

CHAPTER EIGHT

Susan laid on the couch, her head resting in Tatiana's lap, as the woman watched the evening news. She stared up at the wood beams of the ceiling, as the woman gently stroked her head. She felt like she was in a trance. Her body was completely relaxed and her eyes lazily followed the wood grain of one particular section. The more intently she stared, the more she imagined that she could see figures within the detailing.

"Can I ask you a question, Tee?"

"You can ask me anything you want, my love," the woman replied, turning the volume down on the television and setting the controller on the coffee table.

"Why don't you like your name?"

"What do you mean?" Tatiana asked. "I love my name."

"No, I mean your *real* name," Susan said, sitting up on the couch and looking at the woman.

It had been just over a year since the two women had met that fateful night in Key West. Susan had been immediately drawn to the woman from the moment she had first laid eyes on her at the beachside restaurant.

Tatiana was tall, attractive and seemed to exude equal parts of confidence and sexuality. At first Susan had thought she was just a tourist, down in the Key's for Spring Break, and someone she could have a quick fling with, but soon she learned that they shared a much deeper bond.

During the ensuing months Tatiana's role had run the gamut from lover to teacher to maternal figure, but, for as much as they had shared, Susan still felt that she purposefully kept a part of herself from her.

"That part of me is dead," Tatiana said with a frown, as she picked up her drink from the end table and took a sip.

They'd been down this road so many times before.

"I know," Susan replied. "I get it. My past is dead as well, but that doesn't mean that it is dead to you."

When they had first met each of them had lied to the other about their true identities. At the time Susan was using the identity she had stolen from one of her victims, Hannah Kurtz. Over time, as their relationship moved from just a sexual to a more intimate one, she had dropped the alter-ago and had reverted back to Susan, at least when it came to her. She had shared her story, even the ugly parts. It was her attempt at being completely honest; exposing herself to her companion, but Tatiana had never reciprocated. In many ways, Tatiana still remained an enigma to her.

Hannah knew her story, but sometimes she really questioned whether or not she truly knew the *real* story. Tatiana had shared the details about the abandonment, the love, the abuse and the torture, but it was almost as if she was telling someone else's story. Even finding out her real name, Patricia Browning, had been something Susan had stumbled upon by accident.

She had pieced together enough clues that one day she started doing a search. It didn't take too long before she's found articles about the accident. She followed one link after the other; like she was uncovering some long lost family history. In many ways it seemed like she was reading about someone else.

In fact, the only one she ever seemed to talk about with any real semblance of affection was the one person who seemed to have hurt her the deepest, Keith Banning. It seemed odd to her that Tatiana would hold him in such reverence, but even when she talked about how he had broken her it was never with any remorse. In a way, it was Banning who she credited with setting her free from what she had been. Tatiana always said that being under his tutelage was like her *chrysalis* and that when she emerged on the other side she had been transformed into a beautiful butterfly of death.

Unfortunately, a part of Susan craved to know the real Patricia Browning, to have her share something truly intimate with her. She felt that it was the last remaining barrier to the two of them having a true relationship and that was something she feared would never happen.

"You know I love you, baby," Tatiana said. "It's just that there is too much ugliness in my past and I don't want to bring that into our present or our future."

"But everyone, even your enemies, knows you as Tatiana, why can't I have something different?"

"You have something they will never have," Tatiana replied. "You have me."

"That's the point, Tee," Susan said, her voice tinged with exasperation. "I don't have you, I have *Tatiana*. Please don't get me wrong, I love you, but there are times I crave something deeper, something more meaningful than what everyone else has."

"You're asking me to bring something into our relationship that I feel is tainted," Tatiana said.

Susan got up and stood in front of Tatiana. She rested her hands on the woman's shoulders, straddling her legs, and sat down.

"Nothing about you is tainted, Tee" Susan said, looking into her eyes. "I love who you are, the good and the bad."

"You're so sweet," Tatiana said, as she brushed a strand of hair from Susan face.

"I just want you to trust me enough to give me that part of you as well," Susan said.

"I will," Tatiana lied, "one day. Just be patient with me."

"Promise?"

"I promise."

Susan kissed her softly, feeling Tatiana's arms wrap around her waist, pulling her close. She began to playfully grind herself against Tatiana.

"Don't start anything you don't plan on finishing."

"Have I ever *not* finished anything I started with you, Tee?"

"Mmmmmm," Tatiana purred.

She was just about to suggest they move into the bedroom when something on the television screen caught her attention.

"Where's the controller?"

Susan sighed, reaching behind her, and grabbed the controller.

"Here," she said dejectedly, giving it to Tatiana, as she climbed off her lap.

A pretty looking auburn haired reporter, wearing a drab grey pantsuit, was on the screen doing a live shot from the front of Penobscot City Hall.

"Our sources say that the officer involved in the shooting, Chief Alexandria Taylor, has been with the Penobscot Police Department since July of 2012. Prior to that we are being told she was with the New York City Police Department, but we are still trying to confirm that, Chet."

"What do we know about the shooting, Kristin?" the studio anchor asked.

"Well, according to a press release issued by the State's Attorney's Office, Chief Taylor had entered the Quick Mart convenience store this morning when she encountered the suspect, identified as eighteen-year-old Chase Akins, of rural Ellard. At some point an altercation occurred and Mr. Akins was killed."

"Have the authorities indicated if he was armed."

"That's the issue at hand, Chet," the woman replied. "According to her statement, Chief Taylor said she observed a gun, however none was recovered at the scene. Chief Taylor is currently on leave, pending the outcome of the investigation. Police are asking anyone who witnessed the incident to please contact their local law enforcement agency."

"Kristin Stuart, reporting live from Penobscot," The anchorman said, as the camera panned to him and his female co-host.

"This incident appears to be the second *questionable* police shooting in the past two weeks, Chet," the anchorwoman said. "If you remember, an unarmed Chicago teen was gunned down by police who were responding to a report of a robbery."

"Yes, Liz, at some point we need to ask the question if we are doing enough to prevent these types of senseless murders. Next up, our meteorologist, Tom Beatty, will let us know if we are going to need the umbrella this weekend."

"Well isn't that an interesting turn of events," Tatiana said, turning off the television.

"Why?" Susan asked.

"It looks like you screwed her over pretty good by picking up that gun."

"Sucks to be her, I guess."

"Yes, but it is also something we can exploit."

"What do you mean?"

"I mean that an unarmed target is a lot more attractive than an armed one."

"Dear God, Tatiana, you can't be serious."

"Why not? She's not immortal."

"She's a cop," Susan protested, "she's not like our usual marks."

"Granted, there is a bit of a risk," Tatiana replied, "but it's not something we can't overcome."

"I don't believe this."

"I thought you said you wanted to go after her?"

"And I thought you were the one that questioned me if it was wise," Susan replied.

"I did," Tatiana said, "but what's life without a little risk? I mean it isn't like we haven't gotten our hands dirty before."

"But this is different, Tee. She's a cop."

"Not anymore she isn't," Tatiana replied. "She killed a kid and, thanks to you, no one is ever going to find that gun. Face it, she's never going to carry a badge again. Hell, she'll be lucky if they don't put her ass away in prison."

"You think they will?" Susan asked.

"They might. Things seem to be decidedly anti-police these days. If a grand jury indicts her they might easily move forward with a manslaughter case."

"Damn," Susan exclaimed, as she considered the cops potential fate.

"Yeah, that's going to be fucked up," Tatiana mused. "Imagine going to jail for something you're innocent of, huh? Oh well, it's not like that shit never happens, right?"

Susan sat on the couch, staring at the blank television screen, a mixture of emotions competing for her attention. There was a part of her that enjoyed playing this game with the cop, but she never actually intended for it to ever get to this level and that struck her as a bit odd.

How many innocent people had her and Tee killed? she wondered.

Dozens and she'd never felt any remorse over any of them.

She admitted that in the beginning it was personal for her. She'd targeted people who'd personally hurt her, like her parents, Lou Jenkins, that little cock whore Paige Wilson. Once she had settled up old scores with her past, the majority of her later *victims* were just perverts, older men or women, who had a thing for young girls. She'd pick them up and give them a taste of what they wanted. Then Tee would come in to ship them off to the afterlife, but when it came to Tatiana's chosen victims, she was a bit different and there didn't seem to be any rhyme or reason. Tee had shared with her, early on, that she had also targeted people who'd hurt her, but lately it seemed she'd go after people who just wore the wrong colored shirt to the bar. She just seemed to enjoy the act of killing.

"It's a tough thing," Tatiana mused.

"What's that?" Susan replied.

"Knowing someone will spend the rest of their life behind bars because of something you did."

"I never wanted that," Susan said. "I just wanted to screw with her head a little."

"Look, I know you don't like the idea, but maybe putting her out of her misery is the more humane thing to do."

Susan thought about that.

The topic of prison was one they had both discussed at length. Neither of them was a big fan of the idea, nor did they have any illusions that they would be serving anything less than life in prison without the possibility of parole. It was one thing to actually be guilty, but she couldn't imagine how it would feel for someone who was innocent.

"What are you suggesting?" Susan asked.

"We scope things out," Tatiana said with a smile. "If it doesn't look feasible then we walk away and let karma dictate her fate."

"And if it does look feasible?"

"If it does look feasible then we do what we always do," Tatiana replied, as she brought her hand up, her fingers mimicking the shape of a gun, and fired off an imaginary bullet. "We send her off with a bang."

CHAPTER NINE

Alex laid in the darkened bedroom, staring up at the ceiling fan, and watched as it spun around methodically; its blades eerily lit up by the moonlight streaming through the window. She glanced over at the alarm clock. It was just after 2 a.m.

She had gone to bed hours earlier, mentally and physically exhausted, but she laid in her bed afraid to go sleep; wondering if her dreams tonight would be visited by Cory Childers or would Chase Akins now take his place.

When she closed her eyes she could see the young man's face, the pale skin, and the cold, lifeless eyes staring up at her. A kid, who was barely old enough to shave, was now dead because of her.

Alex got up and sat on the edge of the bed. She felt like shit and she desperately wanted a drink, but her cupboard was currently dry. She grabbed the pack of cigarettes off the night table and lit one up.

Had she really seen a gun? she wondered. *Could her mind, in its exhausted state, have played a trick on her?*

No, she knew what she had seen. Now it was up to the investigators to identify the witness who had been in the store and track them down. Maybe one of them had picked it up.

But why would anyone take a gun from a robbery and not turn it in?

It seemed that the deck had been cruelly stacked against her; missing witnesses, no video and no gun. On top of that she'd been hung out to dry for political expediency.

"You had to see that one coming," she said, taking a drag on her cigarette.

Alex was never one to back down from a fight; not when she was a kid and certainly not when she'd become a cop. An unfortunate side-effect was that she routinely knocked elbows with everyone from school officials to her superiors within the police department. However, she was also smart enough to know that if she was going to fight, not only did she need to win, but she also needed to be right.

Unfortunately, it was also this defensible *righteousness* which often led to her biggest blowouts; case in point, the Penobscot Town Board. On one hand Alex enjoyed it, especially the vociferous go-rounds with Sheldon Abbott, but on the other hand it did very little to win her friends. She used to openly mock the ass-kissers, those who acquiesced to petulant little bosses, in order to further their careers, but at the end of the day they had all kept their asses while Alex routinely had hers chewed-out or in some instances chewed-off.

Tonight she was reminded that, while she had been on the winning side of most of the battles with the board, no one was going to go out on a limb to come to her aid.

"Well you certainly showed them, didn't you, Alexandria Marie?" she said sarcastically, as she crushed the cigarette out in the ash tray.

Alex got up and headed off to the bathroom to take a shower. There was no use pretending that she was going to be able to sleep. If she was going to be an insomniac at least she was going to be productive. One of the joys of living in a quaint, rustic house in the country was that there was always shit to be done.

●●●

"Do you see anything?" Susan asked, as she sat in the back seat of the car.

"No, it's all quiet," Tatiana replied, gazing out the back window toward the darkened house through the night vision monocular.

They were in the same parking lot on Lake Moriah that Susan had taken them to a few months earlier. It was the very same lot where she had first seen Alex since the cabin incident. To quote Yogi Berra, 'It seemed like Déjà vu, all over again.'

Tatiana gazed intently through the lens, even though there was nothing to see. She loved playing the part of voyeur. Sometimes she and Susan would come up here, when the lot was filled with wayward lovers looking for a quick sexual release, just to sit and watch. It was like going to some erotic play where the actors and actresses were only a few feet away. There was something much more visceral about watching it live than seeing someone perform in an X-rated movie.

"You sure this is the right thing to do?"

"Please don't tell me you're developing a conscience at this stage of the game, darling," Tatiana replied.

"Please don't be so dismissive of my feelings, Tee," Susan said angrily.

Tatiana turned around, sitting back down, and looked at Susan.

"Believe me, I'm not," Tatiana replied. "It's just that I have never seen you so hesitant before. You're always the one jumping at the chance to have some fun."

"I know," Susan said. "That is what is so strange. I just get this really bad feeling."

"Do you trust me?"

"Of course I do, you don't even have to ask that. If I didn't trust you, Tee, I wouldn't be here."

"Then just go along with me on this one and you'll be able to sleep at night without having to worry if she is going to come looking for you."

Tatiana did have a point. This cop wasn't like the rest of them; she actually had her shit together. If it had been old Chief Parker, she could have sat down on his porch, lit a joint and flipped him the bird before he'd ever come up with the answer to 1 + 1. As far as she was concerned, the cops in Penobscot came with two speeds: slow and reverse.

But this one was different, she was a thinker. Susan had managed to stay one step ahead, but just barely. She thought about how quickly the cop had tracked her down to the apartment in Yardley. She'd barely had enough time to write the letter and split before the cops came knocking on the door. And judging from the way she lit up that fucker in the Quick Mart, if she ever did end up in her crosshairs, it was unlikely that she would miss.

Susan surmised that she might remain safe, if she stayed out of state, but as long as she continued to pop back into town, she'd never be able to relax. Tatiana was right; it was time to clear up this loose end once and for all.

"Oh shit, change of plans," Tatiana said, as she looked out the back window.

Susan turned around and saw what she was talking about. A light was now shining brightly inside the house. "Shit."

The original plan was to wait until the middle of the night, when she would be asleep, then go in and quietly pop her. Clearly that wasn't going to happen tonight.

"Now what do we do?" Susan asked.

"Now we move to Plan 'B'," Tatiana replied.

CHAPTER TEN

Maguire reached over and picked up the cell phone off the desk.

"Hey, angel, is everything alright?"

"Yeah, can't a girl call her man?" Melody Anderson said.

"You can call me anytime you want, but I thought you were heading out to D.C. this morning."

"We are, but we got delayed due to weather," she said. "Kat is waiting for things to clear up over New Jersey before we head down. So we are probably looking at around noon."

"Ah, so I'm your second choice."

"Actually, you're my third choice," she replied, "but don't take it personal."

"Why, who came before me?"

"Peter Bates," Melody replied.

"Peter Bates?" Maguire asked. "Alex's Peter?"

"Yes, he called me and asked if I would relay a message to you to call him," she said. "He said it was pretty important."

"Did he give you a number?"

"Yeah," Melody replied and read it off to him.

"He didn't say what it was about?" Maguire asked.

"No, but I have a bad feeling if he is calling here that it involves Alex."

"Yeah," he replied. "I talked to her the other day."

"Oh?" Melody asked. "Is there anything wrong?"

"No," he said, "well, nothing that I thought was major. She was talking about having problems sleeping. She said she kept having this reoccurring nightmare about the little boy that was murdered up there."

"Oh, God," Melody replied, "that's horrible. Do you think this is what it's about?"

"Don't know, could be," Maguire said. "My fear is that things might have gotten bad and she fell off the wagon."

"That won't end well."

"I'll give him a call and see what the heck is going on."

"Okay and please let me know," Melody said.

"I will."

"Love ya, cowboy."

"Love you too, angel. Have a safe trip and call me when you guys land."

"I will, bye."

Maguire ended the call and dialed the number that Melody had given him. It rang a few times and then he heard Peter's voice.

"Dr. Bates," the man said.

"Peter, its James Maguire, how are you?"

"Commissioner," the man said. "I am so sorry to bother you."

"No problem, what's going on?"

"Obviously this isn't a professional call," Peter said. "It's about Alex."

"I kind of figured as much, what's the problem?"

"Have you heard the news?"

"No," Maguire replied, "Is she alright?"

"There was a shooting here," Peter explained. "Alex interrupted a robbery at one of the stores in town. She shot and killed the perpetrator."

"When?"

"Monday," Peter replied.

"Christ, I talked to her Monday morning. Is she okay?"

"I don't know" he replied. "They placed her on leave and she's not taking my calls. I went by the house, but there was no answer; although her car is still parked in the garage."

"Don't take it personal, Peter. Alex is rather *complicated*. Sometimes she needs space to sort things out."

"I know," he replied. "That's why I reached out to you. You're the only one she seems to listen to and I was hoping you could find out what is going on with her."

"I'll call and talk to her," Maguire said. "When I know more I will let you know."

"Thank you."

"No problem."

Maguire hung up the phone and immediately dialed Alex's number.

It rang several times and he assumed it was going to go to voicemail, when she answered.

"Let me guess, Peter called you?"

"You were in a shooting and you didn't call me?" Maguire asked, his voice laced with anger. "What the hell, Alex?"

"Wow, good news travels fast," she replied. "I'm alive, he isn't, what's the issue?"

Maguire's jaw clenched tightly and he purposefully counted to ten before he responded. This was classic Alex. The worse the situation was the bigger and the more cold-hearted bitch she became.

"Do you want to tell me what happened or should I call the local news station and have them send me the video?"

"Not much to tell really," she replied. "I walked in on a stickup; he pulled a gun and I shot him."

"Is that why you were placed on leave?"

Now it was her turn to be quiet.

"Look, Alex, we can play this stupid game where you make me pry everything out of you or you can just shelve the tough-as-nails act and start talking to me."

A tense silence gripped the phone line.

"I'm screwed royally, James."

"Jesus, what happened?"

"The perp's gun took a *Brooklyn Bounce*," she said, swallowing hard. "They're insinuating that I shot an unarmed kid, but I didn't. I know what I saw."

"Are you fucking serious?"

"Yeah, I tend not to joke about things that could end up getting me indicted, rookie."

"Were there any witnesses?"

"Yeah, a bunch, but they've only been able to identify a few who were pretty much useless. One was an old woman who couldn't see clearly and the other couldn't even tell them what was going on, just that they heard a *commotion* and hid."

"What about the rest?"

"In the wind," Alex replied. "State cops are trying to track them down, but I'm not counting on it."

"Video?"

"Apparently the video age hasn't reached Penobscot yet."

"Jesus Christ," Maguire replied.

"Yeah, if I wasn't so intimidated by the thought of God laughing hysterically, I might be inclined to pray right about now."

"I'll send Monsignor O'Connor up; he'll get you straight with the big guy."

"It may be too late for me, partner," Alex replied. "You just might want to send up some lawyers, guns and money, cause it looks like the shit has hit the fan for little old me."

"Tell me exactly what happened, Alex."

"Honestly, I wasn't sharp," she said. "I walked in without looking; next thing I know I see these folks hugging the floor and the light bulb goes off. I drew my gun and heard a noise to my right. I went in that direction and saw movement. A hand came up with a gun and I fired. When I got to him I kicked the gun away and heard a noise in the back. Thought it was a second perp, but the back was empty. By the time I got back to the front the witnesses had fled and the gun was gone."

"So one of the witnesses picked it up?"

"Or I just fucked up."

"Did you?"

"I've been asking myself that question," she replied. "Penobscot isn't Brooklyn, James. I can't imagine one of the church ladies getting all *gangsta* and snatching up a hot *gat* on their way out."

"So you think you imagined it?" he asked. "Do you think the lack of sleep screwed up your head?"

"That's just it, I don't," Alex replied. "I keep playing it out over and over in my mind. I can *see* the gun, hell I even remember feeling it under my foot when I kicked it away. There isn't anything fuzzy about that."

"I believe you," Maguire said.

"You do?"

"I do."

"Well, you might be the only one," she said.

"Who's running the investigation?"

"A captain from the state police," Alex replied. "His name is Tom Blackshear."

"You know him?"

"Yeah, he's solid, but I also know he has a job to do."

"I'll reach out to him and let him know that if there is anything he needs that the NYPD will be happy to assist."

"I appreciate that, James."

"I'm also sending you up an attorney."

"That's not necessary; I don't have anything to hide."

"I don't think you do," Maguire replied, "but this isn't about hiding anything. If they don't come up with a witness who will put a gun in that kid's hand, you're gonna be screwed in a really *bad* way. You need someone to protect your rights."

Silence held the line for a moment. "Look, I'm really scared."

The admission struck Maguire hard; in part due to its simplicity and also because he couldn't recall Alex ever admitting to being scared about anything.

"Don't be," he replied. "You know I won't let anything happen to you."

Alex had never once doubted him. She had trusted him with her life a countless number of times, but this time it was different.

"Just promise me you'll send me a cake with a file in it," she said.

"You're not going anywhere that you'll need a file, Alex" He replied. "Just do me a favor and call Peter, he's worried about you."

"Yeah," she said. "I will, I just hadn't felt like talking. I was trying to sort this shit out first."

"You're not alone," Maguire said. "People care about you and you need to start opening up to them, not just me."

"I know."

"So call him and I will let you know more after I speak with Blackshear."

"I will," Alex replied, "and thanks again."

"That's what partners are for," he said. "We'll talk as soon as I know more."

Maguire ended the call and hit a button on his desk phone.

"Yes, Commissioner?" Detective Amanda Massi said, when she answered the phone.

"Amanda, have Operations reach out to the New Hampshire State Police and get in contact with a Captain Tom Blackshear. I need to speak with him."

"Yes, sir," the woman replied.

He hung up the phone and pressed another series of numbers.

"Deputy Commissioner, Legal Matters, Officer Quintana speaking, how may I help you?"

"This is Commissioner Maguire; I need to speak to Deputy Commissioner Washington."

"One moment, sir," the cop replied, placing him on hold.

A moment later he heard the phone connect.

"Yes, Commissioner, what can I do for you?"

"I need some advice, Angie," Maguire said.

"About what?" the woman asked.

"Regarding who the best criminal defense attorney there is for someone who is facing a potential homicide charge."

CHAPTER ELEVEN

Alex stared aimlessly out the bay window, clutching a cup of hot coffee in her hands, as she watched the waves breaking on the lake.

After her bout of late night cleaning, she'd taken refuge sitting on the couch. She had kept a silent vigil, watching as the night surrendered its hold to the day. Minute by minute the night sky turned from black, to deep blue and finally to brilliant streaks of pink and gold.

If only your mood could change as quickly, she thought.

Alex felt *odd*.

It was as if her mind and body were both rebelling against her. She felt sluggish and was having a hard time processing her thoughts. It was like she was pressing the gas pedal, but the car wouldn't accelerate. She knew that right now the lack of sleep was her main issue, but with everything going on she just couldn't bear the thought of having to deal with the dreams as well. Still, if she didn't get some sleep soon, they'd be hauling her ass out in an ambulance.

Alex glanced over at the cell phone on the coffee table. She knew that James was right and that she should call Peter to let him know she was okay. Yes, it would be a lie, but it was an acceptable one. It wasn't his fault that she was fucked up and he shouldn't have to pay for it.

The problem was that he would want to try and *help* her, but he couldn't. There was just too much baggage in her life and she didn't have it in her to deal with it. Twenty years ago, maybe, but now, no. Besides, it wasn't like it was going to change anything. She wasn't going to get some magical, mystical do-over that would correct all the ills in her life. It wasn't going to make her mother any less of a fucking bitch and it certainly wasn't going to restore her career back with the NYPD.

Abby's comment about seeing someone wasn't the first time that she'd gotten that advice, but she had always found an excuse not to. The bottom line was that she just didn't want to talk about it. Besides, the relief she had found in a bottle of whiskey was a helluva lot cheaper than a shrink.

Well, unless you factored in the problems that were caused by the whiskey bottle, she mused.

She picked up the cell phone and typed a message to Peter: *I'm okay, just trying to come to terms with some stuff. I'll call soon.*

Alex questioned whether she was lying to herself or lying to him. He deserved better. He deserved a girlfriend who wasn't so screwed up. Maybe that was just the way it would be. He wanted her, but she wanted Maguire, so neither of them would ever be happy.

"Screw it," Alex said, as she got up from the couch.

She walked into the kitchen and set her coffee cup on the counter. Then she grabbed the keys for her car and headed toward the door.

She knew what she needed to do.

CHAPTER TWELVE

Blackshear read through the report then leaned over and picked up the desk phone.

"Hey, Scott, this is Tom Blackshear," he said, when the call connected. "Just got some information I thought you would want to know."

"Anything good?" Nichols asked.

"Yes and no," Blackshear said. "We came up with another witness, but it doesn't really help Alex."

"Who'd you find?"

Blackshear looked at the top of the report. "Say's here the witness is a Deborah Booker, 43, of Penobscot."

"What's her story?" Nichols asked.

"She's a history teacher over at the high school," Blackshear explained. "She said she had stopped by the Quick Mart to pick-up dessert for the teacher's luncheon."

"Did she see anything?"

"Ms. Booker said that when she first walked into the store everything appeared to be fine. She saw a neighbor of hers, Eleanor Woods, who was one of the witnesses we previously spoke to and was chatting with her when they heard a loud commotion. She was about to look when an unknown man grabbed her and pulled her down to the ground. The man told her it was a robbery."

"So what we have is another witness who didn't see anything?"

"It appears that way, but at least we know that there was one other person who knew it was a robbery and might have seen something to corroborate Alex's account."

"The unknown male?"

"Yeah," Blackshear said. "I'm going to reach out to the local news stations later today and see if they can run something on the evening news."

"Why didn't she stay at the scene?"

"She said she was afraid, so when everyone ran out she did as well and she just kept going. She figured since she hadn't actually seen anything there was no reason to stick around. It wasn't until she was talking to one of her colleagues over at the school that they told her she needed to contact the police.

"Unreal," Nichols said with a laugh. "How fucking stupid can you possibly be that you don't think you should go to the police with this information?"

"More importantly, they are teaching our kids."

"Another reason why I'm not having any," Nichols replied.

"Smart man," Blackshear replied, "and one of the reasons I send mine to private school."

"So where does this leave us?"

"Not much different than where we were, but at least we have a new lead to go on."

"Do you believe her, Tom?"

"I do, Scott."

"Why?"

"Because it's the only thing that fits," he said. "Alex is right; this little shit wasn't buying a carton of milk for his mom. He isn't even a local. He's a career criminal who made it to the first round of the playoffs and lost."

"It's still a hard sell for the grand jury."

"That's your bailiwick, Scott. You asked me if I believed her, you didn't ask me if I thought it was going to be easy to prove, but we're still investigating."

"I wish I was as convinced as you."

"What reservations do you have?"

"I can't get over this missing gun," Nichols said.

"It's a tough one, but I don't think she made that up."

"But what if it wasn't a gun? What is it was something else, something she thought looked like a gun?"

"What do you mean?" Blackshear asked.

"The interior in the store was strewn with debris," Nichols said. "What if the little fucker had pointed a candy bar at her? In the flash of an eye could she have mistaken it for a gun? It wouldn't be the first time some idiot was shot for pointing something as innocuous as a wallet."

"If you're that stupid...."

"That's what I mean, Tom. What if it was something as dumb as a candy bar with a silver wrapper and we can't find it because it was lying with the rest of the merchandise. We may have seen it, but we just passed over it because it belonged there."

"It's an interesting theory," Blackshear replied, "but it's just a theory."

"And until we find a gun, or a witness who says they saw a gun, then Alex's story is just a story," Nichols replied. "Look, Tom, don't get me wrong. I like Alex, I really do, but that won't play out well in court."

"Then we better keep digging and hope something pops."

"Good luck," Nichols said. "You might want to do a follow-up with that witness, just in case."

"I planned on that," Blackshear replied. "I tried calling earlier, but it went to voice mail. I figured I'd give it a little bit and try again."

"Ok, keep me posted, Tom."

"I will."

Blackshear hung up the phone and stared down at the witness statement. He picked the phone up again and dialed the number listed for the witness. The phone rang several times and again went to voicemail.

"Ms. Booker, this is Captain Blackshear again. Please call me back as soon as possible. I need to follow-up on the statement you gave regarding the robbery. Thank you."

He hung the phone up.

Something has to give, he thought, as he stared at the stack of reports on his desk.

As much as he wanted to believe Alex, he also knew that Nichols was right about the possibility of mistaken id on the gun. There were numerous accounts of cops shooting people who'd pointed guns at them, only to find later that it was something as innocuous as a wallet or a cell phone.

Why anyone in their right mind would point anything at the police seemed incongruous to him, but in the heat of the moment people did dumb shit. Maybe that was the real problem, maybe they weren't in their right mind. It reminded him of criminals who pointed toy guns at the police. That took stupid to a whole different level.

The worst part was the aftermath of these shootings, when the cops were vilified for the actions of the people they had encountered. Like in Alex's case, most of these incidents were over in a matter of seconds. Cops had the unenviable position of having to decide in the blink of an eye whether that *gun* was, in reality, just a wallet, phone, candy bar or other innocent item. If they made the wrong call someone was likely to end up dead, either themselves or the person pointing the item.

As many stories there were of cops shooting these unarmed individuals, there were many more where cops didn't, hesitating for that one split second longer, that ultimately led to their deaths.

Damned if you do, dead if you don't, he thought.

His musings were interrupted by a knock on the door.

Blackshear looked up to see a uniformed trooper standing in the threshold.

"Sorry to bother you, Captain, but there is a call on line four," the trooper said. "It's the NYPD."

"NYPD?" Blackshear asked.

"Yeah, it seems their police commissioner wants to speak to you."

"You're shitting me?"

"No, sir," the trooper replied.

"Thank you," Blackshear said, as he reached over, picking up the phone and hit the button for line four.

"Captain Blackshear," he said cautiously.

"Sir, this is Sergeant Mulligan, please hold for the police commissioner."

Blackshear waited for the call to be transferred.

"Captain Blackshear, I hope I'm not bothering you," Maguire said when he got on the line.

"No, sir, what can I do for you?"

"Actually, I was calling to see if there was anything I could do for you," Maguire replied. "I know you're handling Alex Taylor's investigation."

"Yes, sir, I am," Blackshear replied. "Do you know the chief?"

"Alex and I were partners years ago."

"Are you aware of the details?"

"I found out this morning," Maguire replied, "and just for the record Alex did not ask me to call you. In fact, she said that she has the utmost confidence in you and your agency, but I also know how tough things can be in terms of manpower and resources, so if there is anything we can assist you with, please let me know."

"Thank you, sir, that is very much appreciated," Blackshear replied. "Do you mind if I ask you a question?"

"Sure, shoot."

"You said you were partners with Alex. How would you describe her as a cop?"

"She can be moody and cantankerous at times, that's especially true when she is right, but she is a solid cop."

"It's a little bit different down in New York City than the way it is up here," Blackshear replied. "We don't have nearly the workload, so it is hard to figure out how someone handles things when the shit hits the fan."

"I'll save you the traditional dance routine, Tom," Maguire said with a laugh. "I don't believe in beating around the bush so I guess it is safe to assume you are trying to find a gentle way of asking if she could have screwed up, the short answer is yes. I'd be lying if I said otherwise, because the reality is that none of us are immune from making mistakes. However, that being said, I wouldn't bet on it. Alex, for all her faults, does know her shit. In all the time I worked with her I never saw her screw something up based solely on a reflexive response. Alex has good intuition. She is also extremely effective at reading situations and people."

"That's what I was looking for, sir. Thank you. It's kind of refreshing to get a straightforward answer in this line of work."

"My old boss in the Navy wasn't a big fan of beating around the bush."

"You were in the Navy?"

"Yep, a lifetime ago," Maguire replied.

"No shit," Blackshear said. "I'm a plank owner of the *Big Stick*."

Maguire knew the *Big Stick* well. It was the nickname of the U.S.S. Theodore Roosevelt, CVN-71; a Nimitz-class aircraft carrier. A plank owner was an old Navy term that meant that Blackshear had been aboard the ship when it was commissioned back in 1984.

"Really, I used that taxi service a few times," Maguire said. "The mess deck was pretty damn good. When did you get out?"

"Ninety-One, after we shipped back to *No-Fuck, Vagina* following the first Gulf War. I was a *grape* and got tired of humping *go-juice* for the fighter jocks, so when I came back home I took the test for the state police. I've been here ever since."

"I was just coming in when you were getting out."

"What adventure story did your recruiter tell you?"

"Oh, the usual, join the Navy, see the world, meet interesting people, etc."

"How'd that work out for you?"

"It was working out pretty good till I got *blowed up*," Maguire said with a laugh.

"No shit," Blackshear said. "What happened?"

"Humvee I was riding hit a Hajji IED.

"Sorry to hear that."

"I guess it worked out okay. I'm still here, they're not. Like you, I decided that I might try my hand at civilian work."

"Just another fine Navy day."

"Amen to that," Maguire replied. "Anyway, I thought I would make the offer. If you guys find yourself in need of anything, don't hesitate to pick-up the phone."

"Much appreciated," Blackshear said. "You have any wizards down there that can conjure up missing guns?"

"No, but I have known a few of them to take a mysterious bounce. Are all the witnesses accounted for?"

"Not even close. Alex put's the count at a half dozen, possibly more. So far we have located and identified three. We were trying not to sound desperate, but at this point it looks as if we are going to have to go to the media and ask for people to come forward."

"Then there is still hope," Maguire replied.

"I'm going to channel your optimism."

"Sometimes it's the only card you have to play."

Just then the trooper reappeared in the doorway. "Captain, line three, a Ms. Booker for you."

"Hey, Commissioner, I hate to cut you short, but you might have brought me luck, that's one of my witnesses calling."

"Go," Maguire said. "Call me if you need anything."

"Will do and thank you."

Blackshear ended the call and hit the blinking button.

"Ms. Booker, this is Captain Blackshear, thank you for calling me back."

"I'm sorry I wasn't available to take your call earlier," the woman replied. "I had to substitute for one of our teachers who called in sick."

"No problem," he replied. "I just wanted to go over the statement that you gave regarding the robbery."

"Oh, it was so dreadful," the woman said. "I'm still having nightmares about it."

"I'm sorry to hear that," Blackshear replied. "I know these events can be very traumatic, which is why I wanted to speak with you. I know sometimes little details come back that might have been missed earlier."

"It all happened so fast," she replied. "One minute I was on the floor and the next there was shooting. A moment later I was running for my life."

"Actually, I'm interested in that period of time before the shooting. I was wondering if you might be able to walk me through the events that happened just before it."

"Well, like I explained to the nice officer, I had stopped at the store to pick-up some food for our luncheon at the school."

"Did you notice anything unusual before you walked in?"

"No," she said. "Everything appeared to be quite normal."

"What about when you went into the store?"

"I really wasn't paying much attention," Booker replied. "I guess you'd say I wasn't very observant."

"Was there anyone in the store you recognized?"

"Oh yes, Eleanor Woods, she's a neighbor of mine. We were talking when it happened."

"Where were you in the store?" Blackshear asked.

"Oh, on the left side; over by the bread aisle."

"Do you know how long you talked for?"

"Oh it was probably not more than a minute, maybe two at the most."

"Did you see anyone else in the store?"

"Yes, there were a few others, some in different aisles, but I really wasn't paying much attention."

"So when did you first know what was going on?"

"Well, we heard this commotion up near the front. I was about to go and take a look when some man came around the corner. He told me it was a robbery and told us to get down. So we hid behind one of the displays."

"Did he say why he thought it as a robbery?"

"No and there really was no time to ask. A moment after that is when I think Chief Taylor walked in. How is she doing? The poor thing must be going through a very tough time."

"She's doing as well as can be expected."

"I imagine that has to be hard on a person, even when you think you are doing the right thing."

"Police work is never easy," Blackshear replied. "And you had never seen this man before?"

"No, like I told the officer he was younger than me, but he wasn't a kid. He had that look of real fear, so I just did what he told me."

"So you never actually saw the suspect, correct?"

"No," she replied. "It seems us old people live in our own little bubble most of the time."

"So besides Ms. Woods, you didn't actually recognize anyone else in the store."

"I'm afraid no. I wish I could be more help."

"No, you have been very helpful."

"Wait a minute. There was one other person I do recall seeing."

"Really? Do you remember who it was?"

"No, I actually don't, but she was a young girl, with blonde hair, and I remember thinking that she looked vaguely familiar. I guess that's the teacher in me."

"Could it have been a student of yours?" Blackshear asked, as he made notes on a pad.

"Oh, I don't know," Booker replied. "Like I said, she looked familiar in that brief moment I saw her, but I couldn't recall where I had seen her."

"If you had to guess how old the girl looked, could you give me an idea?"

"Oh, young, maybe late teens, early twenties at the most," she replied. "Like I said though, I only saw her for the briefest of moments.

"Can you describe her?"

"Probably not enough to help you," she said. "She wasn't that close. Blonde hair, cut short, with a tee shirt and jeans. What you would call your typical young girl fashion."

"How long have you been teaching at the school?" Blackshear asked.

"September will be my twentieth anniversary."

"Okay, well if you can think of anything else, please don't hesitate to call me. Even the most inconsequential thing could prove very useful to us."

"I will," she replied.

"Have a good day, Ms. Booker."

"You too, Captain."

Blackshear hung up the phone, looking down at the notepad. It might be a wild goose chase, but Penobscot wasn't that big of a town. He reached over and picked up the phone.

"Penobscot Police Department, Officer Simpson speaking."

"Abby, it's Captain Blackshear, how are you?"

"Doing well, sir," she replied. "Any progress?"

"Not much, but I have something I was hoping you guys might be able to follow up on."

"Sure, what do you need?"

"One of the witnesses is a teacher over at the high school, a Ms. Booker, do you know her?"

"She was my history teacher years ago, why?"

"I just got off the phone with her and she recalled seeing another person in the store at the time of the robbery," Blackshear explained. "A young girl who she thought looked familiar."

"You think it might have been a former student?"

"The thought crossed my mind," he replied. "I was wondering if one of you guys could go over and talk to her, maybe look through some old yearbooks. She said she was in her late teens or early twenties, so it's a small window. Besides, she might be more inclined to be chatty with a familiar face as opposed to a *just-the-facts* trooper."

"Sure thing," Abby replied. "I'll get someone over there right away."

"It might be nothing," he said, "but at this point I'm willing to roll the dice and hope something comes up."

"When you have nothing, you have nothing to lose by trying," Abby said. "I'll call you back and let you know how we did."

"Thank you."

CHAPTER THIRTEEN

Alex pulled her 2006 silver Jeep Rubicon into the parking lot and turned off the engine. She lit up a cigarette, as she stared out the window; wrestling with the emotions that had haunted her since the shooting.

How many times had she been here? she wondered. *How many times had she been left to wrestle with her inner demons all alone?*

It never seemed fair.

Most folks had someone they could reach out to; someone they could depend on to be there for them, when things in their life got out of control. Ironically, as a cop, she had spent most of her adult life being there for someone else. She was the one that the despondent turned to; when everyone else had abandoned them. She was the one that answered the last phone call they made, their last cry for help, before their fatal plunge into the abyss. She'd comforted them, wiped the tears from their cheeks, brought them back to life and sadly, in some cases, held them as their lives came to an end; so that in their final moments they were not alone. And she carried all of those memories tucked neatly away inside her.

The worst part was that, for so many cops like her, there was no 911 for them to call. Cops were supposed to be tough, they were expected to have all the answers, but they were also not immune to the problems that everyone else faced. Sadly, too many felt that admitting they had problems was a sign of weakness; it was their kryptonite. The thought of having their guns removed and being placed on a medical leave for psychological issues was repugnant to them. It was also a stigma that never went away. No one wanted to be labeled as the one who couldn't hack it, so many of them fought their demons in quiet solitude until they could simply no longer fight. Then, like the disconsolate civilian who feared dying alone, many of them would make their way to the one place they found safe, the police station. Whether it was in the locker room or their patrol car, they knew they would be found by a brother or a sister who would understand. If you asked, most cops could recall someone they knew who had killed themselves.

Alex recalled an admonition, from the 19th century German philosopher, Friedrich Nietzsche, which hung on one of the locker room doors like a warning. It read: *Beware that, when fighting monsters, you yourself do not become a monster... for when you gaze long into the abyss. The abyss gazes also into you.*

How long had she been staring into that abyss?

She wanted someone to turn to, but she didn't have anyone.

Yes, it was true that she had James, but the very thought of unloading anymore of her baggage on him repulsed her. Besides, he already knew too much; had already bailed her ass out on occasions too numerous to count. Deep inside her she held onto the notion that maybe, one day, they might have something more and she wasn't going to ruin that chance with a confession that confirmed that she was fucked up more than he might already believe.

Peter was another story altogether. He was kind, caring, handsome and a very successful doctor. He was everything a woman could want and more. Maybe things would be different if she was a civilian, but she wasn't. As nice as Peter was, and as much as he cared for her, he still couldn't understand what she had seen and what she had gone through. The reality was, she was a warrior and he was one of the people that she protected. How could he ever possibly be able to relate to what she had faced in her life? It was a dynamic that was complicated even further by the fact that she was a woman.

When they went out to dinner she was always scanning the room, watching the doors. Half the time she'd make him switch seats with her, just so she could watch the front door. Often his conversations went unheard because something about another customer didn't *feel right*. He would be rambling about something that happened at the office and she'd be looking for signs of weapons, any potential innocents in her line of fire, and where the exits were situated. She wished she could be like him, like all the rest of them. They had the luxury of going through life with blinders on, unaffected by the chaos around them, but she didn't have an *off* switch. There was no button to push when you clocked off at the end of the shift that turned you from cop to civilian.

Alex knew that she needed help to get through this. She could put it off, continuing to try and fight it on her own, but she knew that she would only be prolonging the inevitable. She took a final drag on her cigarette, got out of the car, and walked toward the building.

From the moment she stepped inside, she felt as if everyone's eyes were on her, following her. They all knew who she was; which made it even harder. She could feel her face begin to flush and it seemed like the heat had suddenly been cranked up to a hundred and ten degrees.

This is such a bad friggin' idea, she thought, as she smiled, putting on a brave face.

It only took a moment to find what she needed.

She reached down, grabbing the one liter bottle of Jack Daniels from the shelf and quickly headed back upfront toward the register. Along the way she grabbed a 2 liter bottle of Coke. In her mind she figured that adding a mixer made it look slightly less bad than the idea she was drinking it straight.

"Will that be all, chief?" the young man working the cash register asked, as he placed the bottles into a brown paper bag.

The *chief* part probably wasn't a dig, but at the moment it certainly felt that way.

"Yeah, give me a carton of Marlboro reds," she said. "I've got a party to go to and it's a long drive."

She wasn't sure why she added that part in at the last minute, but it sounded good.

That's the guilt speaking, asshole, the voice inside her head said admonishingly. *Because God forbid that the guy who sells you your alcohol thinks that you're a lush.*

"Sure thing," the man said, as he reached around, grabbing the carton of cigarettes, and then rang up her order.

Alex paid the man and picked up bag.

"Take care, chief."

"You too," Alex replied, as she headed toward the door.

Outside, the cool spring air was a welcome respite from the heat of the liquor store. She felt herself begin to calm down, as she made her way to the Jeep. Alex set the package down on the seat next to her and pulled out of the parking lot.

One day she would have to seek out a professional to help her confront the demons, but now wasn't the time. She had no illusions that an appearance at a psychologist's office, even with all the patient / doctor confidentiality bullshit, would eventually make it to Nichols' office or worse to the attorney representing the perp's family in the inevitable civil rights violation law suit that was bound to follow. Folks wouldn't bat an eyelash if their little Johnny got whacked on the street corner by another thug, but let a cop shoot them and they all acted like they just hit a royal flush in a Vegas poker tournament.

So for now, her trusted confidant would be the incomparable Doc Daniels from Tennessee, who always made house calls.

She pulled up to a red traffic light and glanced over at the bag. It was silly, but just having it so close made her want to take a sip.

Jesus, you do have a problem, she thought.

She turned away quickly and stared up at the light impatiently.

This was the part of the job they never warned you about; the Monday morning quarterbacking that happened after an incident like this. Where the life and death decision, that you made in the blink of an eye, was examined under a microscope for weeks and months afterwards, as they looked for the one mistake, the one petty violation, on which to hang you.

Well, if they warned you about it, idiot, no one would ever take the job.

She thought back to her junior year in high school, where she had briefly flirted with the idea of being a marine biologist. The thought of scuba diving in the crystal clear waters of the Aegean Islands seemed a pretty epic way of making a living. That was until she watched a documentary about a marine biologist who had been attacked by a great white shark off the coast of South Africa. The idea of being chowed down for lunch, by a beast more than 3x her size, made the potential career choice seem very unappealing. Actually, it wasn't the idea of being killed it was the thought of losing some important body parts and living to tell about it that quickly killed that idea.

In retrospect, it might have been safer in the water, she thought, as she considered her current predicament.

Whoop, Whoop.

The noise startled Alex and she physically jumped in her seat. She turned to her left and saw Abby sitting in her patrol car.

"Wow, you were zoned out."

"You scared the shit out me," Alex said.

"So what are you going to do, write me up?" Abby said with a laugh.

"Is this what you do when I'm gone? Harass the poor innocent civilians in Penobscot?"

"Oh please spare me," Abby replied. "You're not so innocent."

"Speak for yourself."

"Pull over, before I get some pain in the ass who actually will complain about me."

Alex steered the jeep over to the curb and watched as Abby came to a stop behind her.

Is this how it feels to get pulled over? she wondered.

She had to admit that it was a particularly unnerving experience, as she watched Abby get out of her patrol car and walk toward her.

"So how are you doing?"

"I've been better," Alex replied, "but I've also been worse. So I guess that means I'm batting a solid .500 average."

"I don't even know how you can keep a sense of humor with everything that's going on," Abby said. "You're a better woman than me. I'd be at home, curled up in a corner."

"Oh cut the crap," Alex said. "You'd do what you have to do, we all do. It's just part of the game."

"If you say so," Abby replied.

"So how are things going in the office?" Alex asked.

"I don't know," she replied. "Hutch might be curled up in a corner of your office. I don't think he is adapting to his new role very well."

"What the heck? It's only been two days."

"I think Sheldon Abbott has been pushing his buttons," Abby replied.

"Sheldon can't help himself. It's all part of the little game of *who has the biggest balls* that he likes to play; especially with folks he thinks might be weaker than him."

"Yeah, but Hutch doesn't have your knack for playing the game or, to be honest, your balls."

"Well he and you better grow them quick," Alex replied. "I won't be around forever. Hell, I might not last till the end of the month."

"Hush your mouth," Abby replied. "This shit will all get squared away soon."

Alex rolled her eyes. It was a nice sentiment, but it was naïve.

"I'll call him and give him a little pep talk."

"I think he would appreciate that. It also doesn't help that we still have a bunch of state guys running around."

"Oh yeah, how's that going?"

Abby looked around conspiratorially, as if making sure no one was around that could hear her, and then back at Alex.

"There nice enough, but mostly they keep to themselves," Abby replied. "Hutch had a meeting with them and told us to help them with whatever they need, but not to ask any questions directly related to the case."

That made sense, she thought. They were still the lead investigating agency and the local cops were still her people. It was always best, from an investigative standpoint, to keep that wall between the two.

"Oh, but I actually did hear them talking about a possible witness."

"Really?" Alex asked, perking up a bit. "They interview her?"

"Not sure, like I said they kind of keep to themselves."

"Well, if you do hear anything let me know," Alex said, "but don't do anything that's gonna get you in trouble,"

"I will and I won't," Abby replied. "Hey, why don't I stop by on Saturday? I'll bring a chick flick and some popcorn."

"Make it an action flick, along with some Chinese take-out, and you have yourself a deal."

"Sounds like a plan."

"Stay safe, Abby."

"You too, Chief."

Alex watched the woman walk back to her patrol car and hook a U-turn. She started the Jeep back up and pulled away from the curb. She had two good days of drinking ahead of her before she'd have to entertain anyone.

CHAPTER FOURTEEN

"Hello, Earth to Tom," Jacqueline Blackshear said to her husband across the dinner table.

"Hmmm?" Blackshear replied, a confused look on his face. "Did you say something, Jackie?"

"No, you just agreed to pay for me and Lisa to go on an all-expense paid shopping spree vacation to Manhattan."

"I did what?" he replied, a look of panic spreading on his face, as the image of his wife and daughter on 5th Avenue played in his mind.

"Take it easy, there Tommy-Boy," she said with a laugh. "I was just messing with you. You haven't said more than two sentences the entire dinner."

"You damn near gave me a heart attack," Blackshear replied.

"Well, I certainly don't want to cause that."

"Why?" Blackshear asked. "Is it because you love me so much?"

"No, it's because we need to finish paying off Lisa's college, silly."

"How romantic," he said.

"But seriously, where the hell is my husband's mind?" Jackie asked.

"Trying to make heads or tails of this shooting in Penobscot."

"Oh, I take it that things aren't going so well?"

"It's going well if you're looking to build a case for a homicide prosecution."

"Well that's not good."

"No, it's not," he replied. "The problem for me is that I honestly believe she saw what she saw, but I just can't get anyone to corroborate it."

"I thought it was a robbery?"

"Theoretically it was," he replied. "The only problem is that, while all the witnesses claim *something* was happening, I still have no one that can corroborate that a gun was involved."

"So what's going to happen to that poor cop?"

"Kid's family is already pressuring the state's attorney to pursue charges," he replied. "They just hired some hot-shot attorney from New York who's been making the rounds at the television stations claiming we are covering things up."

"What is the state's attorney going to do?"

"His job," Blackshear replied, a frown on appearing on his face. "They're empaneling a grand jury to look into it."

"But you believe her? You think she saw a gun?"

"Yeah, I do."

"Will you have to testify?"

"Most likely," he replied.

"How does that work?" she asked. "If you believe her story can you say that?"

"No," he said. "I'm going to be asked specific questions based on the investigation and I have to testify to the facts, not my feelings."

"Well, your opinion should count for something," his wife replied. "You have certainly been doing this long enough."

"The only thing that counts is whether you can prove it or not."

"I wonder how many guilty people go free because of that."

"You don't even want to know," he replied.

"I don't envy you," she said, as she got up and picked up the dinner plates from the table.

"I don't envy me."

"You want another glass of wine?"

"I would love another glass of wine," he answered.

"Go relax and I'll bring you one."

"Bring it to my office, please," he replied. "I've got a bunch of reports I have to finish reviewing."

Blackshear got up and headed off to his office. He sat down behind a large mahogany desk and began going through the most recent reports that had come in from the Penobscot investigation. A moment later his wife entered the room and placed the wine glass onto the desk.

"For the record, I'm going to submit a bill to the state police for all the lost time I have endured since you've been with them," she said.

"Good luck with that," he replied sarcastically. "The way the state is racking up debt they'll be lucky if they can afford to pay the electricity bill this month."

"I thought things were getting better?"

"They were," he said, "and then they went on a spending spree to celebrate their success."

"If I ran our household like this they'd throw me in jail."

"Just wait a few years and they'll just have you do home confinement because they won't be able to afford to keep the jails open."

"I was actually hoping to get a break from cooking and cleaning."

"You'd never survive the dress code," he said with a laugh.

"Are you kidding me?" Jackie said, putting her hands on her hips. "I make everything look good and don't you forget it, mister."

Blackshear eyed the sensual curves of his wife's very attractive body. If anyone could pull off making correctional orange look good it would be her.

"You certainly do, my dear."

"You're a very smart man," she replied. "I'm going to finish the dishes and go take a nice warm bath. Lisa doesn't get off work until nine, so if you want to get lucky don't play detective for too long."

"I thought you liked playing cops and robbers," he said with a knowing look.

"I do," she smiled seductively, "but we don't have time for the handcuffs so just bring your nightstick, big boy."

Blackshear laughed, as he watched his wife slip out of the room, her hips swaying back and forth seductively, while whistling the theme song from the show COPS.

He leaned back in his chair and rubbed at his eyes. His job was generally tough enough, but this case was being particularly brutal. Under normal circumstances he would have let his people run with the ball; however this was anything but normal. For one thing, he felt as if he had the fate of another cop in his hands and if he failed at his job then she just might end up being the one wearing the correctional orange.

"No pressure," he mumbled to himself, as he put on his reading glasses and perused the latest report.

An hour's worth of reading later he was no better off then when he had first started. He looked down at his watch. He still had another hour and a half until his daughter came home. That was more than enough time to take his wife up on her offer. He closed the folder and turned off the desk lamp.

Just as Blackshear stood up he heard the cell phone vibrate. He glanced down and read the display: Troop E.

You've got to be shitting me, he thought, as he hit the button and accepted the call. "Blackshear."

"Captain, this is Trooper McCormick over in Troop E. I'm sorry to bother you while you're off-duty, sir."

"It's okay," Blackshear lied. "What's going on?"

"I just got a call from Trooper Miles Kennedy. He's processing an arrest for felony possession and he said that he might have some information regarding your shooting in Penobscot."

Blackshear sat back down in his seat. "You have a number for him?"

"I do, are you ready to copy."

"Let me just grab a pen," he said, as he rifled through the desk drawer. "Okay, go."

Blackshear wrote down the number the trooper supplied him, thanked the man and then quickly called it.

"Trooper Kennedy," the man said when he answered the phone.

"Kennedy, this is Captain Blackshear from Major Crimes. I was told you might have something related to the shooting in Penobscot?"

"Yes, sir," Kennedy replied. "I stopped a 19-year-old kid named Floyd Peters for speeding just outside Ossipee. He was doing 71 in 35. During the stop he was being very evasive. He's from up around Dummer, but he couldn't say exactly why he was down here. He was acting really squirrely so I had a K9 unit come over and sure enough the dog hit on the car. I got him for a gram of cocaine along with some marijuana inside the center console."

"Nice arrest, but what does that have to with my shooting?" Blackshear asked.

"Well, we impounded the car and when we were inventorying it we found ten packets that tested for heroin," Kennedy said. "Once we told him we were hitting him with an *intent to distribute* charge he started talking about how he wanted to make a deal. He said he might know something about what happened up there."

"He has information on the shooting?"

"That's what he is claiming, sir," Kennedy replied. "It's his second narcotics arrest and the intent charge is going to have him looking at serious time. The state's attorney up here is coming up for re-election and he is coming down heavy on all drug arrests."

Blackshear leaned back in the chair and took a deep breath.

"Do we know if he has a lawyer?"

"He said he does," Kennedy replied. "He gave me the name George Reid, but it's late and I haven't been able to corroborate that."

"Where was that first drug arrest?"

"Up in Coos County."

"Okay, listen I don't want you asking him any questions about Penobscot," Blackshear said. "In fact, I don't want you to ask him anything. Just process the paperwork and wait to hear back from me. I'm going to reach out to the state's attorney and find out what the story is."

"Will do, sir."

Blackshear ended the call and immediately dialed the number for Scott Nichols. He listened as it rang several times.

Am I the only one that doesn't have a life? he wondered.

He was waiting for the call to go to voice mail, when he suddenly heard it connect.

"Nichols," the man said quietly.

"Scott, it's Tom Blackshear, can you hear me?"

"Yeah," he said, his voice still coming through quietly.

"Where the hell are you?"

"My daughter's recital, this better be important."

"Get to somewhere you can talk."

"Seriously?"

"Seriously," Blackshear said. "Call me back quick."

Blackshear ended the call and set the phone on the desk. He drummed his fingers on the desk top, as his mind tried valiantly not to guess at what information the kid might have.

"Did you forget something?"

Blackshear looked up to see his wife standing in the doorway wearing a white robe and a towel wrapped around her long brown hair.

"Oh, God, I'm so sorry."

"I'd almost be happier if it were another woman instead of this damn job," Jackie said. "At least I could get the satisfaction of kicking her ass."

"I know," he replied sheepishly, "but I just got a call from a guy down in Troop E. He arrested a guy that might have information about the shooting. I'm just waiting for the state's attorney to call me back."

"Hmmm, is that what it takes?" she said, as she walked over and sat down on the edge of the desk facing her husband.

He watched as she opened her robe just enough to expose the upper part of her breasts to him.

"Well, maybe I have some information that I'm willing to share with you," she said coyly.

"Oh really?" he replied, pulling on the edge of the robe playfully. "And what might you be holding out on me?"

Jackie tugged on the material, pulling it free from his grasp, an evil little smile emerging on her face.

"Tsk, tsk, tsk, *Mr. Detective*," she said with an admonishing tone. "I'm not that easy."

Blackshear reached out, grabbing his wife by the hips and pulled her onto his lap, as she squealed gleefully.

"No, stop," she said in mock protest. "I'm not that kind of girl."

"Oh yeah, what about that time...."

"You shut your mouth, Thomas Blackshear," Jackie said, as she placed her hand against her husband's lips, muffling the remainder of his comment.

"But baby, I was just going to say..."

"Oh, I know *exactly* what you were going to say, mister."

Just then their playful moment was interrupted by the vibration of the cell phone on his desk.

"Aww, too bad," she said with a pouty smile. "Duty calls."

Just before she got up, she playfully rubbed her bottom against his lap.

"Tease," he replied, as he reached for the phone. "I'll be up soon."

"Oh, you just take your time, darling," Jackie said, as she paused in the door, looking back at him, "You don't have to worry about me. I have something upstairs that vibrates too."

Blackshear rolled his eyes as he answered the call. "Scott?"

"This had better be good, Tom," the man said. "You have no idea how much shit I am about to get from my wife."

"Yeah, well I might argue that point," Blackshear replied, "but, more importantly, we might have a break on the shooting."

"You're kidding me?"

"No, I just got off the phone with a trooper down in Carroll County. He arrested a guy with felony weight and tagged him with an *intent to distribute* charge. Kid's a two time loser and he knows that the state's attorney down there is most likely going to drop the hammer on him so he wants to cut a deal."

"Do we know what he has to say?" Nichols asked.

"Not yet," Blackshear replied. "Trooper says the kid told him he had an attorney, some guy named George Reid, so I told him not to ask any questions because I didn't want to jeopardize anything. I don't know who the attorney is, but the kid's old arrest was in your jurisdiction, so I figured you might know him."

"I know George," Nichols replied. "He's a bit of an ambulance chaser, and I question his morals at times, but he has some decent litigating skills. What's the kid's name?"

"Floyd Peters."

"You've got to be shitting me," Nichols replied. "Not that little shit bird."

"I take it you know him?"

"Yeah, he's a piece of redneck trash," Nichols responded. "He's been causing problems since his mother kicked him off her tit to raise up the next societal misfit she'd given birth to."

"Sounds like a lovely family," Blackshear said.

"You don't know the half of it. His brood actually gives rednecks a bad name. They're original from just over the border in Maine, but apparently mom and dad Peters had to relocate rather quickly because they were bouncing checks all over the place. The town there was ready to string them all up."

"How come no one put them behind bars?"

"I tried, at least with Floyd," Nichols lamented. "When he turned eighteen I caught him on that drug charge. I wanted to hit him with some time, based on his juvenile record, but the judge bought into the kid's BS story and just gave him probation."

"Well, he's certainly nervous about something because he's looking to talk."

"He's nervous because his ass graduated to the big leagues and now he's afraid he's going to actually have to do time with a second drug charge."

"The real question is will his attorney let him?"

"No, the real question is what does he know?" Nichols replied. "I'm betting if it is something good George will be more than happy to have a chat with us to discuss a reduction in charges."

"When do you think we will know?"

"I'll call him, but I know he's going to want to talk to his client first. But before I do that I want to reach out to Paul Mitchell, the state's attorney down in Carroll. I'll explain what we have going and make sure he is willing to work with us on this."

"You think he'll push back?" Blackshear asked.

"I'd like to say no," Nichols replied, "but he's got himself in a tough race down there. His opponent has a solid family name and some serious financial backing. He's been beating up Paul on his record so Paul has been pushing for heavier sentences."

"Yeah, but this is a police involved shooting," Blackshear countered. "Surely that has to carry a bit more weight."

"You would think, but it's not that simple. You see Mitchell has a bit of a checkered past when it comes to law enforcement."

"How so?"

"Let's just say that when he was in private practice he had a run in that almost cost him his career. Ever since then he has been a tad bit *anti-cop.*"

"You're fucking kidding me."

"I wish I was, but it is what it is. I think he takes a bit of enjoyment in running roughshod over the cops down there."

"Great, so we are fighting a defense attorney as well as a prosecutor."

"Mitchell is a political animal," Nichols replied. "I'll try and appeal to that side of him. See if I can get him to work with us."

"And if that fails?" Blackshear asked.

"Let's hope it doesn't, because I don't exactly have a Plan 'B'."

"I hate small town politics."

"Don't we all?"

CHAPTER FIFTEEN

Alex took a drag on her cigarette, listening to the sound of the kitchen clock ticking in the background, as she sat at the island and stared at the bottle of whiskey.

In front of her, the growing stack of cigarette butts in the ashtray bore silent witness to the epic struggle that was going on inside her mind. She had been resolutely staring at the bottle since she had first come home; fighting the demons that beckoned her to crack open the top.

Goddamnit, you're stronger than this, she chided herself, as she crushed the cigarette out in the ash tray.

What does strength have to do with it? a voice inside her asked.

Alex wrestled with the question.

What did being strong have to do with anything?

With everything she had been through in her life, both personally and professionally, she knew she was strong. This had nothing to do with strength and everything to do with desire.

So what was so terribly wrong with desiring something?

After all, everyone desired something. Some people desired wealth while others desired power. Some women desired the bad boy while others wanted a respectable man. Some folks desired a good meal while others wanted junk food.

Wasn't that what made life enjoyable? she wondered. *Why did it have to be wrong to desire something?*

Alex grabbed the pack of cigarettes and lit up another.

"You're rationalizing it," she said, as she took a drag. "It's a bottle of whiskey, not a fucking bullet to the head."

In a remarkable display of mental fortitude, she put the bottle away and poured herself a coke instead.

CHAPTER SIXTEEN

Tom Blackshear and Scott Nichols sat on the other side of a large wooden conference table staring back at George Reid, while the man professed the innocence of his client.

"George, please stop," Nichols said, halting the man's monologue. "I honestly don't give a rat's ass about whether or not your client is innocent or guilty, although I am inclined to believe the former over the latter. Your client was the one who said he had information on the shooting, so my question is, does he?"

"Yes," Reid replied. "He has information that he will gladly provide if and when the state's attorney in Carroll agrees to a lenient plea deal."

"C'mon, you know that's not how this works. If I go to the state's attorney with that he's going to laugh me out of his office and rightfully so. I'd do the same thing to him if the roles were reversed."

"It's not my job to sell this to the state's attorney," Reid replied. "You want information; my client has that information, so now you get to convince Paul Mitchell that it would be in the best interests of your investigation to cooperate."

Blackshear shook his head, fighting the urge to laugh. The argument Reid was making bordered on insanity.

"George, that's like asking us to buy a car without even knowing if it runs. You're going to have to bring a little more to the table than that wishy-washy bullshit."

"Look, Scott, for the record, I'm not saying that my client was there at the time of the shooting, but I am saying that he has firsthand knowledge of what went on inside that store just prior to and including the shooting."

"And he is willing to make a statement about that and testify in court?"

"Yes, in return for a bail reduction on the current drug charge and leniency in sentencing," Reid replied, "both in Carroll as well as Coos."

"If you're looking for leniency in Coos, I take it that his appearance inside the store was not accidental?" Blackshear asked.

"He was there," Reid replied, "but I won't say anymore until I at least have a working agreement that my client will not be facing overly onerous charges."

"I'm going to tell you a story, George," Nichols said. "Please feel free to correct me at any point, if you feel as if my tale lacks any credibility."

"By all means," Reid replied.

"This is the story of little Johnny," Nichols began. "Johnny went on a trip with his good friend Billy. They'd traveled a long time when they realized that they needed to stop for food, but they had no money. So one said to the other 'I have an idea, we will just stop at a place where we can get everything that we need.' Does this sound like a plausible story so far?"

"I don't see any glaring problems, please continue."

"Well, the two men came upon a place where they could get what they needed, but to their surprise a large ogre stood in their path preventing them from getting what they needed. Billy tried to fight the ogre, but he was too strong and it struck Billy down, so Johnny fled out of fear because he knew he couldn't beat the ogre by himself."

"Quite an interesting fairy tale," Reid said. "I think it could be a best seller if offered to the right people."

"You know that I can't speak for Paul Mitchell, but I will say that if your client was in the store in Penobscot, for any potentially unlawful reasons, that I would be willing to accept a plea agreement that theoretically would not call for any jail time, providing your client agrees to give a complete written statement and testify in court."

"And what do you suggest we do about Mitchell?"

"You're going to have to give me something more to sweeten the pot with him," Nichols replied. "You and I both know your client is not so innocent. He's managed to rack up quite an extensive criminal record in the few shorts years he has been on the streets."

Nichols opened a folder and removed a computer printout, reading a litany of charges that stretched over a six year period.

"And your point is?" Reid asked. "My client is a victim. He grew up in a shitty home, was sexually abused by a relative and got hooked on drugs to cope. Besides, most of that stuff is juvenile."

"And some of it isn't, including a prior drug charge, which means he is potentially looking at some serious time in Carroll, which Mitchell will gladly pursue, so you had better give me something more substantial to work with."

Reid leaned back in the chair. He knew that he'd already won half the battle, which was a lot more than Floyd would have done on his own, and he was reasonably sure that he'd be lucky in getting the charges dropped or at least any potential jail time reduced on the Carroll County charges. He'd got them with the bait, now it was time to set the hook.

"Let's just say that, using your quaint analogy, little Johnny is willing to testify that he accompanied Billy to the place for the purpose of liberating some items and that Billy was indeed armed when they arrived."

"And he'll testify to that?" Blackshear asked, trying hard to contain his excitement.

"Yes," Reid replied. "But, Johnny will also state that he was there under duress."

"Under duress?" Nichols asked. "Oh, I can't wait to hear this part of the fairy tale."

"It turns out that Billy was little Johnny's drug supplier," Reid explained, "and Johnny owed him some money. Billy said he knew a way that he could make things even. He told him about the store and that he needed a ride. Johnny didn't want to go, but Billy forced him to."

"A drug user with a conscience, how anomalous," Nichols said.

"There's no need to be condescending, Scott, even fairy tale characters can have a tough life."

"Alight, enough with the fairy tale, make believe BS," Blackshear said. "It's making my head hurt. Can we all just agree that what we are talking about is strictly off the record for the purpose of establishing how we get from A to Z?"

The three men looked at one another and nodded.

"So if he was only the driver, why did he go inside?" Blackshear asked.

"Apparently Akins didn't trust him to stick around so he forced him to go inside with him."

"What happened to the clerk?" Nichols asked.

"He was in the backroom when they entered and Akins hit him from behind, knocking him out."

"What about the gun?" Blackshear asked.

"You want the gun, you give me a deal," Reid replied.

"What are you looking for?" Nichols asked.

"Drop the intent charge," Reid said. "Floyd isn't a seller; he was just acting as a deliveryman. He'll accept a plea deal on the possession. Like I said, Floyd is a victim here as well. Akins got him hooked on drugs in the first place and now he just wants to get help. In return for pleading guilty he is willing to accept court ordered treatment at a substance abuse facility in Manchester and probation."

"Jesus Christ, George," Nichols replied. "You don't just want the pot of gold at the end of the rainbow; you want the state to provide the transportation to the damn thing."

"Let's be honest, Scott. Without my client's testimony, he'll be out free long before your cop is."

"How the hell do you sleep at night?" Blackshear asked, his voice tinged with disgust.

"Quite well, Captain," Reid replied. "So do we have a deal?"

"Just one more thing," Nichols said. "He's also going to give up the name of who he was delivering to."

"He'll give up the name, but he won't testify in court," Reid said. "If he does, he'll never live long enough to complete the treatment program. In fact I'd prefer to get him out on bond before the wrong people find out that he is even incarcerated."

"Be realistic, George, its Friday afternoon."

"All the more reason to get this ball rolling as quickly as possible."

"I'll talk to Mitchell."

"Make it convincing, Scott," Reid said. "For everyone's sake."

CHAPTER SEVENTEEN

Alex sat on the couch, her feet propped up on the edge of the coffee table in front of her, clutching the bottle of whiskey between her thighs.

She took a drag on her cigarette, as she stared out the window, an impassive look on her face. In her mind she had put up a valiant fight. She had made it almost the entire day before she had ultimately fallen victim to her desire.

Her conscience, whom she'd long ago christened *Angel Alex, was* always the voice of reason. It was the voice that was always whispering in her ear, cautioning her about the latest ill-advised endeavor that she was preparing to undertake, and arguing for restraint. Alex knew that she was right, she always was, but that never seemed to make it any easier. *Angel Alex* was her optimistic, the sun is always shining, side. She envisioned her clothed in long-flowing white robes and wearing a shiny gold halo. She was always encouraging her, telling her what a strong woman she was and just how far she had come in her life. *Angel Alex* was the one who was always prompting her to make better decisions and to achieve greater things, whether it was in her personal or professional life. It was not the first mental conversation the two of them had ever had and Alex was reasonably confident that it wasn't going to be their last. In fact, the only problem was that inevitably *Devil Alex* appeared to bust-up their little party.

Devil Alex was the disembodied voice of pure evil. Unlike her angelic counterpart, *Devil Alex* had never heard of a bad idea or a bad time. If *Angel Alex* was the one wearing the white robes then *Devil Alex* was the one wearing black leather with thigh-high stiletto boots. Just like *Angel Alex*, this voice was always championing her as well, but she played to a different part of Alex's psyche. She acknowledged that Alex was indeed a strong woman, but that she was strong in-spite of everything that had been thrown her way and that she didn't have to defend her actions to anyone.

Devil Alex was always the one urging her to just do what felt good and to hell with the consequences. Life was too short to play nice. If she wanted to get shit-faced drunk she didn't need anyone's approval. If anyone had a problem with that it was *their* issue, not hers. For *Devil Alex* the act of burning bridges took too long; she preferred using explosives. Hers was the voice that always seemed to be egging Alex on when she got into arguments. *Devil Alex* was a hard drinking, fun loving, *zero-fucks-to-give,* kind of girl.

In the end she did what she had done so many times before; she told *Angel Alex* to fuck off as she opened the bottle; choosing to party with the ever fun *Devil Alex*. She comforted herself with the notion that sometimes she just needed to feel numb for a while; to be able to just not care, but she ultimately knew that it was a lie. Alcohol only served to fuel her emotions; it never numbed them.

Now, as the effects of the whiskey began to take hold, she grappled with her decision. It seemed as if everyone around her had someone or something that brought them happiness. Abby had her bodybuilding, Hutch had his Vanessa, and James had his.....

Alex let the last part of the thought trail off, as she felt the anger build inside her. She grabbed the bottle and took a long drink.

While the whiskey had long ago numbed her physically, it had done very little to numb her mentally. In fact it had only served to amplify the foul mood she was currently experiencing.

"Fucking bitch!" she screamed, as she grabbed the pack of cigarettes and lit another. "That's what James has, a blonde-haired fucking bitch with her perfect little fucking body and her perfect little fucking life"

It annoyed Alex to no end having to get along with his girlfriend, Melody.

"*Fiancée*," she corrected herself. "They're getting married and they're going to have a perfect fucking happily-ever-after life. She'll probably want you to be a fucking bridesmaid too, just so that she can throw the bouquet at you and torment you one last time."

The sad thing was that she knew Melody had no idea about her feelings for James. Hell, she'd only just shared them with him a few months earlier, but that didn't mean she still couldn't hate the woman.

Alex often fought the urge to *think* about them together, but that generally proved futile, especially when she was drinking. As much as the images repulsed her, she still couldn't help herself. She found it rather disturbing that the very idea of them together both angered and aroused her.

She took another swig of whiskey, than set the bottle on the coffee table, as her mind played out a reoccurring scene with the two of them in bed, as Alex stood in a darkened corner watching.

It should be me, she thought, taking one last drag on the cigarette before crushing it out in the ashtray.

Knock, Knock, Knock.

Alex closed her eyes and gritted her teeth.

She didn't need this, not now. This was her pity party and it was a private affair.

You should have turned off the lights, she thought.

Knock, Knock, Knock.

"Oh for fuck's sake," she exclaimed, as she got up from the couch and stormed down the hall to answer the door.

"Hey there," Peter said, when the door opened.

"You should have called first," Alex said, the words coming out a bit slurred. "You could have saved yourself a trip."

"Are you okay?" he asked, a concerned look on his face.

"I'm freaking awesome," she replied. "Thanks for asking and have a good night."

As Alex began to close the door, Peter grabbed it.

"Take your hand off my door, Peter." Alex said slowly, an angry edge to her voice.

"I'm worried about you," he replied.

"Your concerns are duly noted," she said. "Now take your hand off my door."

"Why do you do this?"

"Do what?"

"Shut everyone out of your life when you are going through a rough patch?"

"Rough patch," she replied with a laugh. "You think this is a *rough patch*? I'd call looking at twenty-to-life as a little bit more than a goddamn fucking rough patch, Peter."

"Okay, maybe that was a poor choice of words, but you know what I meant."

"No, I don't know what you mean, Peter. I don't know what any of you mean, with your *aw shucks, oh my goshes,* and *rough patches.* What the hell does any of that mean? That's not real life, no one talks like that. That's Mayberry shit."

"I hate when you drink," he said.

"Fuck you," Alex replied. "You invited yourself to this party, no one asked you to come around with your sanctimonious, holier-than-thou bullshit."

"I'm not holier-than-thou, Alex," he said indignantly. "We all have our demons that we battle with."

"Is that what you think I'm doing out here?" She asked with a smile, her voice taking on an almost sing-song tone. "Battling my demons?"

"Yes," he replied, "and losing."

"Oh, baby, you have no idea. I don't battle my demons, I party with them."

"I can't do this anymore, Alex," he said somberly. "I can't help you if you don't let me and I can't watch you destroy yourself."

"Then don't, Peter." she replied. "Go find yourself a nice, demure little girl. It shouldn't be too hard. As I recall it's been brought to my attention numerous times just how lucky I am because half the women in town would kill to be banging *Dr. Hunk.*"

"I don't want them," he said angrily. "I want you."

"No you don't," she snapped. "You think you do, but you don't."

"Yeah, well if you think you know me so well why don't you tell me what I want, Alex."

She smiled seductively, as she held onto the edge of the door for support.

"You want what every boy wants, Peter. You want the *bad girl*. You want the girl that you're ashamed to bring home to mommy; the wild one in the sheets who fucks you back, but you only want her on your terms and behind the bedroom door. The rest of the time you want someone who doesn't drink or curse like a sailor. You want to find a girl who'll fawn over you and say things like *aw shucks* and *oh my gosh,* at least when she's not standing quietly behind you; in her proper place. One who can walk into church without running the risk of Christ falling off the cross, and God knows I'm not her. You may think you want me, Peter, but make no mistake, you only want to change me and that is something no man will ever do."

Peter stood silently, staring impassively at Alex.

"Introspections a bitch, isn't it?" she asked with a wink.

"I've got to go," he said.

"Yeah, me too," she replied. "I'm about to go do body shots with my demons. Drive safe."

Alex watched as the man walked back to his car and drove away.

She closed the door behind her and made her way back to the couch.

"Asshole," she muttered, as she picked up the bottle.

Who the hell did he think he was to judge her? she thought, as she took another drink. *For that matter who the hell were any of them in this pissant little town?*

None of them had any idea who she was or what she had been through in her life, and they certainly had no right to judge her.

She lit another cigarette, as she sat on the couch and fumed. She didn't belong here; she didn't fit in with this *clickish* community. In many ways she felt like an alien watching some primitive life form evolve and, just like that little extraterrestrial shit, she just wanted to go home.

But you can't, she scolded herself, *because you're a bad girl and you've been exiled.*

It seemed that even among her own people she was a pariah.

She knew that she didn't have to drink, didn't have to curse like a drunken sailor, but that's who she was and she didn't want to change.

Alex took a drag on the cigarette and began blowing smoke rings, as she lamented her current situation. The blissfully ignorant buzz that she had been working so hard on was gone now, replaced by a sense of drunken awareness.

A part of her was angry, knowing that her relationship with Peter was pretty much over. Maybe after he got elected he could be like Sheldon and find himself his very own *Juggs* Montgomery. Someone like her would be the perfect woman for him; eye candy that would never embarrass him. He could even take to church without having to worry about a stray bolt of lightning wiping out the congregation.

*Plus she's one of those Penobscottitarians......
Penobscottian..... fuck, she's a local bitch.*

It wasn't that she didn't care for him, but they were truly from two different worlds. If she was the *Harley* chick he was the *Vespa* guy. She was straight whisky and he was a crisp chardonnay. She felt at home among cops, he felt at home among........ well, refined people like Melody.

"Prissy little bitch," she said, as she crushed out the cigarette in the ashtray.

The words had formed perfectly in her head, but they came out as a slurred, unintelligible jumble; which somehow seemed quite hilarious to her. Alex soon found herself giggling uncontrollably at her inability to speak clearly, but then the room began to spin violently.

"Oh crap," she exclaimed, as she felt her body begin to topple over.

The last thing she saw was the image of James and Melody locked in a passionate embrace and then she passed out.

Devil Alex was so proud.

CHAPTER EIGHTEEN

Alex let out an audible groan, as she gingerly lifted her head up off the throw pillow and opened her eyes. The inside of her head felt as if a troop of circus clowns with large mallets were running around inside it, beating every square inch of her skull.

"You're not sixteen anymore, asshole," she said dryly, as she slowly crawled up into a sitting position.

She sat cross-legged on the couch and took a moment to allow her brain to process the scene in front of her. The living room had that old familiar smell of cigarettes and whiskey. A near empty bottle of Jack sat on the coffee table alongside an overflowing ashtray. Halfway across the room her jeans lay on the floor in a crumpled heap along with one sock. The only thing missing from the whole sorority party scene image were a bunch of other bodies passed out on the floor.

When did I take my pants off? she wondered, as she stared down at her one bare foot.

Alex gave up trying to remember, as she rubbed at her face; trying to shake the cobwebs free. She would have liked to have said that this was unusual, but the truth was that the scene was an all too familiar one for her.

She reached over and picked up the pack of cigarettes from the table. She lit one up and leaned back, staring out the window. Darkness still held its grip on the outside world.

For all intents and purposes this was her customary fallback position. Whenever the shit hit the fan in her life she'd find a place to hole up in till things settled down; somewhere that had an ample supply of booze and smokes. In fact the only thing that was different now, from when she lived in New York, was that she had a better view to keep her company.

She got up and slowly made her way into the kitchen. Her body was still suffering the effects of misguided folly and she held onto various pieces of furniture for support, as she moved along. She slumped over the counter, laying her face on the cool ceramic tile, and hit the switch on the coffee pot. A moment later the stale air was replaced with the aromatic smell of the dark coffee being brewed.

By the time she had finished her cigarette the coffee had completed brewing. She poured a cup and used it to wash down the aspirin that her aching head so desperately needed.

She walked over to the front door and put on her jacket, before stepping outside. This was one of the things she enjoyed about rural living: *no neighbors, no worries*. Sitting on your porch drinking coffee, while half-naked, was something that was generally frowned upon in the suburban enclaves of Long Island. Alex took a seat on the porch swing and cradled the hot cup of coffee in her hands.

The evening sky was flooded with an expanse of brilliant stars. The imagery never ceased to impress her. Back on Long Island you would be lucky to see one star, but up here there were millions. Having spent her life surrounded by urban sprawl, the life she lived now seemed like a blessing.

Well, maybe not after last night, she thought.

The cold air felt so good against the bare skin of her legs. She took a deep breath, filling her lungs with fresh mountain air. She took a sip of her coffee as she contemplated her current situation. Her latest rock-bottom moment had probably destroyed her relationship with Peter. She didn't remember all of the alcohol fueled venom she had spewed, but the things she did recall weren't all peaches and cream.

She knew that she couldn't survive this way and that she had to make some serious changes in her life. In many ways the alcohol was like an abusive lover. The one you loved to hate, but who you still couldn't stay away from. It was always there to comfort in her times of trouble, but more often than not it was the original source of her problems in the first place. To be fair, she had always been a willing participant. It was never the alcohol that sought her out, she was always the one pursuing it.

"Prison will probably change that for you," she said dryly, as she patted the outside of the jacket, thankful when her hand hit the rectangular box in the pocket.

She reached inside and pulled out the cigarette pack. It seemed a bit incongruous that on one hand she would enjoy the fresh air, yet only to then light up a cigarette and fill her lungs with smoke, but that was her life. Like the alcohol, her smoking was simply a crutch to help her get over the *issues* in her life.

The chilling dreams of Cory Childers had been replaced by something new. A nightmare that wasn't just limited to when she was asleep and one that chilled her to the core. No one ever wanted to imagine themselves in jail, relinquishing their freedoms, and that held doubly true for a cop. Just the very thought of being among the same people that she'd arrested terrified her. It wasn't that she was afraid for her safety; she'd always held her own with the boys so the idea of being around women really didn't faze her. What really bothered her was the fact that she might end up there even though she had done nothing wrong. She knew that she had seen a gun and nothing could convince her otherwise.

Yeah, but will a jury buy that? she wondered.

The unfortunate answer was no. Even if they only found her guilty of manslaughter, the odds were that she'd end up in prison, at least for some length of time. She was pretty sure that she could survive incarceration, but what worried her was life afterward. Her career would be over and then what? Most likely she would lose everything in the subsequent civil law suit, not that she had all that much. She'd be an ex-con and, with the battles she'd waged against Sheldon Abbott, her job opportunities would probably be quite limited.

"Maybe Sheldon will give you Jugg's' job," she said. "Then he can leer at you with impunity."

Just the very thought of Abbott ogling her day in and day out made her shudder. She'd slip on a pair of neon orange hot pants and a tight t-shirt to serve burgers before she'd stoop low enough to accept that job.

Then you had better put more time in at the gym, she chided herself. *No one drops tips to look at a middle-aged woman's saggy ass.*

She closed her eyes, listening to the sound of the birds chirping off in the distance.

Maybe that isn't such a bad idea, she thought.

Maybe if she hit the gym today she would feel better. At the very least she could work off a bit of the pent-up frustration that she'd been carting around inside her. She took a final drag on the cigarette, crushing it out in the ash tray, before getting up and heading inside.

As she made her way through the kitchen, she set the coffee cup down on the counter and continued to the bathroom. She turned the shower on and got undressed. Alex paused for a moment, examining her reflection in the mirror. She cupped her breasts in her hands and turned to the right, checking herself out in profile.

"I can still give them a run for their money," she said approvingly, although deep down she knew she needed to quit making excuses when it came to the squat rack.

Alex turned around, opening the shower door and stepped inside. The hot water felt wonderful as it cascaded down her head and across her back. She placed her hands against the wall and just relaxed. After a few moments she reached over to grab the shampoo and began washing her hair. The summer was coming and she'd been toying with the idea of cutting it short. It'd be a lot easier to wash if she went with the biker chick look and she reasoned that if she did end up in prison there wouldn't be much to grab hold of in a fight.

You always got to think ahead, she thought, as she slid her head under the water and rinsed her hair out.

When she was done she grabbed the soap and washed off. She allowed herself a few extra minutes, feeling the tenseness leave her body, before grudgingly turning off the water. She knew that if she waited any longer that the dream of hitting the gym would remain just that, a fleeting dream.

She got out of the shower and grabbed a towel to dry off. She thought about blow drying her hair, but if she was going to the gym there was no point. She pulled her hair up into a pony tail and headed off to the bedroom. She emerged a few minutes later wearing a pair of black colored Lycra leggings and a bright pink sports bra. On her way out to the living she slipped her cell phone into her pocket, then grabbed her sneakers, a pair of socks and an athletic shirt that sported the PPD logo. She took a seat on the couch, glancing around at the mess she had made, as she put them on.

You need to get your shit together, girlie, she thought. *Even on your worse days back in New York you would have never left the house looking this way.*

Alex made a promise to herself that as soon as she got back from the gym she would clean things up. You couldn't unclutter your mind if you were living in a cluttered home.

She reached over to pick up the top to the whiskey bottle just as *Devil Alex* made a reappearance.

One more time, for old time's sake? she heard the voice whisper in her ear.

Alex pushed away the thought, as she finished screwing the top back on and stood up.

But one more really wouldn't hurt, would it? she though.

"Oh for Christ's sake, you're an adult, just have one more drink if you want and be done with it."

Alex sat back down and opened the bottle.

She hesitated, feeling the struggle raging inside her. In the end, just like always, *Devil Alex* won.

She raised the bottle to her lips and took a drink.

There, now you have it out of your system.

She set the bottle back down and screwed the top back in place.

That was the key, wasn't it? You could do anything you wanted, as long as it was in moderation.

Even as the words came out she knew she was lying. It was always the same hollow platitudes. There was no moderation with her, just another excuse for the abhorrent behavior. She hated herself for giving in, yet it was the only thing she had, the only thing that never betrayed her and it frustrated her so damn much.

She got up quickly and then sat back down, as she felt a sudden rush.

"That's what you get, asshole."

The long, hot shower and whiskey didn't make for good partners. She leaned back on the couch and closed her eyes, as she waited for the moment to pass; only it didn't. She tried to get up, but she had no control over her body.

"Fuck me," she said, the words coming out slurred, as she gripped the edge of the couch.

Alex opened her eyes, but she had a hard time bringing her vision into focus. Instinctively she knew that something was terribly wrong.

Am I dying? she wondered, as her sight began to narrow and she slumped backward.

Just before her vision went completely black she saw a figure emerge from the darkness and at that moment she knew that dying would have been the preferred choice.

CHAPTER NINETEEN

"What the hell was that?" Susan asked

"What?"

"That noise?"

"I didn't hear any noise," Tatiana replied.

"I swear I heard a noise, like a buzz."

"Are you sure you didn't just hear road noise?"

Susan glared at the woman behind the wheel. "I didn't imagine it; stop the car."

Tatiana sighed and pulled the car off to the side of the road. When the car had come to a complete stop, Susan got out and opened the rear passenger door.

"What are you looking?"

"Whatever made the noise," she said.

"Why don't we just go back to the cabin and we can look for it there?" Tatiana asked.

Susan ignored her, and began running her hands methodically over the unconscious body in the back seat.

"Jesus H. Christ," she muttered.

"What?"

"This, Tee," she said angrily, as she slipped the cell phone out of the shirts interior pocket and held it up.

"It's a cell phone, big fucking deal."

"It *is* a big fucking deal!" she exclaimed. "They can track these things."

"I already covered that base, babe," Tatiana replied. "You're worried about nothing."

"What the fuck, Tee?" Susan said, as she opened the back of the phone and proceeded to remove the battery and SIM card. "Lately you're acting as if you're not even using your brain."

"Well maybe if you stepped up to the plate and started pulling a little more of your weight, I wouldn't have to think about everything!"

"What the hell is that supposed to mean?"

"Just get back in the damn car," Tatiana said tersely.

Susan spun around and chucked the disassembled phone off into the nearby field, before she got back into the passenger seat. Tatiana gritted her teeth, as she tried to calm down. She put the car in drive and slowly pulled away from the curb.

"Why did you do that?"

"Because now any possible trail ends here," Susan said.

A few minutes later they made their way through one of the sleepy little towns that dotted the landscape up here. A bright blue neon sign advertised the town's only bar.

God, I could really use a drink right now, Tatiana thought, as they continued their drive in awkward silence.

CHAPTER TWENTY

Tom Blackshear, Scott Nichols and Paul Mitchell sat across the conference table, in the Carroll County Court House, listening as Floyd Peters recounted his involvement in the robbery of the Quick Mart. George Reid sat next to him, listening intently, as a court reporter sat in the corner taking notes.

To say that the kid appeared unremarkable would have been a gross understatement. He was neither short nor tall, hitting the tape at a mere five foot, five inches. If he weighed in at one-hundred and thirty pounds it was most likely because someone was stepping on the scale. He had brown eyes, collar length brown hair and sported a scraggly looking mustache. In essence he would have blended in with any crowd, anywhere.

Paul Mitchell had reluctantly agreed to the deal in exchange for a seat at the interview table. In addition, he got a promise that Nichols and Blackshear would issue a pre-election glowing endorsement of Mitchell's invaluable investigative assistance in clearing Chief Taylor.

"So whose idea was it to rob the store?" Nichols asked.

"It was Chase's idea, sir," Peters replied.

"Why did he want to rob that particular store?"

"He said that he knew someone in town who had told him that there was only one cop who worked during the daytime. He figured that if we went in quickly, first thing in the morning, that we'd be long gone before they could respond."

"Why did you agree?" Mitchell asked.

"I didn't have a choice," Peters replied. "I screwed up. I got behind on some payments to him and he told me that he'd let them slip if I drove him to Penobscot."

"Payment for what?" Nichols asked.

Peters looked over at his attorney, who'd nudged him under the table.

"Floyd had borrowed some money from the decedent," Reid said. "I'm sure you are all aware the financial situation we are facing these days, unfortunately he struggled to find gainful employment in order to make proper restitution."

Nichols eyed him skeptically.

"At this point what difference does it make, Scott?" Reid asked. "My client owed him money and he didn't have a choice."

"He could have said no," Mitchell chimed in.

"You don't know Chase," the young man said, his voice cracking a bit as he spoke. "I might not be an angel, Mr. Mitchell, but that kid was flat-out nuts. And I'm not talking crazy, but I mean *crazy*. Once he had you, he *had* you. I saw him take a blowtorch to the face of a kid's sister, because the kid told him he wasn't doing drugs anymore. I was there, I heard her screams. That little girl didn't do anything to him, but it didn't matter. You tell me what kind of person does that?"

Blackshear frowned at the image, as a hush fell over the room.

"Why didn't you go to the police?" Mitchell asked.

"To do what?" Peters replied with a laugh. "If anyone asked her what had happened she'd just say that she had an unfortunate accident. When someone takes a torch to another human being's face you honestly think that anyone is going to testify against him? If you hadn't noticed, the system isn't just broken, it's completely fucked up. I'm not the smartest person in the world, but even a fool knows you don't fix problems by turning people back out onto the streets to do the same thing."

"It's worked out well for you," Mitchell said.

"Really?" Peters asked. "What do you know about me, Mr. State's Attorney? To you I'm just another druggie, but you don't know or care why I use drugs. So let me ask you a question. Do you remember how your life was when you were ten-years-old?"

"I don't see how that's relevant to this discussion," Mitchell said.

"It's relevant because my life at that age included having my head forced down into a pillow to muffle my screams, as my uncle stuck his dick in my ass. All while my drunken mother was passed out in the next room. He was a product of your criminal justice system and screwing other men was a hobby he picked up while he was a guest of the state. I'd consider that pretty relevant, don't you think?"

Silence gripped the room as the young man spoke.

"So is it any wonder why I turned to drugs to dull the pain?" Peters asked. "But no one ever wants to hear that part, because no one has an answer for it. I'm sure you would all just say 'lock him up,' but would that solve anything? No, not really, because the truth is he was sexually abused as a kid by his mom. It doesn't make it right, but it shows the true extent of the problem. Who do you penalize first? You see, when you dig below the surface you realize the problem just keeps expanding. The system can't really fix anything; so they just slap a Band-Aid on the visible problem and congratulate themselves for being morally superior. Besides, no one really gives a rat's ass about the folks who live out in the Pine Meadows Trailer Park or the tough life they might have."

A sense of uneasiness gripped the men seated at the table; all of whom recognized the truth in what the young man had just said. They, both the prosecution as well as the defense, were all part of the problem, even though they wouldn't admit it.

Crime and punishment was a fundamental principal in a civilized society, but what happened when the criminals themselves were the victims as well? The kid was right; the criminal justice system was broken. Years of revolving court room doors, social justice experimentation, excessive or inadequate judicial sentencing, particularly when it came to unrepentant criminals, and massive overcrowding in jails for people who simply didn't belong there, had led to a system that was on life-support and failing fast.

The problem wasn't a lack of answers, but the sheer volume of conflicting ones. Like spokes on a wheel, everyone had an opinion as to how to fix the problem. Unfortunately, most of those answers were theoretical ones and very few ever came to fruition in the real world.

"I'm sure we can all agree, at this point, that my client was in fear of the descendant?" Reid asked.

"I have no problem with moving ahead," Nichols said, glancing at Blackshear and Mitchell, who both nodded in the affirmative.

"So you drove Mr. Akins to the store, then what happened?" Nichols asked.

"He was really hyped-up," Peters replied. "I'm pretty sure he was high on something. We pulled into the parking lot and that's when I first saw the gun."

"What kind of gun was it?" Blackshear asked.

ANDREW G. NELSON

"It was small," the kid said. "It wasn't one of those normal guns; you know the big kind that everyone carries."

Blackshear pulled up a screen on the laptop next to him and typed in a search of guns. When the images came up he turned it around to show Peters.

"Can you point out what you saw?"

Peters looked through the photos until he had found one that resembled what he had seen.

"This one, it looked like this," he replied, pointing toward a 2" snub-nosed revolver.

"You're sure?" Nichols asked.

"Positive," the kid replied. "Just seeing it scared the shit out of me."

"You didn't think about how he was going to rob the store beforehand?"

"Hey, all I knew was that I was supposed to just be the driver," Peters replied. "I didn't think he was going to have me come in with him."

"Why did he?"

"He got paranoid," Peters said. "Started accusing me of setting him up, said that I was going to leave him there, so we left the car running and he made me come inside with him."

"Then what happened?" Nichols asked.

"We went in through the back door. There was an old man standing in the back room and Chase hit him in the head. The guy

158

hit the ground like a ton of bricks. I thought he'd killed him and I got scared. I turned around to head back out the door, but he grabbed me and dragged me to the front with him."

"Was he saying anything?" Mitchell asked.

"Yeah, but I don't know what. Honestly, I was scared to death and it all sounded like gibberish. Some guy came up to him, but Chase just pushed him to the ground. Next thing I know the guy was crawling up the aisle to get away."

"What happened next?"

"Chase continued up toward the cash register and I started to back away. I just got this really bad vibe."

"Did you hear anything, see anything?"

"I heard someone scream police and then this huge explosion" Peters said. "By then I was close to the back of the store. I just turned around and got the hell out of there."

"Where did you go?" Nichols asked.

"I went out the back door and took off in the car. I don't think I even hit the brakes till I made it to Dummer."

"I need to ask you where you got the drugs, Floyd, specifically the heroin," Mitchell said.

"Just for the record, we are in agreement that any information proffered, concerning any potential narcotics found in my clients vehicle at the time of his arrest in Ossipee, is being offered anecdotally and will not be used against him at any subsequent criminal proceedings, is that correct?' Reid asked.

"Yes, counsel," Paul Mitchell replied. "As long as the information provided by your client, as to how he came into possession of said narcotics, is clear and concise."

Reid leaned over and whispered an approval into Peter's ear.

"I was sent to Ossipee by Eddy Davis to deliver the drugs."

"Who were you delivering to in Ossipee?" Mitchell asked.

"I don't know his real name," Peters replied, "but he goes by the name Ray-Jay and he lives in a grey house over on Fisher and Altamont."

"So where is this guy Eddie dealing out of?" Blackshear asked, as he made notes on the legal pad in front of him.

Peters looked at the cop quizzically. "Not Eddie, Eddy, he's a she."

"Eddy Davis is a girl?" Nichols asked.

"Yeah, she's Chase's cousin," Peters replied. "She's the one that Chase learned his *crazy* from. She took over the operation when Chase got killed, but if you ask me I have a feeling she was already running things. She's crazy, but she's also smart."

"Just when you thought it couldn't get any stranger," Blackshear said, tossing his pen onto the table.

"Where can we find her?" Nichols asked.

"I don't know where she's living; she's not exactly what I would call the trusting type. I just know I was supposed to meet her at the ball field in Dummer at midnight."

"Is there anyone working with her?" Blackshear asked.

"Yeah, she has this big, dark skin guy that's always with her. He's like six-six, biggest dude I've ever seen in my life. I think he's her enforcer. She calls him Kike, but I never heard him say anything."

"What kind of vehicle does she drive?"

"A black Ford F-150 with tinted windows," Peters replied.

"Anything you want to add?" Mitchell asked.

"I just want help," Peters replied. "I just want to get help and get as far away from here as I can."

Blackshear got up and escorted Peters to the door, behind which a deputy sheriff stood waiting to take custody of him.

"Okay, Toni, thank you," Mitchell said to the court reporter. "Please get that drawn up as quickly as possible."

"Yes, sir," the woman replied, as she gathered up her belongings.

"So, are we good here?" Reid asked.

"He'll have to sign the statement, after it's been transcribed," Mitchell said, "but yes, we're good here. I spoke to Judge Myers this morning and he has agreed to come in later this afternoon. We'll do an in-chambers appearance. Your client will plead guilty to simple possession and I, in consideration for his testimony, will recommend in-patient treatment followed by one year probation."

Reid began gathering up his paperwork, placing them back inside the leather portfolio.

"Just for the record, I don't buy half that stuff he said," Mitchell added. "He went along willingly, there's just no one else to refute his tale of woe."

"Does it really matter, Paul?" Reid asked.

"You just might want to remind him that this is the last chance he gets. He either turns his shit around or the next time he messes up in Carroll County I'll drop the hammer on him so hard he'll be old enough to collect social security when he gets released.

"Let's be real for a moment, Paul. The kid's odds are dismal at best and you know it. He has no education to speak of and non-existent family support. Just send him down to Manchester and be done with it. When he fails, and most likely he will, he'll be Hillsborough's problem."

Nichols shook his head, motioning Blackshear to follow him outside.

"Do you believe that shit?" Blackshear asked when they were out of earshot range.

"Nature of the beast, Tom," the man replied. "It's a business, nothing more and nothing less. Everyone just wants to get the best possible deal they can before the ink dries on the paperwork. Mitchell wants to get re-elected and Reid has aspirations for the bench. It is what it is."

Blackshear grabbed Nichols by the arm, stopping him, and faced him.

"No, this isn't business, this is about people's lives, Scott," the man said. "We dodged a major fucking bullet here. If this little shit-bird had done the speed limit you'd be getting ready to try Alex for murder and we all would have been patting ourselves on the back if we managed to walk away with manslaughter."

"I don't make the rules or the laws, Tom, and neither do you."

"So that makes it right?"

"What do you want me to say? You're right, it's not fair, and it has never been fair. For Christ's sake we used to string people up for being witches, was that fair? How about convicting someone just because of the color of their skin, is that fair? The system isn't perfect, Tom, but we try."

"I guess this case has just gotten to me, Scott," Blackshear replied. "I just keep thinking that it could be me in Alex's shoes."

"I know it sucks and I know it all seems a bit too impersonal at times, but you know what? As bad as it is, it's still better than anyplace else in the world."

"That's a helluva consolation prize," Blackshear said. "*Hey kids, check it out, we don't suck nearly as bad as the next guy.*"

"Listen, if it will make you feel better, go give Alex a heads up. She won't be able to be reinstated until the ink on the judge's signature is dry, but at least she can quit worrying."

"I'm sure she'll be grateful to hear it."

"And then I'll get the enjoyment of telling Sheldon Abbott; whom I am reasonably sure will not have the same enthusiastic response."

"Politics," Blackshear said, as they made their way out of the court house building. "I'm so glad I'm just a cop."

CHAPTER TWENTY-ONE

Susan sat on the edge of the small wooden dock, which jutted out over a large, tree-lined stream in the northern foothills of the Nash Stream Forest area, with her feet dangling over the side, but even this beautiful scenery could do nothing to counter the rather foul mood she found herself in this morning.

She lit another cigarette and took a drag, as her mind struggled to make sense of the new topsy-turvy direction her life had recently taken. She leaned back, closing her eyes, and felt the warmth of the sun radiating down on her face; as she listened to the cheerful sounds of nature. It took a little while, but eventually the stress began to ease from her body.

This was how it was supposed to be, she mused.

They'd been planning their current *adventure* for months now. As much as they both enjoyed the thrill of the unplanned, anonymous victim, each of them also had a *thing* for something a bit more familiar. There was just something about looking into the eyes of someone you knew at the last minute, seeing the immediate recognition, and then watching as they died in front of you. It was such an incredibly powerful turn on for both them; the intimate intermingling of sex and death.

Generally they took turns selecting targets; indulging each other in their respective hunt for prey. Often they went shopping for their victims at local bars that were situated just off a highway. Those were generally like candy stores for them. They would simply walk in and find someone to their liking. The simple truth was that if you were in a bar at nine o'clock on a weekday you were probably looking to score. Much of the time it would be men, who were looking to have some extramarital fun, although women now seemed to be gaining a strong foothold in the burgeoning affair market.

They'd walk in, make eye contact and after a few drinks invite them outside to have some fun. As they were basking in their post-coital bliss, the other would end the life of the unsuspecting victim. But they'd gotten a bit bored with their anonymous victims and decided to spice things up.

Tatiana had been up last, taking out her victim back in New York City. Even though Susan went along for the ride on that one, she was still up next on the game board. The idea had been to come back here, find a nice secluded place in the country and then begin to stalk her old Algebra teacher, Mr. Goodridge.

Goodridge had been one of those lecherous male teachers, the ones who were continually trying to peer down their female student's blouses. Most girls hated it, but Susan got a perverse thrill out of it. He wasn't a bad looking guy, but just creepy. So she decided to finally give him what he wanted. Spring was the perfect time of the year, because it allowed them to track him fairly easily due to school being in session. There was something inherently exhilarating about surveillance. It was like being a voyeur into someone's life. Over the course of two months they'd been able to figure out his routines to the letter.

Adam Goodridge was a creature of habit. He got up every day at the same time, including weekends, and he went to bed at the same time. He wasn't married and there hadn't been any hint of a girlfriend or other romantic interest. He lived just outside of town and every day before work he would hit the coffee shop on the square. If he had any hobbies they clearly didn't include any that took place outside the home.

He was probably jerking off to yearbook photos, she thought.

The idea was that they would catch him after the school year had come to an end. She wanted to be able to take her time with this one, to draw it out, and make this one a bit more special. It seemed only appropriate considering all the attention he had paid to her. By waiting for school to officially end he wouldn't be readily missed until it started back up again in September and she could have her fun. Everything was going perfectly, until the robbery.

Why the hell did you even take that stupid gun?

It had seemed like such a simple thing when it happened, but it had changed everything. She couldn't understand why Tatiana seemed obsessed with snatching the cop. She'd chalked it up to her hatred for the guy back in New York, but it was almost as if the woman was one of Tatiana's marks.

It was even like when they had gotten back to the cabin. Once they had brought the unconscious woman inside, Tatiana seemed to just zone everything else out. She'd come up with this elaborate plan to keep the cop alive, to drag out her punishment, even though that went against everything they'd ever done before.

Susan took a final drag on the cigarette and then flicked it into the air; listening to it hiss for a moment when it hit the water.

"Are you okay?"

She turned around startled and looked up at Tatiana who was standing behind her.

"Yeah," Susan said. "I'm fine."

"I don't believe you," Tatiana replied, taking a seat next to her on the dock. "Here."

Susan took the offered bottle of beer and took a sip.

"I'm just not feeling it," she said. "I thought we were just going to have our fun with Goodridge and then get the hell out of here."

"I know and we still will, but we also have to be adaptable to the moment," Tatiana replied. "After all, weren't you the one who went looking for her?"

"Yes, but only because she intrigued me," Susan replied, taking a sip of her beer. "I hadn't come to a decision on what to do about her."

"Sometimes the targets come to you."

"Did she really come to me, Tee?"

"When an opportunity presents itself, you need to recognize it for the gift that it is," Tatiana said. "Would you rather just eliminate the threat or would you prefer looking over your shoulder for the rest of your life; waiting for her to pop up behind you?"

"Killing her is one thing," Susan said. "Bringing her here is something completely different."

"You act like we've never kidnapped anyone before," Tatiana argued. "What about that guy in Reno? As I recall that ended up being a pretty good time."

Susan couldn't argue that point.

They'd both decided they needed a guy to liven things up and had found Mitch at a roadside bar feeding a slot machine. He was a pretty good looking guy and it didn't take much too convince him to leave with them.   They were playing the mother / daughter angle with him and when they got back to the hotel found out that he was extremely well endowed. It didn't take much convincing for him to agree to being tied up to the bed frame. Rather than kill him right away, they'd kept up the ruse for several days; literally and physically enjoying the ride.

"That was different," she said softly.

"Are you getting cold feet?" Tatiana asked.

"Oh hell no," Susan replied, "but I just get a really bad feeling about this one."

"Like what? Like she's going to break free and she's going to take us both out of the picture?"

"No, not like that," Susan said.

"Then what?"

"I don't know, it's just different, Tee. It's like I get this bad feeling about *her*. Everything inside of me is screaming 'go inside, kill her and let's get the heck out of here.'"

Tatiana took a drink and stared off across the water. She felt as if she was between a rock and a hard place. She'd never shared with Susan that she'd known Alex; that she had a personal grudge with the woman that needed to be taken care of. There was no attachment with any of their other victims. They had their fun and then they killed them, but she knew this would be different. Tatiana struggled with how she could explain to the young woman how much Alex had affected her physically, without Susan becoming jealous. She'd already lied to her and that would only fuel the fire. Her only plan was to keep them apart until she got what she needed.

"Baby, we are out in the middle of nowhere," Tatiana said. "You'd literally have to get lost in order to find us. There's no way to track her to here. Her phone's in a field twenty miles away from here. Not to mention the fact that I've got her tied up tighter than a BDSM practitioner. Trust me, she's not going anywhere and she's not going to do anything to us."

"Then what's the point?" Susan asked. "Why go through all this trouble?"

"Because I have a plan," Tatiana said.

"Oh really?"

"Yes," Tatiana replied. "One thing I learned from Banning is that psychological torture can be incredibly powerful. It can unlock things in a person that give you invaluable insight into better understanding your prey."

"What does that have to do with her?" Susan asked. "She's a small town cop."

"She is, now, but she wasn't always. I did some research on her and I found out that she came to Penobscot by way of New York City."

"So?"

"So, there might be something I can salvage from her to make my end game a lot more attainable."

"Maguire," Susan replied.

"Exactly," Tatiana replied. "You see, if you want to learn about the king, sometimes you need to have a chat with the pawns."

"I still don't like it," Susan said, fishing out the pack of cigarettes from her shirt pocket and lighting one up.

Inwardly, Tatiana smiled. Those five simple words marked, if not outright acceptance, at least acquiescence on the part of Susan to Tatiana's plans.

"What would make it more to your liking?"

"Just learning what you need to and getting the fuck out of here," Susan replied. "I'm already done with New Hampshire."

"What about Goodridge? All the work we've done?"

"We've always killed and left town, two bodies at the same time breaks the rule," Susan said. "I say screw him. Let him keep staring at teenage titties for a little longer. We can revisit the little perv at a later date."

"Whatever your little heart desires, babe."

"My little heart desires for you to just do whatever it is you have planned for her and let's just get out of this state."

"As you wish," Tatiana replied, fighting to suppress her smile.

CHAPTER TWENTY-TWO

"We're sorry the person you are trying to reach is unavailable or has traveled outside the coverage area. Please try your call again."

Blackshear ended the call and laid the phone on the desk. He glanced up at the large clock that hung on the office wall; it was just after two-thirty. He had tried to call her at least a dozen times since he'd left the Carroll County Court House, but each time he had gotten the same automated reply.

"Where the fuck are you, Alex?" he said, as he leaned back in his chair and drummed his fingers on the desktop.

He reached over and picked up the folder off his desk and looked inside. Then he grabbed the cellphone, dialing the number written on the inside cover and listened as it rang.

"Penobscot Police Department, Officer Simpson speaking, how may I help you?"

"Abby, this is Captain Blackshear from the state police."

"How are you, sir?"

"I'm fine," Blackshear replied. "I was just curious; have you seen or heard from Chief Taylor recently?"

"I saw her Thursday afternoon, why?"

"Because I have been trying to call her since this morning and haven't had any luck reaching her."

"Is there a problem?"

"No, not at all" he replied. "I just really need to speak with her."

"Let me put you on hold for a minute," she said. "I'll try and get through to her."

Blackshear waited, watching the second slowly march its way around the clock.

"Sir?" Abby said, when she came back on the line.

"Yes?"

"There's no answer. I tried her cell phone and it's saying the caller is unavailable."

"Yeah, that's what I keep getting as well," Blackshear replied.

"I also tried the house phone, but it just keeps ringing."

"How was she when you saw her?"

"Fine," Abby said. "We actually made plans to get together this weekend."

"Then it's probably nothing," Blackshear said. "She most likely needed to just get out of the house."

"Well, I do know that cell phone reception out in that area is pretty shoddy at times," Abby said. "It's a nice day, so if she is outside she wouldn't hear the house phone and she doesn't have an answering machine."

"Isn't it amazing how dependent we have become on these damn phones?" he said.

"Well, if you'd like, I can stop by her place on my way home. I'm getting off soon and I can swing in on the way."

"Would you mind?" Blackshear asked.

"No, not at all," Abby said. "I'm going to pass by there anyway. Is there any message you want me to give her?"

"Yeah, just have her call me. She has my number."

"Is it bad news?" Abby asked.

"Can you keep a secret?" he asked.

"Yeah," Abby said apprehensively.

"We've cleared her in the shooting," he replied.

Abby gasped at the good news. "Seriously? How?"

"I'd like to say that it was just good old-fashioned investigative police work," Blackshear replied, "but the truth is we got lucky. A trooper grabbed a kid on a speeding charge down in Carroll and he had dope in the car. He was looking at a pretty big fall so he offered to make a deal. It turns out that he was the second perp inside the store when the robbery went down. He confirmed that Chase Akins did have a gun on him when they went inside."

"Oh my God, that is so awesome, thank you."

"Well, it's not official yet, Abby," he warned. "We are still waiting for the judge to sign off on everything. It'll happen sometime today, but I haven't gotten the word yet from the state's attorney."

"Yeah, but still," Abby said. "Just knowing that she wasn't mistaken is a huge relief, but don't worry, I won't say anything. I'll just have her call you back."

"Thanks," Blackshear said. "It's just that I don't want any word getting back prematurely to Sheldon Abbott. I don't trust that man as far as I can throw him and I don't want him to sabotage anything."

"Trust me, I agree a hundred percent."

"Thank you," Blackshear replied.

"I'll have her call you as soon as I get in touch with her," Abby said.

"Okay, stay safe."

CHAPTER TWENTY-THREE

Alex's eyes twitched, as she started to come to. A heavy darkness engulfed her vision and for a moment she thought it was still night time. Her body physically ached and her head was throbbing.

What a fucking lightweight, she thought.

She started to get up, but couldn't; which only served to further confuse her. It took a second for her to realize that she couldn't move because her hands and feet what tied up.

What the hell? she thought, as she struggled against the restraints.

Now she realized that the *darkness* was merely the effect of a hood over her face and she tried to scream, but there was something large in her mouth which prevented her from doing so. The result was something akin to a barely audible moan.

A wave of panic came over her, but she willed herself to remain calm. If she couldn't see, she could still hear. There was a window open. She could hear birds chipping outside and could feel a slight breeze on the exposed skin of her hand.

She fought to remember everything that had happened, but it was as if her mind was in a fog. She knew she'd gotten drunk the night before, but she also remembered waking up.

I showered, she thought.

She recalled getting dressed for the gym and walking out into the living room. She'd sat on the couch to put her sneakers on and......

The fucking whiskey, she remembered. *You were poisoned.*

Her mind was racing as she tried to pick up any shred of information, any small detail, which would make sense of it all. It couldn't have already been in the alcohol when she bought it and she hadn't left the house, which meant that someone had either come into her home while she was passed out on the couch or while she had been in the shower.

Oh this is so not fucking good.

She tried pulling on the restraints again, but it was of little use. Her arms and legs were splayed apart and there simply wasn't enough give to provide her with any type of leverage.

Just calm down, you're still alive, so you have to play it cool.

Alex listened intently, trying to discern anything that would help her situation. She could barely make out the sounds of a muffled conversation taking place.

Okay, so there are at least two people, she thought. *Now all you have to do is just figure out who they are and what they want.*

CHAPTER TWENTY-FOUR

Abby Simpson made her way out of City Hall and quickly headed toward the waiting patrol car.

"Abby!"

She turned to see Mildred Parker walking toward her.

"Hi, Mrs. Parker," Abby said. "How are you?"

"Oh, doing well," the woman said. "Each day that I wake up I count my blessings."

"That's certainly the right outlook to have," Abby replied.

"Well, I guess I could complain, but that wouldn't help matters much, would it?"

"Unfortunately, there are a lot of folks who still love to do just that."

"Yeah and we have a name for them," Mildred said. "They're assholes."

Abby stifled a laugh. The former chief's wife was quite a pistol, but she guessed that when you got to her age you no longer really had to worry about what you said or how you said it.

"Were you coming to City Hall for a social visit or was there something you needed?" Abby asked.

"Social visit? Here? Oh good Lord no girl," Mildred replied. "If I came here for a social visit I might run into Sheldon Abbott. Then I would most likely end up in your jail and that wouldn't be very social at all."

Abby could no longer contain her laughter at the image of little Mildred Parker beating up Sheldon Abbott.

The man was certainly a galvanizing figure in Penobscot. It seemed like half the folks hated him and the other half loved him, although she wasn't sure if it was love or fear. Either way, he always seemed to have enough of a majority to keep getting himself reelected and no one on the board would dare move against him to challenge him for the city manager position. Abby had always wondered just what kind of *dirt* he had on the other board members that kept them in check.

"I was wondering if you had heard from Alex?" she asked.

"Why do you ask?"

"Because she was supposed to come by my house for dinner last night and she never showed up," Mildred replied. "Normally she'd call, but I haven't heard from her since the morning of the shooting."

As Abby watched, Mildred looked around furtively and then leaned in closer.

"I also ran into Dr. Bates this morning at the Y," she said. "He didn't seem very happy and I asked him what was wrong. He said he went out to Alex's house last night and they had a pretty bad blow-up."

"Well, she's probably got a lot on her mind," Abby said, even as her brain was trying to reconcile what it was being told.

"I'm sure that you are right, Abby, but you know how we *motherly* types get."

"Well, I'm heading out to her place now," she replied. "I'll make sure and let her know to give you a call."

"Do you mind?" Mildred asked. "I would really appreciate that."

"Don't worry; as soon as I see her I will let you know."

"Thank you so much," the woman replied. "Please tell everyone back at the office that I said hello."

"I'll do that Mrs. Parker," Abby said. "You really should stop in one day. I know everyone would love to see you."

"I'll do that, Abby," Mildred said.

"Ok, you have a great day."

"You too, Abby."

Abby watched the woman walk away, wondering what was going on. If Alex had skipped out on dinner, that meant that she was the last one to see her before yesterday and it begged the question of why she was in town in the first place?

She didn't want to think it, but everything in her head told her that she was going to find Alex drunk when she got out to her place.

Can you really blame her? she wondered, as she made her way to the patrol car and got in.

The answer to that question was a resounding *no*.

She started up the car and pulled away from the curb. She made a quick a right onto Atlantic Avenue and headed out of town.

Abby couldn't even begin to imagine what it would be like to have been in a shooting in the first place, let alone one where everyone was questioning whether it was justified or not. The thought of being found guilty had to be weighing heavily on Alex's mind, which made getting out to the house and finding her even more imperative.

During the ride out of town her mind replayed the last conversation they'd had. While Alex had seemed fine to her, she couldn't help recall the distant look in her eyes when she'd first pulled alongside her. She'd dismissed it, thinking that she'd have had the same look if she was going through what Alex was, but now she wondered if she might have missed something.

As she left the confines of the city, she found herself cruising just a bit faster, feeling herself becoming more anxious with every passing minute. By the time she turned off the road, and onto the driveway that led to Alex's house, her speed caused a spray of gravel to fly into the yard as the car's tires fought to stay in contact with the road. A moment later she locked the brakes up and bounded from the car.

The setting sun in front of her caused her eyes to squint as she made her way up to the front door. With her mind was racing and her thoughts becoming darker it was no wonder that she never saw the large, intricately woven spider-web until it was too late.

As to just who was more afraid over the unexpected encounter, was up for debate, but the bloodcurdling scream followed by the flailing of limbs seemed to give Abby a distinct edge. Coming in at just under an inch in size the Cross Orbweaver spider was not what you would exactly call *menacing*, but at that particular moment it certainly looked a helluva lot bigger!

Abby swatted away at her face, as she desperately fought to untangle herself from the silky strands of the once intricate web, while the aforementioned spider crawled up a dangling strand and disappeared behind the porches rain gutter.

"Motherfucker!" Abby exclaimed angrily, her body shuddering, as she continued to pull the strands from her face and hair.

She approached the door cautiously, as if the spider was preparing for a counter-attack.

"God I hate those damn things" she said, as she began pounding on it with a sense of urgency.

"Boss, its Abby, open the door."

When there was no answer, she slowly made her way around the side of the house, scanning for any other surprises that might be lurking nearby, and peered through the garage's side door. Abby felt a sinking feeling in the pit of her stomach when she spied the Jeep parked inside.

"Oh shit," she muttered under her breath, as she returned back to the front of the house.

Abby walked over to a large, rectangular limestone 'welcome' sign, that sat off to the side of the porch step. Actually, the sign read: *Go Away - Trespassers will be shot, Survivors will be shot twice,* which was about the best greeting you could expect if you knocked on her door.

She tilted the stone back and felt underneath for the plastic box. She opened it up and removed the key for the front door.

A sense of apprehension gripped her, and she felt her heart skip a beat, as she slid the key into the cylinder and turned it. As the door slowly opened she paused and took in a deliberate breath. It wasn't by any means scientific, but it passed the *sniff test,* so to speak. Even in her relatively short law enforcement career she had come to know the distinctly sickly-sweet smell of death all too well.

"Boss?" she said, as she guardedly made her way into the home, her right hand resting against the Glock 22's stippled back strap.

"Hello?"

Abby entered the kitchen, scanning it and the living room quickly. Next she moved into the bedroom. The bed was neatly made and everything appeared to be in its proper place. A quick check of the bathroom and the guest room / home office came up with more of the same. Nothing seemed amiss, yet nothing felt exactly right either.

She walked back out into the living room and spied the empty bottle of whiskey sitting on the coffee table.

"Uh oh," she muttered, as she walked over to it.

She noticed a piece of paper next to the bottle with a pen sitting on top of it.

Abby picked it up and began reading it.

With everything going on, I just needed to clear my head. I need some time alone so I'm going for a hike. I'll be back soon.

"A hike?" Abby said quizzically.

She walked out the front door and stood on the porch.

Off in the distance, Mt. Moriah rose up behind an endless expanse of pine trees; its upper ridges still adorned with patches of snow. It was easy to appreciate why Alex lived out here. Living out in the country, there was a sense of tranquility that customarily enveloped you, but not today. As Abby stood there, listening to the melodic sounds of nature, she could not help but feel a sense of dread. It was entirely possible that Alex had indeed gone out for a hike, and cell reception in this area was notoriously bad, but something about the empty bottle just gnawed at her.

She reached into her pocket and checked her cell phone. She was greeted by zero bars on the display screen.

She let out a sigh and headed back into the house. She located the house phone and placed a call to Hutch's cell number.

Abby knew that he was still at the office working. She'd never heard him clear for the day and she knew that Sheldon Abbott was doing all he could to keep him swamped with *busy* work. The phone rang a half dozen times before it switched over to voice mail.

She returned the phone back to its cradle, then reached up and grabbed the mic from her shoulder.

"M-11-6 to base."

"Base on the air, go with message."

"Base is M-11-3 available?"

"Standby."

A moment later she heard his voice over the radio.

"M-11-3, go with message."

"Trying to contact you direct, M-11-3," Abby said.

"I'm 10-73," Hutch replied.

Abby frowned at his use of the code they used for *unavailable due to administrative duties.*

"Copy that, standby on landline."

She picked the phone back up and dialed his cell again. A moment later she heard him pickup.

"This better be important, Abby," he said with more than a slight bit of annoyance in his voice.

"I need you to come out to the Chief's place."

"Now?"

"Yes, now."

"Is there a problem?"

"I'm not sure," Abby said. "I came out here to talk to the boss and she's not here."

"Well, maybe she just went out, Abby," he replied. "It's not like she has to notify us of her every move."

"Look, I really don't want to get into this over the phone. Can you just take a run out here?"

"Can't you just come here and tell me?"

"No, I can't," she replied forcefully. "When was the last time I called you about bullshit, Hutch?"

"Fine," he replied, with an exasperated sigh. "I'm on my way."

CHAPTER TWENTY-FIVE

Alex awoke from her nightmare with a start, her body jerking violently, as the vivid images of being restrained in a cold, dark prison cell slowly fled from her mind. She tried to move, but felt the restraints tugging at her skin.

So much for it all being a bad dream, she thought.

Her brain still felt more than a bit sluggish, as if her thoughts were being muffled inside her head. She chalked it off to being the lingering after-effects of whatever drug they had used to knock her out.

Everything was quite now. The voices she thought she had heard previously were gone now and she was acutely aware of the fact that she had absolutely no time reference to go by.

Was it day or night? she wondered. *Hell, for that matter, was it even the same day or another?*

Without any warning she heard the familiar snap of a Zippo lighter. The sound immediately sent a chill throughout her body, as she realized someone else was in the room with her. She struggled in vain against the restraints, as fear coursed through her body. Then she caught a whiff of smoke in the air.

While she couldn't see, it was as if every other one of her senses had been kicked into overdrive. She could hear the sound of the rolling paper burning, as whoever it was took a drag on the cigarette. Then she heard the slow, deliberate exhale and once agent the pungent aroma of the burnt tobacco filled her nostrils.

If they were watching her then they would have known she was awake. They would have seen her body pulling against the restraints that held her in place.

They're toying with you.

Time passed by agonizingly slow until she heard the sound of the cigarette being crushed out.

A moment later she felt something brush against the back of her head and without any warning the hood was removed. Immediately she shut her eyes tightly as the overhead ceiling light blinded her. It felt like an interminably long time before she was able to slowly reopen them in an attempt to identify her captor. It was only when she was finally able to open them that she understood the true extent of her situation.

"Hey, baby," Tatiana cooed.

As Alex watched, the women leaned over and undid the gag, then slowly removed the large, ball shaped device from her mouth. She fought the urge to scream as she knew it was probably pointless. The woman would have never removed it if there was anyone nearby that could have heard her.

Her immediate instinct was to say something smart, but her jaw ached and she was incredibly thirsty. Tatiana must have sensed her distress, because she reached down, picking up a bottle of water and opened it.

Tatiana leaned over, guiding the opening of the bottle toward Alex's mouth, but she recoiled.

"Oh, stop," Tatiana said admonishingly. "Do you really think I'd knock you out again after waiting all this time for you to wake up?"

Alex watched as the woman took a sip from the bottle.

"See? Are you satisfied?"

Alex nodded her head.

Tatiana leaned over and put one hand under Alex's head, lifting it up slightly, as she brought the rim of the bottle to her lips.

"Drink slowly," she warned.

Alex wanted to desperately lash out, but it would be a futile gesture. For the moment Tatiana had the upper hand and she knew that she needed to obediently play along; at least until she figured out what the heck was going on.

The water felt amazingly good going down her parched throat and tasted even better, as she slowly drank from the bottle. When she had gotten enough she raised her head slightly and Tatiana withdrew it, placing it back down on the ground next to her chair.

"So, did you miss me, darling?" she asked with a big smile.

"I can't believe you're still alive," Alex replied softly.

"Aw, you didn't think that I was going to let you waltz into my life and then just disappear, did you?"

"I'll be honest," Alex said. "I was pretty okay with that."

"Really?" Tatiana replied, as she lit up another cigarette. "As I recall, you were pretty much ready to jump into bed with me back then."

"I'd like to say that absence makes the heart grow fonder, but I'm pretty much over the whole psychotic-murderous bitch infatuation."

"You have no idea how much that saddens me," Tatiana said, as she slowly ran her fingers along Alex's forehead, brushing away several stray strands of blonde hair. "And here all I have thought about was you."

"I'm touched," Alex replied, "but, then again, so are you."

"Eh, I've been called worse," Tatiana replied, as she lit up another cigarette. "Over time you'll grow to adore my idiosyncrasies."

"Sweetheart, there aren't enough therapists in this entire state to deal with all of your idiosyncrasies."

"What can I say? I'm unique."

"Well, I'm sure that we can find you some outstanding accommodations at the New Hampshire Department of Corrections while we look for the person capable of unscrewing your head."

Tatiana smiled and took a drag on her cigarette.

"Somehow I don't think you truly grasp the dynamics at play here," she replied. "The odds of you making any type of accommodations in the near future are between zero and none."

"A girl can dream, can't she?" Alex asked.

"Sure she can," Tatiana replied. "I did and now here you are."

Alex smiled and nodded toward the cigarette.

"You want this?" Tatiana asked, holding it out.

"You mind?"

"Not at all," Tatiana said, as she turned the cigarette around and held it to Alex's mouth, "but you know it's bad for your health."

"I'm gonna go out on a limb and say that right now it's the least bad thing for me."

Alex took a long drag and then exhaled slowly, allowing the cigarette to calm her nerves. She knew who she was dealing with and needed to play the game for as long as she could.

"You know, you could always call us even," Alex said. "You go your way and I go mine."

"What fun would there be in that?" Tatiana asked. "Especially after all the trouble I went through to bring you here."

"You know that they are gonna come looking for me."

"Maybe," Tatiana replied, as she leaned over and let Alex take another hit off the cigarette, "but the real question isn't whether they are going to be looking for you, but where are they going to be looking? Unfortunately I have a sneaky suspicion, based on the clues I left behind, that they are going to be going in the opposite direction."

"Maybe I put a little more faith in my people," Alex said.

"Perhaps that's a bit misplaced," Tatiana replied, as she took a drag on the cigarette. "I've been hanging around this area long enough to know that I'm in no real jeopardy of being caught by the keystone cops."

"I wouldn't go and get too cocky," Alex replied. "As I recall I found your ass pretty easily."

"Yes you did," Tatiana said with a smile, "and that is precisely why you and I are here today. We have so much unfinished business."

"What, you mean like me blowing your brains out all over that wall?" Alex asked.

Tatiana laughed. "Mmmm, I do love a woman who can keep her sense of humor when things are spiraling out of control. It's an admirable trait; you're going to need it in the coming days."

"Oh really," Alex replied. "So what are you going to do, torture me?"

"Oh no, that would be such a waste," Tatiana said, as she reached down and ran her finger playfully across Alex's exposed midsection.

Alex fought the urge to recoil at the woman's touch, realizing that she needed to play the game in order to get as much information as possible. "No I was thinking more along the lines of picking up where we left off. You know, showing you what a good time you missed out on as I'm having my way with you."

"Honey, unless you grew a dick since our last encounter there is no way that you're gonna have your way with me."

"God, you're such a feisty little thing," Tatiana said gleefully. "I really hope that you are able to maintain that cheerful little façade in the coming months. It'll certainly help you cope with what's coming."

Months? What the fuck does this crazy bitch have in mind?

"And if I don't?"

Tatiana leaned back in the chair and smiled.

"Well, let's just say that everything depends on you. I am more than willing to put the ugliness of the past behind us and start over. I'll be as benevolent to you as you deserve, but if you choose to take the hard road than you will leave me with no other choice but to treat you in kind."

"Oh, if I'm bad does that mean you'll send me to bed without supper?"

Tatiana took a final drag on her cigarette and then plunged it into the bare flesh of Alex's exposed side, causing her to scream out in pain. A second later Tatiana was out of the chair and on top of her.

"You think this is all a fucking joke, don't you?" Tatiana snarled.

Alex gritted her teeth, as the pain in her side radiated throughout her body.

Tatiana's face had changed in an instant. Gone was the pretty brunette with the gorgeous eyes. What stared down at Alex was the look of a stone-cold killer, the type she'd encountered back on the streets in Brooklyn. But she had a reputation of being willing to go toe-to-toe with any of them and they gave her a wide berth, but now she was defenseless. Which meant it was even more important to stand her ground. The physical pain would pass.

"No, not everything, just you," she replied angrily.

Tatiana reached down and grabbed Alex by the face roughly.

"God, you have so much spirit in you," Tatiana said. "I'm going to love breaking you; your body first and then your mind. We'll see just how long that spirit lasts."

"You'd better pack a big lunch, lady," Alex said. "Because it'll probably take a while."

"Suit yourself," Tatiana said and released Alex's face. "It's your body, your mind, but I think you're going to find that you're not as tough as you pretend to be."

"Maybe I'm not, but I know that I'm a helluva lot tougher than you."

Alex saw it coming, which did nothing to make it any easier when Tatiana's right hand came crashing down into the side of her face. She felt her head snap violently to the side and, at least for a moment, the pain in her side was gone.

"Fuck me," she muttered.

"Aw, did that hurt?" Tatiana asked mockingly.

Alex smiled, as she slid her tongue against the corner of her mouth, savoring the familiar coppery taste of her blood.

"No, not at all," she replied dismissively. "You hit like a fucking girl."

Tatiana laughed and just like that the evil persona disappeared from her face. Her eyes narrowed, as she gazed down at Alex, taking on an almost smoldering look to them.

"I'm so glad that we reconnected," she said, taking Alex's chin in her hand tightly and kissed her lips. "This is going to be so much fun."

Alex tried to twist away, but it was useless. A moment later she heard the sound of tires on gravel.

"Oops, dinner is here," she said, as she climbed off the bed. "Behave yourself and I might bring you some dessert later."

"I'll have a headache."

"That's your problem, sweetheart, not mine," Tatiana replied, as she forced the gag back into Alex's mouth and covered her head with the hood. "Sweet dreams."

A moment later she heard the door shut and then a click of the lock.

Houston, I think we have a major friggin' problem.

CHAPTER TWENTY-SIX

A half hour later Abby watched as Hutch's patrol car came up the driveway and came to a stop adjacent to hers.

"Okay, I'm here, Abs," he said sternly, as he got out of the car. "So what is so damn important that you couldn't say it over the phone?"

"Look, for the time being this stays between you and I, alright?"

"Yeah, yeah, okay, so what is it?"

"They cleared the chief in the shooting," she said.

"What?"

"Yeah, that's why I came out here. I got a call from Captain Blackshear who said they had a guy in custody who admitted that he had been there at the time of the shooting and confirmed that the dead perpetrator was armed with a gun."

"That's awesome," Hutch replied.

"It is, but no one has been able to reach her. Blackshear said he'd been trying to call her, but he couldn't get through. I even tried the house line, but there was no answer so I said I would drive up and notify her."

"When was the last time you saw her?"

"In town on Thursday," Abby replied.

"Did she seem okay to you?"

"A little spacey at first, but I just chalked that up to having a lot on her mind. Then on the way out here Mildred Parker stopped me and said that Alex was supposed to come out to her place for dinner last night, but that she never showed up and never called."

"That does seem a bit odd, even for Alex."

"She also said that she ran into Dr. Bates this morning. He told her that he was here last night and they apparently got into a fight," Abby explained. "When I got here I checked the house and found this.'

Abby held up the note.

Hutch took it and began reading.

"Hiking?"

"Yeah, that was my response as well."

"I mean it's unusual, but I guess it's not implausible."

"I agree, but something about this just doesn't feel right to me," Abby said. "That's why I called you up here."

"Well walk me through it."

"Okay, so when I got here I knocked on the door, but there was no answer. So I thought maybe she might have gone out, but I checked and her car is still in the garage. So I got her spare key and opened the door," Abby said, as she led Hutch inside the house. "Since I didn't get a response I decided to check the house, you know, just in case. I went room to room, but there was nothing amiss."

"Where did you find the note?" Hutch asked.

"There on the coffee table," Abby said, as they walked into the living room. "Right next to the empty bottle of whiskey."

"That's not a good sign."

"No, it isn't," she replied.

"Here's the thing, I saw her at around four o'clock Thursday afternoon. I assume she came into town to get that bottle."

"Why do you assume that?" Hutch asked.

"Because she has been on the wagon since the beginning of the year," Abby shared. "I'm thinking this pushed her off."

"Well, you're probably right about that."

"So she goes through an entire bottle since then and decides to go for an evening hike? I don't buy that."

"Why do you think she went out for a hike at night?" Hutch asked.

"Because when I showed up here I walked into a spider web on the front porch the size of a semi tire," she explained. "Damn near gave me a heart attack."

"So?"

"So, most spiders usually build their webs at night," she said. "If Dr. Bates was out here last night that means that Alex would have had to have left the house after he left, but *before* the web was built."

"It's Alex," Hutch said.

"Precisely," Abby replied. "When she falls off the wagon she doesn't climb back on and she sure as hell wouldn't quit after one bottle. She'd head back to the liquor store a whole lot quicker than she would go for a hike. Call it a woman's intuition, Hutch, but I am telling you something's not right," Abby said.

"You think Dr. Bates is involved?"

"I don't know what I think. I just get this feeling something isn't right with this picture."

"I need some time to process all of this," he said.

"Okay," she replied. "I'm going to have a cigarette."

"You smoke?" Hutch asked with a shocked look.

"Only when I'm stressed," she replied.

Hutch watched as Abby turned and walked out the front door.

"This day is getting stranger by the minute," he said, as he walked into the kitchen and sat down at the island.

He'd known Alex for almost two years now and he understood that she was a very *complicated* person, but there was always an underlining method to her madness; whether that involved her job or her personal life.

Hutch scanned the room, hoping something would click with him that would make sense of it all. Nothing seemed overtly out of place, which wasn't that unusual considering that Alex had a tendency of being a bit OCD, but she had always told him that the clues were there, you just had to know where to look and what to look for.

Where do I even begin?

He got up from the chair and began going through the house, room by room.

At first he felt dirty, like a voyeur peering into her private space, and he just wanted to get it over with. He walked into the bedroom and looked around. Everything appeared orderly, including the bed which had been made. He walked over to the closet and opened the door. He peered inside and once again nothing seemed out of the ordinary. All of her clothing was neatly hung up. Even her shoes were stacked nicely in the shoe rack. He was just about to shut the door when he abruptly stopped.

"Hello," he said, as he stared back at the shoe rack, focusing on the pair of tan hiking boots. "Who goes hiking without their boots?"

Now Abby's suspicions had grabbed a hold of his attention and he began looking in earnest. It didn't take too long before he found her personal gun and her wallet hidden in the back of the dresser.

Now he knew that Abby was right. Alex would have never intentionally left home unarmed or without her wallet. He kept looking, but the only things that actually seemed to be missing were Alex, her cell phone and her keys.

Hutch made his way outside.

Abby was leaning back against the push-bumper of her car finishing her cigarette.

"Well, what do you think?"

"I think we have a problem," he replied.

"That's what I was afraid of," Abby said. "Now what do we do?"

"Let's go back to the office and call Blackshear," Hutch replied. "Alex's cell phone is gone. Maybe they can ping it and we can at least get an idea of where we should be looking for her."

CHAPTER TWENTY-SEVEN

"Headquarters Security, Officer Quick, how can I help you?"

"Hi, I'm trying to reach Police Commissioner Maguire," Hutch said.

"Who's calling?"

"This is Officer, erh, I mean Chief Hutchinson from the Penobscot Police Department."

"Hold on please."

On the other end of the phone line, Hutch covered the mouthpiece and looked over at Abby. "Wow, that was pretty easy. I expected it to be a lot harder."

A moment later another voice came on the line.

"Police Commissioner's Office, this is Sergeant Eberhard, how may I help you?"

"Uh, I'm trying to reach Commissioner Maguire," Hutch said.

"What is this about, sir?"

"I have a missing person case that I think he will be interested in," Hutch replied.

"Well, that's not really something the police commissioner handles. I'm going to transfer you to the appropriate unit."

"Hey, wait...." Hutch said, before he heard the line go silent. "Oh for crying loud."

"What's wrong" Abby asked.

"They transferred me," he replied, as he heard it begin to ring. "Maybe it isn't that easy."

A moment later he heard another voice come on the line.

"Missing Persons, Detective LaBarbara."

"Hi, this is Chief Hutchinson, from the Penobscot Police Department in New Hampshire. I'm really trying to get through to the police commissioner, but they transferred me to you."

"What is this in regards to?"

"I have a missing person case that I think he will be interested in," Hutch said.

"Well, we handle missing persons for the NYPD, sir. Can you give me a little more information?"

"Actually, the missing person is our chief," Hutch said.

"I thought you said you were the chief?"

"I am," Hutch replied. "Well, I'm the *acting chief,* but the actual chief has gone missing and I'm pretty sure the commissioner will want to know."

"Not to be rude, sir, but the police commissioner is a very busy man and he usually doesn't take a personal interest in matters like this. Is there anything I can help you with?"

"Look, the chief used to be with you guys," Hutch said exasperatedly. "She's a former New York City cop and she was partners with Commissioner Maguire."

"Excuse me? Did you say his partner?"

"Yes, I did, now she's the chief up here and she's gone missing."

"What did you say your name was?"

"Hutchinson, Acting Chief Hutchinson."

"Hold on for one moment."

Hutch closed his eyes and let out a loud sigh, as the line went silent.

"What's wrong now?" Abby asked.

"They put me on hold," Hutch said. "I think they're transferring me again."

"Maybe I should start doing that when people call here to complain."

"Yeah, transfer them up to Juggs," he said. "She'd lose her mind if she had to do actual work."

"Sheldon would just go and hire an assistant for her," Abby replied.

A moment later heard a voice come on the line.

"Chief Hutchinson?"

"Yes, I'm here."

This is Sergeant Eberhard," the man replied. "Who is it that you're calling about again?"

"Alex Taylor," he said. "She's the chief of police here in Penobscot and she knows your police commissioner."

"Hold on for one moment," he said and the line went silent again.

"I'm glad I'm not calling to report something *serious*," he said sarcastically.

"You can keep the city," Abby replied. "It's way too impersonal for my tastes."

"I went down there once when I was a kid," Hutch replied. "I never heard my father use so many cuss words. It seemed like half the trip was spent sitting in traffic."

"Your dad used a curse word?"

"Even the Baptist preacher has his breaking point I guess," Hutch said with a laugh, and then heard the man come back on the line.

"Chief Hutchinson?"

"Yes?" Hutch replied.

"Can I have your number please?"

Hutch gave the man his number.

"Is this a number that you can be reached at shortly?"

"Yes, I'll be here for a while," Hutch replied.

"Okay, I'll pass this information on to the police commissioner."

Hutch returned the phone to its cradle.

"Well, now what?" Abby asked.

"I guess now we wait."

CHAPTER TWENTY-EIGHT

"Whatcha doing?" Melody asked, as she walked into the salon.

Maguire looked up from the paper in front of him. "I'm reviewing transfer requests."

"Sounds absolutely titillating," she said, taking a seat next to him on the couch.

"How was D.C.?"

"Incredibly boring," she replied. "There was a time I liked the game of politics, but now I am just weary of it all."

"I take it things didn't go well with the Armed Services Committee?"

"Oh no, that actually went fine," she replied. "The committee is extremely happy with the progress that is being made on Dragon's Breath. It was meeting with the individual committee members that was utterly draining."

"Trust me, I empathize with you," Maguire said. "I like McMasters, but the City Council is filled with mindless idiots. How they ever managed to get elected confounds me."

"It does make you wonder, doesn't it?" Melody asked. "I mean were they really the best candidate or does party politics trump everything?"

"Do you really need to ask that question?"

"No, I already know the answer," she said.

"Well, at least it's over with," Maguire replied.

"For now."

"What's that supposed to mean."

"Well," Melody said. "I ran into Peter Constantine at the Hay-Adams,"

"Eliza Cook's campaign manager?"

"Yep," she replied. "I was having a drink with Senator Mays and his chief of staff. He acted like it was a coincidence, but I get the feeling that it was sort of a set-up."

"You know all too well that nothing happens by accident in D.C.," Maguire replied. "What did he want?"

"After the usual pleasantries he mentioned that Eliza was coming up for a fundraiser at the end of May and wanted to know if I was free to meet with her."

"I told you," Maguire said smugly.

"I don't think I can do it," Melody said.

"Well, you're the only one that can make that decision, angel, but you probably should at least hear her out before you do."

"I don't even like politics."

"Which probably makes you a very attractive choice," he said. "Either way, it doesn't hurt to at least listen to the spiel."

"I guess," she replied.

"In the meantime, do you want to review transfer requests?"

"You're on your own with that, cowboy," Melody laughed, as she got up from the couch and headed to the elevator. "These old bones are aching for some *me time* in the hot tub."

"That's evil," he replied.

Melody paused at the elevator and looked back at him.

"You do realize that this is your last night of quiet, don't you?" she asked.

"Oh crap that's right," he replied. "Have they been gone a week already?"

"Yep, Gen and her boys come back tomorrow so why don't you come join me in the hot tub and see just how *wonderfully evil* I can be."

Just then his phone began to buzz on the coffee table. He peered down at the number.

"It's the office," he replied glumly.

"Aw, duty calls, cowboy," he heard her say, as the elevator doors closed.

"Maguire," he said with slight annoyance, as he answered the call.

"Commissioner, this is Sergeant Eberhard. I really hate to bother you at home, but I think you might want to hear this."

Notifications generally came through the Operations Unit, so this call was more than a bit unusual.

"What's the problem, Sarge?"

"Do you know an Alex Taylor?"

Hearing the words, Maguire felt like he had just been sucker-punched.

"Yes," he replied, "She's my old partner, what's wrong?"

"Well, we just got a call from a cop up in Penobscot, New Hampshire, he said she's gone missing, sir."

"Missing?" Maguire said. "When? How?"

"I don't know the particulars, sir," the man replied, "but I have the name and number for the acting chief up there if you're ready to copy."

Maguire reached over and grabbed a pen and pad from the end table. "Yeah, go ahead."

A moment later he ended the call and immediately dialed the number he had been given.

The phone rang twice and then he heard it connect.

"Hello?"

"Yes, this is Commissioner Maguire. Who am I speaking to?"

"Sir, my name is Chris Hutchinson; I'm the acting chief of police in Penobscot."

"What happened to Alex?" Maguire asked brusquely.

"Well, sir, that's why I reached out to you," Hutch replied. "I have reason to believe that she has gone missing."

"What? How?" Maguire replied. "Wait, just start from the beginning and tell me what you know."

Hutch spent the next thirty minutes explaining everything that had transpired since the last time that Alex had been seen, including their observations at the house and the fact that she had been cleared of the shooting.

"I'd like to say that it is entirely unusual, but Alex has been known to do so *unusual* things from time to time," Maguire replied.

"Yes, I've noticed that as well," Hutch replied.

"Did anyone check her cell phone?"

"Yes, sir, I had the state police check it. The last ping was at approximately four thirty this morning and then nothing since."

"You have a location?"

"Yeah it was off of a cell tower that is located about thirty minutes outside of town."

"And she left a note that said she was going hiking?"

"Yes."

"I understand your concerns," Maguire replied, "but knowing that it is Alex, is it possible that she actually could have gone hiking?"

"Possible? Yes," Hutch said. "Probable? I really don't think so."

Maguire didn't believe it either.

"Have you done a missing persons report? Are the state police doing anything?"

"Well, sir, that's where we get into a bit of sticky issue," Hutch replied. "We've notified Captain Blackshear from the state police's major crimes unit. They've taken it as an informational for the moment, but have asked us to do everything we can to determine if this really is a *real* missing person's case before they take it further."

"Why is that?" Maguire asked.

"Well, with Alex's penchant for not backing down and sometimes doing *unusual* things, she hasn't exactly garnered a whole lot of support from the folks at city hall. In fact, we're a bit concerned that, between this and the shooting, they might try to use any excuse to justify keeping her out of the chief's chair permanently."

Maguire rubbed at his face, as he processed the information.

He knew all too well Alex's proclivity for pissing off folks in authority. What usually irked them more than anything else was not that she had pissed them off, but that she was usually right and left them no other recourse but to grudgingly acquiesce to her.

Having your chief of police going off for moonlight strolls through the New Hampshire countryside, legal as it might be, was just the excuse some might use to make the argument that she was emotionally unfit for duty.

"What are you guys planning on doing now?" Maguire asked.

"Well, sir, to be honest, that's the reason I called you," Hutch explained. "To be quite frank, I'm a bit out of my element here. I've never had a missing person that I've had to deal with in such a sensitive manner. We're a small town force. Ninety-nine percent of the people in the department love the chief, but it only takes that one percent who are looking to score some brownie points with the board to screw things up. Up to this point, this information has been limited to just three people and now you make four.

"Alright, if you don't mind I am going to send you up one of my top detectives to give you some discrete help."

"Thank you," Hutch replied. "I was hoping you might be able to provide us some help, sir."

"Just do your best to keep things under wraps till he can get up there and assess the situation."

"Will do."

"I'll call you back and let you know when to expect him."

"Thank you again, sir," Hutch said.

Maguire ended the call. Then he quickly scrolled through his contact list and selected a number. He listened to it ring several times before he heard it connect.

"I take it this isn't a social call is it, Commissioner?" Detective Angelo Antonucci said.

"No, Ang, it isn't," Maguire replied. "Please tell me I'm not going to ruin your weekend."

"No, sir, the Met's are going to be fully responsible for that," the man answered. "What do you need?"

"Have you ever been to New Hampshire?"

"No, I can't say as I have," Antonucci replied. "I'm not really the whole *Mother Nature* kind of person."

"Well, I'm about to expand your horizons," Maguire said. "I have a missing persons case I need you to take a first-hand look at."

"With all due respect, isn't this something *Missing Persons* should be able to handle?"

"The missing person is a former member of the service," Maguire replied, "and she's my old partner. She's also the chief of police in Penobscot, New Hampshire. The acting chief up there has asked for our help and this all needs to be done under the radar for the time being."

"Say no more," Antonucci replied. "When do you need me to go?"

"We probably have a very short shelf life on this one. How much time do you need to get ready?"

"An hour," he replied.

"Okay, I'll make arrangements to have a helicopter pick you up over at Nassau County Aviation in two hours."

"Okay, I'll be waiting."

"Thanks, Ang," Maguire replied.

He ended the call and then called Melody.

"OMG, how lazy can you get?" Melody said, when she answered the call. "Are we just going to have phone sex now?"

"Listen, I just spoke to a cop from the Penobscot police," he replied somberly. "Alex has gone missing."

Melody sat up in tub, all levity gone from her voice. "What? When?"

"They think sometime last night," he replied.

"Oh my God, what are they doing? Are they looking for her? What's going to happen?"

"They are reaching out for help," he explained.

"What do you want you to do?"

"I'm sending Angelo up," he replied, "but since this is an off the books kind of job, I really don't want to send him up in one of the NYPD's birds. I can just imagine the scene that would create and potentially the front cover news it might generate."

"You want me to call Bob Miller and ask him to fire up the helicopter?"

"If you wouldn't mind," Maguire said.

"Of course not," she said. "Are you going too?"

"I hadn't thought that far in advance."

"You'd better go, James," Melody replied. "God forbid anything has happened to her; you'll never forgive yourself for not being there."

"What about you?" he said.

"What about me?"

"I hate leaving you home alone," he said.

"Good Lord, I'm not a fragile little china doll," she said with a laugh. "I can handle being alone. Hell, I might even be able to get some actual work done."

"Are you sure?"

"Positive," she replied. "Go do what you do best and I will be praying for her."

"I'll be up in a few minutes to get ready," he replied.

"I'll call, Bob," Melody replied. "When do you want him to pick you up?"

"As soon as possible," he said. "I told Ang that I'd have him picked up in about two hours."

"Okay, I'll have him get everything ready for you."

"Thank you, angel."

CHAPTER TWENTY-NINE

Alex heard the door unlock and the sound of footsteps padding lightly across the floor.

Here we go with round two.

A moment later she felt the hood being pulled from her head. She'd expected to see Tatiana, but instead she stared up at the face of a young girl.

What the fuck? she thought, her mind racing as she tried to process this latest twist.

The girl stared down at Alex for a moment, an impassive look on her face, before pulling up the chair and sitting down.

Who the hell are you?

The girl didn't say a word, she just stared, and Alex got the feeling that she was waging an internal battle inside her head. She decided not to make it any easier; so she held the woman's gaze with the same unflinching eyes.

Seconds slipped by and then minutes, as the two women sized each other up. In the end it was Susan who finally gave in. She broke eye contact, as she reached down and removed the gag.

Alex stretched her lower jaw, feeling the ache radiating thought her jaw.

"Thanks," she said once she was able to talk.

"You're welcome," Susan replied.

"So who the hell are you?" Alex asked.

"I'm the one that you let get away, Chief Taylor," she replied coolly.

Now it was Alex's turn to have the battle in her head, as she fought to figure out who this woman was. Obviously the woman knew who she was. There was something vaguely familiar about her, but, try as she might, Alex just couldn't place the face.

"Not that it means anything," the woman continued. "In fact, all that really matters is that I didn't let you get away."

Alex continued to stare at her, her mind struggling to put the pieces together. She was young, maybe in her late teens and quite pretty. Her light blonde hair was worn in a short bob cut that framed the sides of her face and she had piercing blue eyes. In a way, she reminded Alex of her younger self.

Much younger self, she conceded.

The woman smiled, clearly taking enjoyment out of Alex's inability to figure out who she was.

"Drawing a blank, huh?' she said with a slight giggle. "You know, I'd probably start to question your cop abilities, but the truth is that I've changed my appearance a bit."

"Well then, why don't you help me out a bit?" Alex asked.

"Mmmmmm, you need my help, huh?"

"It's your game, baby," Alex said. "If you want to play your gonna have to give me something more to work with."

"Well, let's just say that we were like two ships in the night," Susan replied. "Back then I was filled with the whole angst-ridden, *daddy didn't love me* bullshit, but I've moved on."

"I hate to say it, but considering your age group, that isn't the most uncommon of traits."

"True," Susan replied. "These years can be particularly brutally for some of us, especially when you squirrel yourself away in your closet, reading some really profound, but incredibly dark shit some teacher told you about. Part of me thinks they do it just to see how many of us they can fuck up in the head before they try and fuck us in bed."

No, it can't be, she thought.

But the more she stared at her the more she realized exactly who she was talking to. The brown hair and eyes were gone, as was the happy smile that had been captured in the school photo; which was completely understandable, considering all that she had gone through.

"Susan?"

"*Ding, Ding, Ding*," she said with a laugh. "It looks like the chief isn't a complete idiot after all. Thank you for restoring my faith in law enforcement."

"Glad I could help," Alex replied.

"I have to admit, you're much better looking up close," Susan said. "Most of my observations of you have always been at a distance, at least until the shooting, but as you can imagine, things were a bit chaotic that day and I didn't feel like whispering sweet nothings in your ear while the lead was flying."

That's why she looked so damn familiar!

In a moment of clarity Alex recalled seeing the girl, the flash of blonde hair, as she turned around at the end of the aisle, just before her world went to shit.

"That was you at the back of the store," Alex said. "You walked around the corner as I started down the aisle."

"Right again," Susan replied. "Damn, you are good. Yep, that was little old me playing hide and seek."

"Oh, lucky me, do I win a prize?" Alex asked with a tinge of sarcasm.

"Oh you want a prize, huh?"

"Yeah, how about you untie me and we go our separate ways?"

"Let me think about that, *Nooooo...........*" Susan said with a pouty face. "But you do get extra points for a nice try."

"Oh come on, you said it yourself, you think I'm good looking, untie me and we can have some fun. I certainly know you're not opposed to that sort of thing."

"True," Susan said. "I can't say the thought isn't appealing to me, but I also have no illusions that the minute I untied you my dreams of pleasure would turn into a reality of pain. I'm reasonably certain that you'd kick my ass long before I could even begin to enjoy it."

"You know what they say, *nothing ventured, nothing gained,*" Alex replied.

"Hmmm, let me sleep on that and I'll get back to you," Susan said. "I must say that you were fucking incredible the other day. The way you lit that prick up gave me such a rush. I'd have stopped to give you a pat on the back, but I was too focused on getting the hell out of there. Cops and I don't mix, for obvious reasons."

"Killing folks does put a strain on those types of relationships."

"On some relationships," Susan said, "but not on all."

"Clearly," Alex replied. "So how did you and Little Miss Psychopath come to be BFF's?"

"Mmmmmm, as luck would have it our stars aligned and we met on the beach," Susan said. "It was paradise. Tatiana is an amazing lover and a wonderful mentor."

"Awww, how romantic," Alex said. "Hopefully when this is all over I can arrange for the two of you to get the bridal suite at the prison."

"That sounds good, and I'm sure you believe it, but the truth is that the future is looking rather bleak for you right now."

"Maybe, but I also get the sense that there is something else going on here," Alex replied. "I mean if it was simply a matter of wanting to get rid of me then it makes no sense to kidnap me."

Susan stared at Alex and she could see the tension in the young woman's face, the muscles rippling along her jaw, as she clenched her teeth. The faux sweetness was gone now, replaced by a darkness that chased away her prettiness in favor of something that resembled pure evil. At that moment, most people would have been gripped by a sense of fear, as they felt an icy chill run through them, but Alex only felt an opportunity being presented to her.

"You see, Susan, you normally just kill people you don't want around and yet here I am. So there's probably another reason why I'm not lying in a ditch somewhere."

"You don't know what you're talking about," Susan said angrily.

Now Alex knew that she had the woman exactly where she wanted her, the point where she was beginning to question things.

"I just mean that it makes no sense," Alex replied "Experience tells me that there must be more to the plan; perhaps something you might not even be privy to. I mean there has to be a reason why I'm still among the living. Don't you at least wonder why that is?"

"Shut up," Susan said.

"Why? Did I hit a nerve, cupcake?" Alex asked. "Am I sensing a bit of jealousy?"

"Jealous? Me? Of you?" Susan said with a laugh. "I don't think so. I mean, don't get me wrong, you're good looking for *your age*, but don't flatter yourself."

"Perhaps," Alex said, "but the truth is that you can only speak for yourself. The last time I looked there was another person here."

"Tatiana and I are just fine," Susan replied. "Maybe she just wants to make you suffer a bit longer before she ends your miserable life."

Susan had taken the bait and now it was time to set the hook.

"Maybe making me suffer isn't exactly what she has in mind," Alex said. "I mean the last time Patty Ann and I were together she seemed to have,...... Hmmm, how shall I say this delicately, more *pleasurable* things on her mind?"

Alex watched as the young woman's eyes went wide and the color drained from the face. The darkness was gone now, replaced with a pained look that was more akin to having been sucker-punched. A painful silence hung in the room, as Susan desperately tried to process what she had just been told.

"Wait,...... What,......" Susan asked stunned, the words coming out a bit choppy. "What did you just say?"

"Just that she seemed to have more pleasurable things in mind."

"No,..... No,...." She stammered. "What did you call her?"

"Patty Ann?" Alex replied with feigned innocence. "That's her name, isn't it?"

"How the fuck do you know her name?" Susan replied angrily.

"What, Patty never told you about us?"

"Us?....... What fucking *Us*?

"Oh, baby, I'm so sorry," Alex said, with manufactured empathy. "I thought you already knew. It's just that Patty, I mean Tatiana, and I go way back."

"How way back?" Susan asked

"Before you, I'm afraid, but I am sure it's nothing; all water under the bridge, as they say. Although, I'm not exactly sure why she wouldn't have told you?"

"What did you guys do?" Susan asked.

Alex could tell from the look on her face what she was thinking. The green-eyed monster had already made its appearance in her head and Susan had begun to fill in the blanks. Jealousy in the head of any woman was bad enough, but in the formative mind of a young girl it was downright dangerous.

"You really don't want to hear all the sordid details," Alex replied, "and it's really not my place to kiss and tell. You're better off asking her yourself. I don't want to get between you two love birds."

"Fuck you," Susan said angrily, as she forced the gag back into Alex's mouth and pulled the hood back over her head. "Enjoy your remaining time alive, *Chief*. When the time comes you can be certain that you'll be staring into my eyes as I put an end your miserable little life, bitch."

A moment later Alex heard the angry slamming of the door, following by the metallic sound of the lock closing.

Well, that went remarkably easy, she thought.

CHAPTER THIRTY

Hutch took a sip of coffee then glanced over at the car's digital clock display, as he and Abby sat in the radio car over at the Earlton International Airport.

It seemed to him a bit of a *stretch* to call the single, gravel runway location an airport, let alone an international one, but the occasional flights in and out of Canada probably qualified it as such. Still the place seemed more suited for the single-prop type of planes than anything you'd see in a traditional airport. For the moment, it would serve its purpose nicely.

They'd selected the airport for two reasons. Number one it was far enough away from Penobscot that it wouldn't attract any attention and number two it was a suitable landing place near to where the last ping was received from Alex's cell phone.

"They did say six o'clock right?" Hutch asked.

"Yeah," Abby replied, "but I guess even helicopters can get delayed in traffic."

"I guess," Hutch replied. "You don't think I did anything wrong by calling him, do you?"

"Who? Maguire?"

"Yeah, I mean if this turns out to be nothing, and she did just go for a hike, she's going to kill me."

"No she's not," Abby replied. "Under the circumstances I think it was completely reasonable. Didn't you say he agreed with you that it didn't feel right?"

"He did, but still......"

"Don't over analyze it, Hutch. You're acting chief and you did what you thought was prudent to do. Besides, it was his idea to send someone up to look at things."

"I know, but I'm *acting* only till we find her," he replied. "I just hope I'm not unemployed after we do."

"Stop it, Hutch. You know Alex would never do that. Besides, she actually does like you."

"How do you know?" he asked.

"We talk," Abby said. "It's a girl thing. Now if you don't mind, I need a cigarette."

Abby got out of the car, walked around to the front, and leaned on the fender, as she fished out the pack of cigarettes from her shirt pocket. A moment later, Hutch joined her.

"I'm sure you're right," he replied. "I guess I just don't want her to think I'm a screw-up."

"Let's just focus on finding her first," Abby said. "She has to be here in order to be angry."

"With all this stress maybe I should take up smoking too."

"You probably should wait."

"Why?"

"Because if Alex *does* fire you; you won't be able to afford them."

"That's not funny," Hutch replied.

"No, it was pretty funny," Abby said with a laugh.

Just then the quiet evening air was interrupted by the faint *thump, thump, thump* of a helicopter, as it approached the airport, its roar growing louder with each passing second.

Hutch and Abby watched as the big Sikorsky S92 cleared the end of the field and began its approach to the helicopter landing pad.

"Wow, talk about arriving in style," Hutch said.

"Must be nice," Abby replied. "Maybe we can talk Sheldon into buying one for us."

"I don't think he'd even spring for a photo of one to hang on our wall."

"This is true."

As they watched, the helicopter set down effortlessly on the small pad and they heard the whine of the engines as they began to throttle down.

"God, I hope whoever he sent isn't an arrogant prick," Hutch said. "I've seen how they are on television and I'd hate to be treated like some dumb redneck cop."

Abby turned to look at him with a frown on her face. "Are you serious? You're being stereotypical about city cops because of the stereotypical performance of Hollywood actors?"

"Be nice to me," he said. "I'm having a tough week."

Abby was about to say something when they saw the door open on the helicopter and a small set of stairs unfold. A moment later a man appeared in the doorway and stepped down.

He had dark hair and a swarthy complexion, which Abby figured made him Italian or at least from some other

Mediterranean country. Ironically, he looked like he had stepped out of a Hollywood casting call for the stereotypical hot police detective.

God, please don't let Hutch be right, she thought.

She was about to walk forward to greet the man, when another person appeared in the doorway and she let out a gasp, immediately feeling her knees go slightly weak.

"Holy shit, is that......? "

"Yes,....." Abby said softly, as she continued to stare at the man coming down the stairs. "Yes it is."

"Hi, I'm Angelo Antonucci," the first man said, as he approached them.

"Nice to meet you, I'm Chris Hutchinson," Hutch replied, shaking the man's hand. "This is Abby Simpson."

"Hi," Abby said with a smile, as she shook his hand, even as her eyes peered past him at the other man approaching them.

In the beginning, she had thought that Alex was exaggerating about just how good looking he was, so she had checked out some photos online and found out she wasn't lying. Never did she expect that the photos of Maguire wouldn't even do him justice.

"Nice to meet you," Antonucci said, as he stepped to the side. "This is Police Commissioner Maguire."

"It's a pleasure to meet you, Commissioner," Hutch said, shaking the man's hand. "I'm Chris Hutchinson, we spoke on the phone. I just wish it was under different circumstances, sir."

"Likewise, Chris," Maguire replied.

"Oh, please, call me Hutch," he said, "and this is Abby Simpson."

"Pleasure to meet you, Abby," Maguire said, taking her hand in his.

For a brief moment Abby was mesmerized, as she stared up into the most amazing blue eyes she had ever seen, and then realized she hadn't responded.

"Oh, I'm sorry, I was just thinking about something," she said. "It's very nice to meet you as well. Alex speaks very highly of you."

"Only believe half of everything Alex says about me," Maguire said with a laugh.

"Oh, it's all good," Abby replied.

"Well then, if it's all good, believe even less."

"Where would you like to go first, sir?" Hutch asked.

"It's your show, Ang," Maguire said, deferring to Antonucci. "I signed on to be Detective Antonucci's assistant on this one, but the truth is I just needed some fresh air."

"Well, we have plenty of that up here," Hutch replied.

"I know it's late," Antonucci said, "but can we go and take a look at the area where the last cell phone ping was picked up at?"

"Sure thing," Hutch replied, as he motioned them toward the waiting car. "It's just down the road."

They loaded their bags into the trunk of the car and got inside. Fifteen minutes later Hutch pulled the radio car onto the shoulder of a particularly desolate stretch of Route 26.

"Here we are," he said, putting the car in park. "Not much to see, but the tower is just over there."

Antonucci got out of the car and acclimated himself to his new surroundings. The cell phone tower sat out in a large, empty farm field, about fifty yards from the two lane road. He did a three hundred and sixty degree turn, taking in his surroundings, but there was little if anything to be seen. There were no visible signs of any homes or other structures from what he could make out.

"How far away from here does the chief live?" he asked.

"About a half hour drive in that direction," Abby replied, gesturing with her hand toward the east.

"Without sounding too much like a city-slicker, are there some areas around here that are more prone to hiking than others?"

"If you're asking whether she would need to drive to one, then the answer is no," Hutch chimed in. "Her house is out in the country, almost at the base of Mt. Moriah, so she could actually walk out her front door and start hiking."

"So the odds are pretty good that when the ping came in she was probably on the road and not walking."

"Yeah, but her car is still in her garage," Abby said.

"Could someone have picked her up?"

Hutch and Abby looked at one another. It was a question neither of them had truly considered.

"To be honest, Alex doesn't really have many non-cop friends out here," Hutch said, "and those she has I wouldn't consider as being the hiking type."

"What about the non-hiking types?" Antonucci asked. "I mean we're all adults here. Could she have simply gone off with someone to get away?"

"There's only one person *here* that she would go off with," Abby said, glancing over at Maguire, "but I really don't think that happened."

"Why?" Antonucci asked.

"Because he and Alex supposedly got into an argument last night," Hutch replied.

"Oh really," Antonucci said. "Has anyone spoken to him?"

"We spoke to him earlier today," Hutch said. "He seemed pretty upset about the whole thing."

"You mean Peter Bates?" Maguire asked.

"You know him, boss?" Antonucci asked.

"Yes and no, Ang," Maguire replied. "He came to my house last Christmas with Alex. He seemed like a pretty stand-up guy from what I could tell. I guess you could say they're dating."

"They are," Abby said, "but it's sort of an on-again, off-again thing relationship."

"Why is that?" Antonucci asked.

Abby glanced over at Maguire wondering what she was supposed to say. That Alex couldn't commit to anyone because she was still hung up on her old partner?

"Because Alex isn't exactly the easiest person to get along with," Maguire replied.

Antonucci took the moment in, knowing that there was something missing from the equation and it appeared to be intentional. Clearly there was more to the story, but he would need to tread with caution. It did after all involve his bosses' old *partner.*

"What did he tell you?" Antonucci asked.

"Just that he was concerned about her, because of the shooting, and that he went out to check on her. He said that she'd been drinking and was being a bit *belligerent.* So he just decided to leave and deal with things when she had sobered up. Before he could come back out we talked to him."

"How did he seem to you?"

"Concerned, upset," Hutch replied. "I understand why you're asking, but Dr. Bates is a really nice guy."

"I'm sure he is," Antonucci replied. "Unfortunately, experience has shown me that nice people still do bad things to other nice people, even the ones they love."

"I understand," Hutch replied. "I guess that's why I asked for help."

"Well, before we go rounding up folks for interrogations; let's see where the evidence leads us first," Antonucci said.

He gazed around at the empty thoroughfare, checking in both directions.

"I guess it would be too much to ask if they have traffic cameras on this roadway?"

Hutch looked at Antonucci, then at the road, and finally back at him.

"We're lucky to have any traffic," he replied with a laugh.

"Point taken," Antonucci replied.

"So if she was traveling west on this road, what's the first town she would hit?"

"Earlton," Abby said. "The airport is back there; we just took the back road to get here."

"Can we go and take a look at the town?"

"Sure," Hutch replied.

A few minutes later they drove into the sleepy little town and Hutch pulled the car into the parking lot of a closed tractor dealership.

"Welcome to Earlton," Hutch said, stepping out of the car.

"It's certainly quaint," Maguire said, as he glanced around at the main drag.

"Population of just over eight hundred people," Abby replied. "It's actually pretty large for this area."

"On the plus side, it shouldn't take too long to survey," Antonucci replied.

"Mind if I join you," Hutch asked.

"Not at all," Antonucci replied.

"How do these towns even stay alive?" Maguire asked, as he watched the two men walk off.

"Most of them survive off the summer rental markets," Abby explained, as she leaned against the car's fender and lit up a cigarette. "The town's residential population may be small, but the area around here is dotted with tons of summer rental places. So the overall population will easily double, if not triple, come July and August."

"Excuse my ignorance, but what's the attraction?" Maguire asked. "I mean it's beautiful and everything, but why here?"

Abby laughed. "It's hard for city folks to understand.

"Actually, I was raised in a place not much bigger than this," Maguire replied, "but we had a major waterway, winter skiing and an Air Force base to explain the draw."

"I apologize," Abby said. "I never would have pegged you for a *country boy*."

"Shhhhh......" Maguire said with a smile. "We all have our secrets."

"Well, the draw here is actually Lake Moriah," Abby replied. "Between the annual boating regatta and an invitational fishing competition, people seem to flock to this place come the summer. The places closest to the lake go quickly, so folks come out here for cheaper prices along with easier access to restaurants and stores."

"Well that makes sense," he replied. "Actually I recall Alex talking about the boating event before."

"Yeah, it's our major *pain-in-the-ass* event, pardon my French," she replied.

"*Je te pardonne, mademoiselle*," Maguire said with a smile.

"*Merci beaucoup, monsieur*," Abby replied with a smile and a wink.

"Ah, so you actually do know French."

"Enough to mangle it," she replied. "At least that was the overall assessment of my high school French teacher."

"It's been my experience that it's pretty much useless; unless of course you plan on traveling abroad," Maguire said. "Then it is useful if only to make illicit laughs from the locals."

"Well, I'd have to travel somewhere first, so I doubt I'm going to make anyone laugh anytime soon."

"Well, take it from someone who has done a bit of traveling, there's certainly no place like home, especially somewhere as idyllic as this."

Abby took a drag on her cigarette and exhaled slowly. Maguire could read by the body language that her mind was already somewhere else.

"You okay?" he asked.

"Yeah," she replied. "I guess."

"That's not really too convincing."

"Please don't take this the wrong way, and I mean no disrespect, but I would have felt a lot better if I didn't see you get off that helicopter."

"Fair enough," Maguire said. "You mind if I ask why?"

"Because all this suddenly became very real," she replied. "I figure if you came all the way up here then you must be worried and if the commissioner of the NYPD is worried......"

"Nah," he said with a smile. "I'm just here to kick her butt when she turns up for making us all come out here."

"That was a nice try," she said with a smile, "but thanks."

"How's she doing up here?" Maguire asked. "Honestly."

"Alex? I'd say she's doing great," Abby said. "Why?"

"She tells me she is acclimating to the new scenery, but I still worry about her."

"You do, don't you?" Abby replied, the words coming out more as a confirmatory statement than a question.

"I just want her to be happy. I just want her to catch a break."

"She's doing really well up here," Abby replied.

"How do the folks around town feel about her?"

"Most of the department loves her, except for the few slackers who she pushes to work. The folks at city hall all think she is trying to bankrupt them and the town folks are generally ambivalent to it all; unless of course something happens to piss them off. So I guess you could say that it's probably the same for her as it is for every police chief."

"Well that pretty much sums up my career," Maguire replied with a laugh. "You have a damn good ability at analyzing things, Abby."

"I can't imagine what it must be like to work in New York City," she said. "Alex will tell me stories and it all seems so surreal. I mean I know she's telling me the truth, her experiences, but it could all be the plot for some outrageous movie or book, as far as what I can comprehend. It is certainly a lot different than we are used to in Penobscot."

"I don't think police work changes too much," he replied. "Maybe the volume is different, but not the crime. It is however a great learning place."

"I can only imagine."

"You should come down for a visit," he said. "I'll make sure you get the grand tour."

"Alex keeps telling me that we should go for a girl's weekend."

"Call me first if she starts talking about taking you to any of her old stomping grounds," he warned. "Some things you need to be eased into."

"Will do," Abby said with a laugh.

"Well that was quick," Maguire said, as he watched the two men walking back toward them.

"It is a *very* small town," Antonucci replied.

"So how'd you make out?" Maguire asked.

"If I was looking to do a crime, this would get high marks," he replied.

"Under the circumstances that's not a good thing," Maguire said.

"No, but we *might* have caught a break. There's a new fishing place just up the road. Hutch told me that it just opened a few weeks back. It looks like they have some surveillance cams on either end of the building. Probably there to cover the parking lot, but judging from the angle of the road in front, they could have picked up something."

"Can we look at them?"

"Dunno," Antonucci replied, looking over at Hutch.

"The store is closed now, it's the off-season," Hutch explained. "Most places don't start staying open late until the end of May. There's just not enough business to justify it. "

"Can we contact the owner?" Maguire asked.

"I tried," Hutch replied. "I called over to the sheriff's office but they don't have a business contact card on file for them yet. We're going to have to wait till the morning."

"Does anyone have any suggestions on where to spend the night?" Maguire asked.

"You're more than welcome to stay at my place," Hutch said. "I've got four bedrooms and it's just me."

"Well, we don't want to be any imposition," Maguire replied.

"It wouldn't be," Hutch said.

"Then we accept your generous invitation."

CHAPTER THIRTY-ONE

The fight had been epic; a regular knock-down, drag-out affair, and had lasted longer than she could have possibly imagined.

At times it was hard to say who was actually winning. Each woman had scored some major blows, as time after time they opened the *vault of history* and began blasting one another with past transgressions.

The acrimony was almost palpable.

Through it all Alex laid there, amused at the level of dissension that she had been able to sow in such a small period of time. It was clear from their willingness to scream at each other that neither woman was afraid of being *overheard*, which led Alex to believe that wherever they were had to be fairly remote.

In her severely restricted environment, Alex could only guess how long they had been going at, but eventually silence overtook everything; prompting her to wonder if the two women had killed each other. That might have been wishful thinking on her part; although in her current predicament it was probably not a good thing for her.

If no one came running with those two idiots screaming bloody murder, then chances are that no one's gonna be tripping over your little ass till you're a broken down corpse.

In the silence she had drifted off to sleep, knowing that she desperately needed to work on a part two of her plan and to do it quick, but that sleep didn't last very long.

Alex was ripped from dreams by the violent removal of the hood. In the darkness she could make out the figure of Tatiana standing over her and she could smell the heaviness of the alcohol on the woman's breath.

"You think you're so goddamn smart, don't you?" she said, slurring her words slightly, as she stared down at Alex ominously.

Even in the dead of night Alex could still make out the visceral hatred in the woman's face.

"That was dumb trying to pit her against me," she continued, as she removed the gag from Alex's mouth roughly.

Whatever type of conversation Tatiana had in mind, it apparently wasn't going to be one-sided.

"So what, you decided to come back and try your hand at being a mean girl again?" Alex asked.

Alex felt the woman's closed fist come down hard across her face, snapping her neck.

Fuck me, that one hurt, she thought.

"Was that mean enough for you, baby girl?"

After she had regained her composure, she looked back at Tatiana and smiled. There was no way she would let her get the upper hand.

"You know, I think they have internet videos that could really help you out in all this."

"I'm glad you think this is all so very funny," Tatiana said, as she sat down in the chair, "but I promise you, that won't last for long."

"Aren't you afraid you're little pet is going to be mad that you're here with me and not with her? Sounds like you two psychotic love birds have some making up to do."

"Oh, don't worry about Susan; she's going to be sleeping soundly for a while."

"You seem to have this thing about knocking people out."

"It has its usefulness," Tatiana said, as she reached out her hand and began to stroke Alex's leg with her fingertips.

"It must really suck that you have to resort to drugging someone to get what you want," Alex said derisively.

"Don't you worry," Tatiana said smugly. "In time you'll be begging for it."

"Only in your twisted little fantasies, Patty-Ann."

The woman laughed, as she fished out the pack of cigarettes from her shirt pocket and lit one up.

"You can call me we whatever you like, Alex, but there's really no point in trying to play mind games with me. In time you'll find that you're way out of your league here."

"We'll just have to see about that now, won't we?" Alex replied.

Tatiana laughed.

It wasn't a funny laugh, nor was it one of ridicule, but the laugh of someone who knew better and it actually sent a chill through Alex.

"I was like you once," Tatiana said. "I was smug, I was arrogant, and I was strong. After the psychological hell that my *husband* had put me though, I naïvely thought that nothing could break me, not even Banning, but I was so very wrong."

"I'm not a weak little girl like you were, Patty," Alex said accusatorily. "I don't bend."

"Oh, you'll bend," Tatiana replied, "or you'll most certainly break. In the end it doesn't really matter to me which one you choose to do."

"What does matter to you? What do you really want?" Alex asked.

"Just to finish what you started," she said matter-of-factly, as her hand gripped Alex's thigh. "Remember, I wasn't the one that sought you out; I wasn't the one who made the first move."

"You know that wasn't *real*."

"Most things aren't real," Tatiana replied. "Just like the pathetic little lives most of us lead."

"Speak for your *pathetic* self," Alex replied. "Putting losers like you, and your warped little *mini-me,* behind bars is pretty damn real for me."

"Is it?" Tatiana asked. "How do you know what is real and what isn't?"

Silence hung in the room for a moment, as Tatiana stared at Alex, her face a mix of pity and contempt.

"I was like you once, thinking that my life actually mattered, but it wasn't until I encountered Banning that I realized that I was just living a lie. At first I thought him to be the essence of pure evil and I fought him with every fiber of my being. In the beginning he would keep me drugged; just enough to not pose a threat to him. It felt so cruel, so inhumane. He would come into the room to use me and there was nothing I could do to stop him."

Tatiana took a drag on the cigarette, staring off into space, as she relived the vivid moments in her mind.

"I came to the conclusion that I might not have been able to resist him with my body, but I could with my mind. Each time I would shut down, go to my *happy place* as they say, until he was done, but after a while I began to wonder why I was doing that. My mind told me one thing, yet my body said something else."

"Why doesn't that surprise me?" Alex scoffed.

"Laugh all you want, but, mark my words, it will be a conversation that you have with yourself one day."

"Just because you're weak, doesn't mean I am."

"Weak? Is that what you really think I am?" Tatiana said with a laugh. "No, Alex, I am far from weak. I will admit that I was, but Banning set me free from that type of life."

"What, like being normal?"

"It's not *normal*," Tatiana said in disgust. "It's a *lie*."

"Oh, so being a rational, well-adjusted member of society is a lie?" Alex asked. "You're crazier than I thought."

"Am I?" Tatiana asked. "If that's the case, then why do we have so many laws and rules? If society is so well adjusted, why do we have folks like you to police us?"

"Because of people like you?"

"People like me?" Tatiana said with a laugh. "That's precious. Humans have been on this planet for hundreds of thousands of years. During that time they have warred, raped, pillaged and plundered. At some point you have to accept that it is who we are, Alex. Have you ever thought for a moment that the ones who established the laws, who sold the theory of *rules* to the masses, were just the weak ones who were afraid that they'd be next? Maybe the lie is that we only pretend to be rational, well-adjusted members of society."

"You're delusional," Alex replied.

"*Au contraire*, my dear," she said, as she took one last drag on her cigarette then crushed it out. "Your very existence confirms my belief. You see, weak people exist, but they do not live. Living life is truly hard and requires freedom, yet the law actually restricts freedom. It tells you what you can and cannot do as well as where you can and cannot go. The weaker members of society require laws to establish what is *acceptable* behavior simply to protect themselves; because they are weak and would not be able to survive without them. Because of this they need other people, like you, to help them. If you removed all laws tomorrow there would be three choices: die, become strong, or serve."

"Freud would have loved you."

"You and I would survive, Alex," Tatiana said, ignoring the jab.

"You and I are not alike."

"Aren't we?" she asked. "You're strong; you're a survivor. You showed that in the store."

"I didn't shoot him for enjoyment," Alex said angrily. "I'm not a cold-blooded monster like you."

"No? Then what are you?"

"I'm a cop," Alex replied. "I protect people."

"Ah yes, the very same people that are lining up at this very moment to lock you away," she replied coldly. "The irony is thick."

"Fuck you."

"I imagine that it has to be cruel living in that world," Tatiana continued, "to know that you are being *used* by the weak simply because they are incapable of doing their own dirty work. Always having to be right; knowing that if you screw up just once those sanctimonious cowards will try and lynch you. If you are honest with yourself, Alex, you will have to admit the truth; which is that they really don't like you."

"You don't know anything," Alex replied.

"You're a mercenary; you just don't want to face it. You sell your gun and your propensity toward violence to the highest bidder. In return they give you a shiny piece of metal, along with a title of legitimacy, so that when you commit the violence in their name it is legal, but it is all an act. You like to pretend you are different from me, but you're not. When you commit violence on their behalf it sickens them, just like when I do it, because they are weak. Your existence reminds them of their own impotence. They suffer you only because they believe they can control you. In the end, you only have to look at them to realize that you have more in common with me then you do with them."

"You and I have nothing in common."

"Don't we?" Tatiana asked. "You know, from the moment I first saw you, I wanted you, but it was you, not I, who made the first move. When things went south I was pissed, but the more I thought about it the more I realized that you are very much an opportunist. You had a goal and you were willing to do anything to advance it. Would you have used your body to further your plans?

Most people would have been repulsed by the very idea, yet you didn't seem to have any qualms. In fact, I think you would have eagerly jumped into bed with me, as long as it meant that you would have gotten what you wanted."

"Go to hell."

Tatiana laughed, as she stood up and leaned over the bed.

"Darling," she whispered in Alex's ear, as her hands reached down and began hiking up her shirt, exposing the bright pink bra. "You're already here."

"Get your hands off me, bitch," Alex said menacingly.

Tatiana grabbed the gag and forcefully stuffed it back into her mouth.

"I won't lie," she said, as she yanked the sports bra up. "At first you're going to hate this, but in time you'll grow to love it."

Alex thrashed about, trying valiantly to resist, but it was useless and she knew it.

"Think of this as the first steps in me liberating you from the lie," Tatiana whispered, nibbling playfully on her earlobe, as she began caressing her exposed breast. "Now that we are finally together, no one will separate us."

Left with no other choice, Alex closed her eyes and went to her *happy place.*

CHAPTER THIRTY-TWO

"Good morning."

Hutch abruptly turned, startled by the unexpected greeting.

"Holy shit," he replied, as he saw Maguire sitting at the kitchen table.

"Sorry, I didn't mean to catch you off-guard."

"No, it's okay," Hutch said, walking over to the coffee pot. "I just didn't expect anyone else up this early."

"I should have warned you that I'm an early riser."

"Early riser?" Hutch replied, staring out the kitchen window into the darkness, as he poured his coffee. "I don't even think the roosters are awake yet."

"You're up," Maguire said with a laugh.

"Eh, I had a rough night," Hutch said, as he took the seat across from him.

"Yeah, me too."

"Was the bed uncomfortable?" Hutch asked with a concerned look.

"Oh, no, the bed was fine, I was just thinking of Alex."

"Hmmm, I'm glad that I'm not the only one," Hutch replied.

"Even when she's not around, she's still around," Maguire said.

"So does that mean you're worried about her too?"

"It's Alex," Maguire said softly. "I'm always worried about her."

"Are you worried that something happened to her or are you worried that we won't find her?"

"I don't know," Maguire replied, "and I think it's that uncertainty that is what's bothering me."

"Clearly you know her better than I do," Hutch said. "Has she ever done anything like this before? I mean is this like her?"

Maguire picked up the coffee cup in front of him and took a drink, as he contemplated the question.

He had known Alex, both professionally and personally, for almost twenty years. During that entire time the only thing he was truly certain of was that she was enigmatic. He would have liked to have been able to give a better answer, but it was the closest thing to the truth he could come up with. To say that she tended to keep things close to the vest would have been a huge understatement. Hell, after all this time, he'd only recently learned that she had feelings for him.

His mind went back to the first day that he had met the young, blonde haired cop in the Seven-Three. He'd watched her arrive in her jeans and t-shirt, hair pulled up in a ponytail, and his first thought was that she was there to file a police report. She looked so out of place to him; a fragile looking girl from the suburbs trapped inside the inner-city, but it didn't take long to realize that it was all just a façade. When she returned in uniform a few moments later, the medals above her shield told a different story. Behind the beauty beat the heart of a tough-as-nails cop.

Maguire might have been the command's newest rookie, but his past experience had garnered him a healthy amount of respect from the other cops, everyone that was except for his new partner. He vividly recalled their first tour together. The patrol supervisor had just given them their assignment and they'd turned out for the four to twelve shift on a warm summer's night in July. Without saying a word to him, she'd turned and walked out the back door; heading to their radio car, which was parked in the lot.

"Don't touch the radio," she said coolly, from behind the wheel of the beat up Ford Crown Victoria, as he got in.

"Okay," he replied.

"All you need to do is look, listen and, unless you see a gun, keep your mouth shut," she said, as they pulled out of the parking lot and turned onto Boyland Street. "Anything else and I will let you know what to do."

"Aye-aye," he replied, unsure what to make of the whole thing.

Alex grabbed the radio off the dashboard. "Three Adam to Central, show us 62 Administrative for a few."

"10-4, Three Adam," the dispatcher replied. "Advise when 98."

Two minutes later Alex pulled up to a Dunkin' Donuts.

"Large black coffee," she said, as she lit up her cigarette. "Get yourself something if you want."

"That's very magnanimous of you," he said gruffly, as he turned and headed inside.

A few moments later he returned to the RMP, handing her the coffee, and she pulled away from the curb. He stared out the window, taking in his new surroundings, as they made their way down Rockaway Ave. The sidewalks were bustling with people, but there was also an uneasiness to the entire scene.

Suddenly; the car crossed over the double yellow line and mounted the sidewalk, coming to a stop just outside the Brownsville Houses.

"What's going on?" he asked, his eyes darting back and forth, as he scanned the scene; searching for some missed threat.

"We're going sightseeing," she replied, as she got out of the car, grabbing her radio and the Styrofoam cup. "Don't forget your coffee."

Sightseeing? he thought. *Are you fucking serious*?

Almost immediately he could feel his body tense up, every one of his senses amped up to the max, as they made their way down the walkway; past a throng of people gathered outside.

Maguire could feel their eyes on him; a mix of suspicion and contempt on their faces. It was a scene that he was intimately familiar with, but one that he had only previously experienced in foreign countries. He wondered if his partner even realized that they were not welcome here.

Without warning she veered off and entered one of the buildings. Maguire followed her inside, looking backward occasionally and checking their six, as she made her way toward the stairwell door.

A powerful, damp mustiness hung in the air of the dimly lit corridor. A mélange of odors, some of them human in origin, fought to overwhelm his senses, as they cautiously made their way up to the rooftop. There was a sense of relief when she opened the rooftop door and they stepped out into the fresh air.

He watched as Alex walked around, checking to make sure that they were alone. Maguire joined her, noting the broken bottles, the five gallon buckets used as make-shift chairs and the glistening, empty brass ammo casings that littered the roof.

When she was done she walked over to the parapet and leaned on the edge, as she sipped on her coffee.

"Welcome to Brooklyn North, rookie," she said, waving her hand out in front of her with a flourish. "The first thing you need to do is take all that social science crap they spoon fed you in the academy and toss it all in the shitter, because none of it matters out here; where anything and everything can and will try to kill you if you're not careful."

"You missed your calling," he said. "You should write travel brochures."

Alex ignored the jab, as she fished the pack of cigarettes out of her pocket and lit one up.

"Let me ask you a question, rookie," she said, after a few minutes. "What don't you see out there?"

Maguire glanced around at the urban sprawl below him. The question was much too vague to warrant a serious reply.

"I don't know," he replied. "Why don't you tell me, *partner*."

"Water," she replied. "There's no fucking water for as far as the eye can see, which means all that Navy SEAL hero bullshit doesn't count for jack-shit out here."

As he watched, she removed her sunglasses and looked over at him, as if she was sizing him up.

247

"Let me ask you another question," she said. "What *do* you see out there?"

Maguire scanned the scene below him.

"Buildings, cars, people," he replied.

"Tell me about the people," she said.

"I get the feeling that they don't like us very much," he replied, "or at the very least they don't trust us."

"Smart boy," she replied cockily. "The truth is that about seventy-five percent of the people out there don't like you and the remaining twenty-five percent *really* don't like you. What you have to do is learn to differentiate between the two."

"This isn't my first rodeo," he said.

"Yeah, but you're not a soldier anymore, you're a cop," she replied. "Things just became a whole lot less cut and dry. There's no *fog of war* here for you to fall back on. Those dickheads in 1PP expect you to know the difference between an airsoft pistol and a real one on a moonless night. They also expect you to be able to make that distinction in some back alley, while your heart is beating a mile a minute, after chasing some thug, who has a rap sheet a mile long, for three blocks, who then suddenly turns on you. If you shoot first and you're wrong, the folks across the river will hang you out to dry in a heartbeat. If you shoot second and you're right, they bury you and give your momma a nice flag; then they hire someone to replace you at a lower salary."

She took a drag on her cigarette and returned back to looking down at the street below them.

"The folks down there don't care about you," she continued. "They've been conditioned over decades to believe that you're nothing more than another outsider sent here to oppress them."

"Sounds a lot like some of the places I've been too," he replied.

"Yeah, but that was some ass-backward village in the heart of *Whogivesafuckistan*," she said dryly. "This is *the* major city in America and you would think that things would be different. For the most part we share the same language and the same history, but for the better part of six decades all the community activists and store-front preaching charlatans have been selling these folks a tale that *we* are the enemy."

"I guess that's a global affliction."

"The truly sad thing is that they couldn't give a rat's ass less about the people down there," Alex replied. "They just sow the seeds of discontent in order to line their own pockets. There's no money to be made in actually fixing problems and most of these folks don't want to be lectured about personal responsibility. So they create a monster to blame it all on and that's us."

"Lovely," Maguire said quietly.

"Truth is that no one wants you here, but they also know that they need you and for that fact they resent you. The enemy is at the gates and you are the last line of defense for a populace who, in many ways, have been taught to believe you are a bigger threat to them. It makes it very hard to work under those conditions and it is very easy to grow bitter."

Alex took a long drag on the cigarette and proceeded to blow several smoke rings into the air.

"You have someone waiting for you at home?" she asked, when she was finished.

"No."

"Good," she said. "Relationships and police work don't mix. There will be days when you sit in your car after the tour is over and wonder what the hell just happened. When you had to comfort some sobbing mother, who's six year old was just killed by a bullet intended for baby-daddy number five, and then watch as one of the vaunted *reverends* comes out of the woodwork to blame the police for not doing more. The very same ones that only a week ago were blaming the police for locking up too many in the community. On those days it's much better to go get yourself a drink instead of going home and listening to some pathetic bullshit sob-story on why little Johnny isn't being treated *special* at school."

"Is this where I'm supposed to quit?" he asked.

Alex turned around to face him. Her face was completely neutral Maguire surmised that she'd be a bitch to play poker against. She dropped the cigarette onto the rooftop and crushed it beneath her boot.

"Quit, stay, I really don't fucking care what you do, rookie. All that matters to me is that when I go through a door that you are with me and that you have my back."

"Fair enough," he replied.

"Then we're good," she replied, as she turned and headed toward the door. "For now."

Maguire shook his head and laughed, as the memory faded away.

On the short list of people he truly respected, Alex was at the very top. For all of her shortcomings, she was a damn good cop. He had hoped that coming up here would be the opportunity she needed to put the past behind her and finally get her life back on track.

Had he been wrong?

"No," he finally said, in response to Hutch's question. "Alex has never done anything like this before."

"Anything like what?" Antonucci asked, as he walked into the kitchen.

"You're up early," Maguire replied.

"How can a person sleep," he remarked, as he poured himself a cup of coffee. "There's more chatting going on here than on a Sunday morning at my *Nonna's* house."

"Hutch was just asking if Alex had ever done something like this before and I told him no," Maguire explained.

"Then I suggest we suit up and go find her," Antonucci replied.

CHAPTER THIRTY-THREE

"Rise and shine," Susan said, as she pulled the hood from Alex's head.

Alex opened her eyes gingerly, giving the impression she'd just woken up when in reality she'd been awake for a while. She'd come to terms with the fact that time was not her friend and she used every available moment to not only formulate her plan of attack, but to listen for anything that might possibly be useful to her in doing so.

Susan removed the gag and set it on the bed next to her.

"Mmmmmm," she said groggily, glancing around the room and then back at Susan. "You're still here? I'm shocked."

"Why's that?" Susan asked, as she sat down in the chair.

"Well, after last night's fifteen-rounder I expected someone else to be doing my morning wake-up call."

"Sorry to disappoint you," Susan replied, as she retrieved a pocket knife from the jean shorts she was wearing and began cutting off slices of an apple. "Nothing but a passionate lover's quarrel, but we are all good now so it looks like you're stuck with me."

"For now," Alex said. "So where is your psychotic girlfriend?"

"Out for her morning walk," Susan said, ignoring the verbal jab. "It's her thinking time."

"Aw, something else she doesn't share with you."

"Fuck off," Susan said angrily. "God, I can't wait till you die."

"Well, like you said before, it looks like you're stuck with me."

"*For now*," she said, with a sarcastic smile.

"So much hate and yet here you are spending alone time with little old me. I'm honored."

"Whatever," Susan replied, taking one of the slivers she had cut and popping it in her mouth.

"Obviously you're here for a reason."

"Maybe I'm just trying to mentally capture the real you, you know, before you leave this world."

"That's pretty funny," Alex said. "I was just thinking the same thing."

"Oh yeah?" Susan asked. "And why is that?"

"Well, it's just that Tatiana and I were getting so close to one another last night that I began to wonder how much longer you were gonna stick around. I imagine it's going to get a bit *awkward* for you."

"Last night?" she asked, as she picked up the glass of water from the table next to the chair and took a sip. "What about last night?"

Alex smiled inwardly.

Susan had tried to sound as casual as possible in her question, and to the average person it would have been, but to a trained investigator it was readily apparent that it was forced. For the second time she had managed to successfully bait the young woman.

"She didn't tell you?" Alex replied.

"Tell me what?"

Time paused, as Alex and the young woman stared at each other.

CHAPTER THIRTY-FOUR

An attractive, middle-aged woman, with long brown hair, sat behind the counter of Junior's Bait & Tackle, reading an outdoors magazine, as the three men walked into the store.

An unseen radio played the local country music station and Maguire stifled a chuckle, as he looked at the tight pink tee shirt the woman was wearing that bore the legend 'Master Baiter' on the front.

"Good morning," she said, closing the periodical and slipping it under the counter. "How can I help New Hampshire's Finest?"

"We were hoping to speak to the owner," Hutch replied.

"You are," she said.

"You're *Junior*?" Hutch asked.

"Marketing: 101, sugar," the woman replied, flashing him a smile. "Lacy's Bait & Tackle just doesn't have the same ring to it. So I decided to name it after my ex. I figured it was the only way I'd ever make any money off of the lousy *sonofabitch*."

"That makes perfect sense," Hutch said, "in a very odd sort of way."

"Well, salesmen don't try to screw you over when they think a man runs the operation, but I don't think you came in to learn business secrets from me, and these two certainly ain't dressed for fishing, so do I need to call my lawyer?"

"No, nothing like that," Hutch replied. "Actually, we were hoping you'd be able to help us out."

"What do you boys need?"

Hutch turned to look back at Maguire and Antonucci, who stepped up to the counter.

"I'm Detective Antonucci, ma'am. We're investigating a missing person."

"Oh dear Lord," she said, eyeing him closely. "You're not from around here."

"No, ma'am," Antonucci replied. "New York City."

"Like NYPD, New York City?"

"Exactly," he replied.

"Oh my God," she replied, her eyes wide with excitement, "and you're investigating something up here?"

"Yes," he replied, moving in closer, "but it's very sensitive, so I would really appreciate it if you would keep what we discuss as a private matter."

"Oh, absolutely," she replied, nodding her head, "mum's the word."

"Thank you," he said. "I was wondering if your camera system was operational."

"Yes it is," she replied.

"How long does it record for?"

"About two weeks, I think."

"Do you still have the recording for the past few days?"

"Yeah, you want to take a look?"

"Yes," Antonucci replied. "I really would."

"Well, then follow me," the woman replied.

"Hey, Ang, we're gonna go and grab some coffee," Maguire said.

"No problem, boss," he replied. "I'll call you when I'm done or if I find out anything."

"The diner up the road is open," the woman said. "Maggie May serves a great breakfast if you boys are hungry."

"Thanks," Hutch replied. "We'll take a walk over there."

"You want anything, Ang?" Maguire asked.

"Coffee is fine," he replied, as he followed Lacy into the back of the store.

A moment later they entered a small office. Lacy sat down at the desk and began tapping the keys on the computer's keyboard.

"I'll get you into the system," she said, as she scanned the monitor, "and show you how to select the cameras."

"I'm mostly interested in the one that faces out front, toward the roadway."

"Okay, that's camera number two," she said, pulling it up. "How far back do you want to go?"

"Take me back to Friday evening," he said. "Around five o'clock."

The woman tapped a few keys and hit enter. A moment later a color shot of the parking lot appeared along with a clear view of the main road; much to Antonucci's relief.

"Hit the 'S' key to begin playing," Lacy said, as she got up from the chair. "Then use the left and right arrow keys to speed up or slow down the video. The system is also hooked up to the printer; so if you see something just hit the 'P' key and it will pause the video. If you want a screen shot all you have to do is select the printer icon."

"Thank you," Antonucci said, as he sat down in the chair.

Outside, the door chime rang, indicating that someone had entered the store.

"Ah, duty calls," the woman said, giving him a wink. "If there's anything else you need, you just let me know."

"I will," he said with a smile.

Antonucci watched her leave and then turned his attention back to the computer monitor. He removed a pad out of his jacket pocket and noted the initial time on the playback display and then hit the 'S' button.

The picture quality was exceptionally good; a lot better than some of the stuff he was used to viewing back in New York. It seemed as if technology in this market was improving by leaps and bounds each day. The primary focus of the camera was on the parking lot, but he could still make out the cars moving along the roadway just beyond it. Even as the sun set, the streetlights provided enough ambient light to make viewing easy.

It might seem to be a mundane thing, but staring at a video screen was certainly not an easy thing to do, especially when it came to monitoring security cameras. It wasn't as bad when there was activity taking place, but after a prolonged period of time behind the screen, watching corridors or other areas with little movement, the viewer simply stopped *seeing* things. They suffered a type of burnout, where the mind checked out and the eyes no longer saw anything. It always struck him as odd that a state of the art security system could be defeated by a bored, minimum wage guard sitting too long behind a video screen.

As a rule, Antonucci made himself get up every fifteen minutes to shake off any cobwebs before they could take hold. It took longer to review video this way, but it helped him not to miss anything.

He scanned the video feed, watching as the clock slowly advanced, looking for anything that stood out. The color imaging certainly helped, as it allowed him to differentiate vehicles by color. By ten o'clock the traffic had died down to nearly nothing and after midnight the only thing he saw on a regular basis was some wildlife.

"How ya doing, sugar?"

Antonucci looked up from the screen to see Lacy standing in the doorway.

"I'm doing fine," he responded.

"Your friends dropped this off," she replied, handing a Styrofoam cup to him. "They said they were going to take a ride to look at something, but that they'd be in the area if you needed them."

"Okay, thanks," he said, taking the container.

"Find anything useful yet?" she asked. "This place doesn't have much traffic during daytime this time of year; so I can't imagine there is a whole lot when the sun goes down."

"No, but I still have a little ways to go," he replied. "So I'm still holding out hope."

"Well if you need *anything*, you just call me," Lacy said with a suggestive smile.

"I will," Antonucci replied.

She was certainly the free spirit type, he thought. *Wasn't that the state's motto? Live Free or Die.*

The clock slowly counted down toward the time they had gotten the cell phone ping and then passed by. After about ten minutes of no activity on the roadway Antonucci began to worry that he had missed something or, even worse, that there simply was nothing more to see.

Any detective would tell you that time was never your friend and this was especially true in missing person investigations. Every passing minute potentially put you further away from your potential victim. Absent alien abduction, people didn't just vanish off the face of the earth. There was always a reason, a motive, whether intentionally or unintentionally.

In this case, the former was certainly an option. The shooting would have weighed heavily on her mind. The prospect of facing a trial, and possibly an extended prison sentence, was certainly a great motivator to make any cop think about *vanishing*, but her case had only been in the investigative stage. Disappearing was usually seen as a glaring admission of guilt and most folks would have waited to at least see what direction the case was going before they took such a drastic step

If it was the latter, and her disappearance had been unintentionally on her part, then she was a victim and they desperately needed something, even the slightest clue, to formulate a direction to move in. Aside from the cell phone ping, they simply had nothing.

Well, that wasn't true, he thought.

They had her keys, her wallet, her gun, her car, her clothes. The fact was that they had everything except her; which brought him back to his belief that her disappearance was an abduction.

As Antonucci stared at the screen, the image suddenly began to grow brighter. A car came around the bend in the road and into the camera's view. He saw two figures sitting in the front seat and then it was gone. He hit the pause button and then rewound it; watching as the tan colored Volvo came slowly back into view.

He could make out the vehicle's manufacturer from the distinctive emblem on the front grill. It was a type of vehicle he'd seen several times before, in his short stay up here, and he noted that the passenger appeared to be a woman with blonde hair, but as he looked closer he could make out that she appeared to be much younger than Alex. Unfortunately, he couldn't tell who was driving because of a glare on the windshield from the street light out front. Still, he had little else to go on so he enlarged the image and wrote down the license plate. When he was done he took a sip of coffee and went back to reviewing the remainder of the tape.

A half hour later he closed out the program and gathered his stuff up. He sent a text message to Maguire saying he was ready to be picked up and headed out front.

"Find what you were looking for, hon?" Lacy asked.

"Maybe," he replied. "Do you know who uses a green colored license plate?"

"Yeah, Vermont," she replied. "Why?"

"I saw a Volvo with green plates in the video and I was just wondering. I guess they aren't uncommon."

"Not really, unfortunately," Lacy said sarcastically. "They're just a bunch of hippie border jumpers. They're not happy unless they are sowing the seeds of their liberal nonsense over here."

"I take it you're not a fan," Antonucci replied with a laugh.

"Eh, they're okay, just a little misguided on most things," she said. "We probably view them about the same way a New Yorker feels about someone from New Jersey."

"Touché," he replied.

"Well, if you ever come up when you're not working, look me up," she said, handing him her business card. "My private cell phone number is on the back. I'd be happy to show you around the back woods."

"I'll do that," Antonucci said, accepting the card from her. "Thank you."

"Anytime, hon."

Antonucci slid the card into his pocket and walked outside, just as the patrol car was pulling into the parking lot.

"Tell me you found something," Maguire said from the passenger seat.

"Not sure, boss," he replied, climbing into the back seat. "I was able to pull off an image of a car passing through at around the approximate time, but it's too grainy to make out the occupants."

Antonucci handed the photo up to Maguire who looked at it and then passed it along to Hutch.

"Can you run the plate for me, Hutch?" Antonucci asked.

262

Hutch looked at the photo and began to enter the information into the in-car computer system.

A moment later he let out a sigh. "System is down for maintenance."

"Timing is everything," Maguire replied. "Any idea how long before it's back up?"

"Probably too long," Hutch said, as he pulled out his cell phone, "but we have a back-up plan."

He dialed a number from memory and listened to it ring.

"Hey Vanessa, its Hutch," he said when the call connected. "I need a favor from you."

There was a pause and Maguire could hear the soft, muffled sound of a female voice. Then he noticed the man's face redden slightly.

"No, not now, Vee," he said, the words coming out with a slight stammer. "I'm working a case with some investigators and our computer system is down. I need you to run a Vermont plate for me."

Again Maguire could hear the voice on the other end of the line; a bit louder this time.

"No, no, it's okay," Hutch replied and read off the tag number. "Call me as soon as you have something."

"Friend of yours?" Maguire asked, as the man ended the call.

"Vanessa? Oh yeah, she's a sergeant with the Vermont State Police. We worked a case together last year."

"It's good to have close personal connections you can reach out to when the need arises."

"Yeah," he said sheepishly. "She's on her way into work right now; she said she'll run it as soon as she gets there."

In the back seat Antonucci looked out the window, a smile growing on his face.

Guess they figured out how to overcome that whole state rivalry thing, he thought.

"Well, I guess all we can do now is wait," Maguire replied.

CHAPTER THIRTY-FIVE

"What about last night?" Susan said coolly.

"That's probably something you should ask her about."

"I'm asking you."

"I don't do the whole *kiss and tell* thing."

"Answer the goddamn question, bitch!" Susan said, exploding in a fit of rage. "Before you're no longer capable of answering."

"What do you want to know?" Alex screamed back. "That your girlfriend has roving hands? That while you were conveniently sound asleep that she passed the time with me getting *reacquainted*."

The look on Susan's face was dark and menacing, as she processed the information. Alex knew she had to tread carefully at this point. Baiting the girl was one thing, but now that she had set the hook it could go wrong very quickly and she was in no position to fend her off.

Alex knew that she had to maneuver Susan's anger away from her and direct it back toward Tatiana. That wasn't necessarily an easy thing to do, but it could be accomplished. You just had to know which buttons to push.

Most people were familiar with the phenomenon known as *Stockholm Syndrome*, which got its name from a bank robbery that took place in 1973 in the Swedish city of Stockholm. It is a condition by which victims can develop loyalty, sympathy and even affection for a captor. This is especially true if the captor provided them a moment of compassion which the captive, under extreme duress, views as a genuine sign of affection.

Additionally, a condition known as *Lima Syndrome* does occasionally occur, although it is a considerably rarer phenomenon. In that instance, the roles are reversed and it is the captor who develops empathy for their captor. The condition was named after an abduction in 1996 at the Japanese ambassador's residence in Lima, Peru. While the overall siege had lasted four months, the terrorists had actually set free most of their captives within days. In the end, the terrorists, who were supposed to kill the remaining hostages, in the event of an assault, could not bring themselves to do it and were killed by Peruvian commandoes.

The key was finding that right empathetic button and pushing it.

"Look, Susan," Alex said, "whatever you think about me, I'm not your enemy."

"It sure as hell looks that way to me," Susan said smugly.

"Look at me," Alex said. "I'm tied to a goddamn bed. I couldn't do anything to resist even if I wanted to."

Susan stared at her quietly.

"I didn't come into your bedroom last night, whispering sweet nothings in your girlfriend's ear, and fondle her. She came in here. I was as much of victim as you were."

"What did she say?"

"Apparently she has some serious long range plans for the two of us and, if I were you, I'd be a little concerned."

"I don't have to worry about anything," Susan replied softly.

"Really?" Alex asked. "I applaud your resolve. It's fucking naïve, but that's your cross to bear. Personally, I'd be a little worried when my girlfriend is knocking me out so she can spend time with her new piece of ass."

"Knocking me out? What the hell is that supposed to mean?"

"Seriously?"

"What the fuck are you talking about?"

"Jesus Christ, Susan," Alex shot back. "Don't be such a friggin' idiot. She drugged you last night."

"Bullshit! You're making this shit up!"

"Oh yeah, it's all me, sweetheart, because you two certainly don't have any fucking trust issues," Alex replied. "Oh wait, yes you do, starting with the fact that she knew about me all along and lied to you about it. Then you conveniently get so sleepy that you pass out while she's in here copping a feel. You're right, my bad, it's all just mere coincidence."

Susan sat there, jaw clenching, as she silently carved another slice of the apple. Alex knew the gears were spinning so fast that they could easily come off the rails at any moment.

"Listen, Susan, I know you have your own shit to deal with, but you have to come to terms with the fact that this isn't going to end well for either of us."

"Why do you say that?" she asked.

"You ever hear the old saying two is company, three is a crowd?" Alex asked. "Right now you're about to take on the role of a third wheel and you don't seem like the type of person who is into sloppy seconds."

"The way you tell it, it seems like you're going to be just fine, so why worry about me?"

"Because I envision myself being in your place one day."

"What do you mean?"

"Tatiana wants me, but she knows she can't trust me. You see the way I am? This is my life. She'll have her fun with me when she wants to and then one day she'll move on."

"So what, now I'm supposed to have empathy for you?" Susan asked sarcastically.

"We're on the same side here," Alex replied. "We are both being played."

"The same side?" Susan said with a laugh. "How the hell do you figure that? You're a cop, I'm a killer."

"Well, to be brutally honest, there's nothing wrong with killing," Alex replied. "Just as long as the right people get killed."

"You've seen some of my work," Susan replied. "I'm not making it into heaven anytime soon."

"Yeah, I have and you're probably right, but I also know that your damaged goods."

"What do you know about *damaged goods*?"

"You didn't get here on your own, Susan, you had a lot of help," Alex said.

"What the fuck is that supposed to mean?"

"You may have scrubbed your past, but your father didn't scrub his."

As Alex watched, the color drained in Susan's face.

"What,….. How,……."

"When the detectives in Yardley closed their case, they had several boxes of your father's belongings that your siblings had no interest in. They knew I still had an open investigation so they asked if I wanted it. Most of it was junk, but inside there were some old business files and I found an envelope that they had overlooked. It had a key to a safe deposit box. Your father kept diaries, Susan, I know what he did."

"You don't know what you're talking about," she said, looking away quickly as she felt her cheeks begin redden.

"Don't I? I could never understand the extent of your anger, your rage, but then it all made sense."

"What the fuck do you know about my anger?"

"Because a long time ago I was daddy's little princess too," Alex said softy.

A look of shock came over Susan's face, chasing away her own anger and shame. "You?"

Alex simply nodded.

"But,…… you're a cop," Susan said, a stunned look on her face.

"I was eleven when he first started, Susan," Alex replied tersely. "It wasn't like I was in any position to say no to him."

Now it was Susan's turn to nod knowingly.

"In the beginning it was just affectionate touching, stroking my hair, when he would come into my bedroom to say goodnight. Then one night I woke up to him touching me inside my pajamas. I was shocked, but I was too afraid to say anything so I laid there pretending I was asleep. After that he began making regular trips into my bedroom. At first I didn't know what to think, but then it kinda felt good. I mean I had hit puberty, so it wasn't like I hadn't been seeing and feeling the changes. You know what I mean?"

"Yeah," Susan blurted out. "Like you know it's wrong, but it still feels right."

"Exactly," Alex replied. "So I figured what the fuck, I might as well just enjoy it. I never opened my eyes, so I didn't actually see what he was doing; I just felt his hands groping me. That all changed the last year of elementary school."

"What happened?"

"The school took us on a field trip to Washington, D.C. He signed up as a class chaperone. Being family, no one batted and eyelash when we shared a hotel room. Looking back it was the perfect opportunity for him."

"Fucker," Susan said angrily.

"Yeah, he was," Alex replied. "I just didn't know that then."

"He was just using you."

"I know and I hate to admit this, but in a way it made me feel special."

"It does," Susan admitted. "But it's just a twisted lie,"

"Well, my bubble burst at fourteen when the cocksucker walked out the door and left me with my bitch of a mother."

"Seriously?"

"Yeah, I found out later he hooked up with a woman with a young daughter. Always felt like I got too old for him and he moved on. So when I got old enough I tried to find him. I probably would have done what you did, but the prick was already dead. Word was that his new wife had found out he'd been tapping her daughter and went to the cops. When they showed up he was swinging from a rope in the garage, so I never got the satisfaction you did."

"I'm sorry," Susan said.

Alex shrugged her shoulders. "It is what it is."

"It's not right."

"I know," Alex replied. "I find drinking helps."

"Does it ever go away?"

"No, never, you just learn to cope, but it's always there. I still have this reoccurring nightmare where he's on top of me, taking me and his hands around my throat. I can't breathe and I'm trying to get him to stop, but he won't. He just laughs as I'm dying and just before everything goes black I wake up screaming."

Susan picked up the glass of water and took a sip. She knew exactly what Alex was talking about. She'd struggled with similar dreams, even after she'd killed her father.

"But you know what the really messed up thing is?" Alex asked. "In a way I miss it."

"You do?"

"Yeah, I'm sure the shrinks would have a field day with me, but the truth is I miss the feeling of being that *special* to someone."

"Like you're so incredible that even a grown man would risk anything to be with you?"

"Exactly," Alex said. "I mean I knew it was wrong, but I still laid there knowing he wanted me so bad that he would risk anything and then it was all ripped from me. As sick as it might sound, I've spent my whole life searching for that feeling again and I'm afraid that it doesn't exist."

"I know what you mean," Susan replied, "and we're not sick."

"Isn't it?" Alex asked, noting how Susan had included herself.

"No, we we're the victims," she argued, "we didn't ask for this to happen to us so it isn't fair that we get blamed for trying to find happiness."

"The world would probably argue that."

"Fuck the world," Susan said angrily. "Where was the world when we were being abused?"

"Can I ask you a question?"

"Yeah, go ahead."

"Just between you and me, how did it feel to kill Paige?"

"Why do you want to know?" Susan asked, becoming suspicious.

"For crying out loud, I already know you killed her, Susan," Alex replied. "It's not like I'm gonna hold that over your head. I only ask because I've had thoughts about it; you know, exacting my revenge on the girl who took my place."

A shock look came over Susan's face.

"You've thought about killing her?"

"I mean, it's hard not to," Alex replied, "but it's not exactly something you can just bring up in a casual conversation. Plus, how often do you get a chance to talk to someone who actually did it?"

Susan paused for a moment, as she contemplated the question. Ironically, it wasn't something she had ever really given much thought about. Paige had betrayed her and she'd killed her. She had a reason and had imagined that it would bring her some level of satisfaction, but the truth was that it hadn't.

"Hollow," she said after a moment.

"Really?" Alex asked.

"Yeah," Susan said thoughtfully. "I thought I would get more out of it, but the truth is I didn't. I mean, don't get me wrong, there was a perverse thrill leading up to it. She'd been on my list, but I didn't expect her to come back to his place. I caught her by surprise. It was so cute how terrified she was. I told her that I was just going to tie her up and leave her there. I gave her something to hold onto, but it was brief. As soon as I started to unload on her, about betraying me and screwing my father, I think she knew that she had fucked up by trusting me."

"Did it make you feel good?" Alex asked.

"In a way I kind of got off watching her beg me to just let her go. I tormented her for a while longer and then I slit her throat. I thought I would get a feeling of satisfaction from it, but the moment was fleeting, like Christmas morning. Then she was dead and it was suddenly very quiet. It felt weird. I still had the anger, but I had no one to direct it at."

"I was afraid you'd say that."

"All of them got what was coming to them, but I was never able to get any satisfaction from it. Honestly, the best part of it all was hunting them."

"What was the real story with your mom?" Alex asked. "I never really fully bought into what you wrote."

"Ah, *mommy dearest*," Susan said with a sardonic smile. "Penobscot's perfect little house wife. Interestingly enough, I always felt a sense of empathy toward her while daddy was fucking me. I imagined it had to suck being so clueless. At least I did until I found out that she was out screwing around on him. Then I actually began to blame her for what was happening to me. I figured that if she had just been taking care of shit at home then he wouldn't have needed to get it from me."

"I remembered my mother being so nice and then after he left us she became a royal bitch," Alex said. "I couldn't take a goddamn breath without her criticizing me. I always felt she wigged out, but later I wondered if she knew what he was doing and then, after he left her, she just blamed me."

"Guess we do have a lot in common," Susan said grudgingly.

"Look, you got played a shitty hand," Alex said. "We both did. If my dad hadn't taken the chicken shit way out I might have found myself in your shoes."

"What do you want me to do?"

"If I had a choice I would say just cut me loose, Susan," Alex said. "I'll walk out the front door and forget I ever saw you. Give you enough time to get far away from here."

"She'll kill me," Susan said.

"I got bad news for you, babe. Chances are pretty good that it's eventually going to happen anyway."

Susan stared at Alex, thinking about what she was suggesting.

"My fight is not with you, Susan. I know you're resourceful so just walk out that door with me. I'll go right and you go left. Just disappear and I'll deal with Tatiana."

"I don't know," she said hesitantly.

"Then just think about," Alex said. "In the meantime I really have to pee."

"You know I can't," Susan said.

"Listen, either you help me out here or you're gonna be left cleaning it up," Alex replied. "Fuck, we've done this before and it's not like I'm not tied up."

Susan struggled with her options. In the past she and Tatiana had always moved Alex together, but it was also true that she was always tied up.

"You're not going to do anything stupid?"

"You have a friggin' knife and it's not like I'm in any position to out run you here," Alex said. "Plus I've given you something to think about and I'm betting that you are a smart girl."

Susan took a deep breath and grudgingly got up from the chair.

As Alex watched, the woman began to adjust the ropes just like they had done before. It was an intricate process whereby loops around both of her wrists drew her hands closer together as her arms were released from the bedframe. When she was done, Alex's hands were clasped firmly in front of her and secured to a rope around her waist. Then her ankles were hobbled before the remaining ropes were removed.

Susan helped her up and cautiously led her over to the small bathroom. Alex turned around in the constrained space and silently waited. Susan reached around, grabbing the edge of the waist band of the leggings and slowly pulled them down.

At first Alex thought about making some smart ass remark, but she resisted the urge. She'd planted a seed in the young woman's head, one that she knew she was struggling with and didn't want to screw that up. So she left Susan alone with her thoughts.

When she was done she stood up and waited as Susan pulled the leggings back up. There was a brief moment, when Susan was still slightly bent over, that Alex dropped down and then exploded forward, knocking Susan backward into the bedroom. As they fell, Alex grabbed hold of the woman, pulling her tight against her. When they crashed to the ground Alex head butted her, knocking the fight out of her for the briefest of moments, but it was short lived. Alex fought to gain control over her, but Susan recovered quickly and they began thrashing about on the floor.

In the ensuing struggle the chair and table next to the bed were knocked violently to the floor. Susan's glass shattered on the ground, but more importantly the pocket knife now lay a mere three feet from Alex.

She fought valiantly to make her way over to it, but once Susan had fully recovered from the suddenness of the attack she quickly regained control of Alex.

"You goddamn bitch," Susan screamed, as she grabbed Alex by the hair and forcibly dragged her back to the bed.

Alex continued to thrash about the bed, until Susan delivered a devastating blow to her stomach, causing her eyes to go wide and knocking the wind out of her. A moment later the woman had managed to secure Alex back to the bed.

She set the chair back up and sat down; breathing hard.

"I should fucking kill you right now," Susan said angrily.

"Hey, I had to try," Alex said with a smile.

Susan reached up and wiped away some blood from her cheek; were a piece of broken glass had scratched her.

"Hey, maybe Tatiana will even kiss your boo-boo when she gets back. You know, when you try and explain how you almost let her precious toy get away."

"Fuck you."

"Sorry, Susan, if you weren't good enough for your own daddy I'm certainly not interested."

"You played me, didn't you?"

"You didn't think I'd ever let someone put their hands on me and live to tell, did you? Christ, for claiming to be such a little badass you are really fucking naïve."

"God, I really hope she makes you suffer before she kills you," Susan said, as she got up and began picking the glass up off of the floor.

"Or I was telling you the truth after all and it's really your days that are numbered and not mine. Either way I wouldn't let myself get too comfortable."

"Shut the fuck up," Susan said, as she leaned over and rammed the gag back into Alex's mouth, then pulled the hood back over her head.

A moment later she stormed out of the room, slamming the door shut behind her.

Alex laid motionless in the bed, her eyes closed, as she brought her emotions back under control. Relieving old memories, especially *those*, was not something she enjoyed doing. In a way, it was rather odd that the only human being she had ever shared them with was someone who wanted to kill her. It took a while to get things wrapped up neatly in her head and stored back away in *bad memory box;* the one which she kept in the deep, dark recesses of her brain. All the while she took solace in the comforting cool feeling of the glass shard that she now held firmly in her right fist.

CHAPTER THIRTY-SIX

"Hey, babe," Vanessa Miller said, when Hutch answered the phone. "Can you talk?"

"Yeah," he replied, as he looked out into the squad room where Maguire and Antonucci were having coffee. "I'm alone right now."

"I am so sorry about before," she said. "I just thought you were calling for a little Sunday morning fun."

"I know," he replied sheepishly. "I lost track of what day it was. I didn't even think about it till it was too late."

"Did anyone hear me?"

"No, not really, I don't think," he said. "Besides, it doesn't matter. I mean we're adults."

"I know, but you were working," she said.

"It's okay, don't worry about it. Were you able to run that plate for me?"

"Yeah," Vanessa said. "It comes back to a 2012 Volvo S60 registered to an Annabelle Birch. No criminal record on file. The address comes back to a residence in Ithiel Falls."

"Where's that?" he asked.

"Over on the west side of the state," she replied. "It's about a half hour from Stowe. You want to tell me what's going on?"

"Alex is missing," he said quietly.

"You're not serious, are you?"

"Yes, I am," he replied. "No one has seen her since Friday night."

"Holy shit," Vanessa replied. "And you think this car was involved?"

"We don't know, but it was in the area around the same time that they picked up a ping from her cell phone."

"Oh my God."

"Listen, can you email me over a copy of that printout?"

"Sure, you want me to run the registered owner and send you a copy of her driver's license as well?"

"Yeah, that would be great, Vee."

"No problem, just give me a few minutes and I will email them over to you."

"Okay, thanks."

"If you need anything else, just call."

"I will," he replied. "Hey, are we still on for next weekend?"

"Oh hell yeah," she said with a laugh. "I'm going through withdrawal."

"Yeah, I noticed that this morning."

"Mmmmmm, just wait till you see what I have in store for you."

"Promises, promises, baby."

"Stay focused, studly," she said.

"I will and I'll talk to you later."

"Okay, hon," she said. "Bye."

Hutch hung up the phone and pulled up the email program on his laptop and waited.

"How are we doing?" Maguire asked from the doorway.

"Sergeant Miller is sending us over the information. The registered owner of the vehicle is an Annabelle Birch."

"Does that name mean anything to you?"

"No," Hutch replied, as he typed the name into the computer, "No criminal record in Vermont and it looks as if we don't have any hits on our local arrest system either."

"So we are back to square one," Maguire replied.

"For the time being it looks that way."

Maguire glanced down at his watch. Time was slipping away from them at a rapid pace. At some point he would have to decide whether they would stay longer or head back to New York. He could manage to be away for another day or two, but after that he had have to make an appearance back in the city. He'd only been in the commissioner's seat for a few months and there was still a lot to learn, especially with the summer just around the corner.

His thoughts were interrupted by the audible ping that signaled an email had come in.

"That was quick," Hutch said, as he clicked the button to open the program.

"I guess this is the part where I say a little prayer."

"Couldn't hurt," Hutch said, as he clicked on the attached files.

"What couldn't hurt?" Antonucci asked, as he walked into the office and sat down.

"We just got the DMV records from Vermont," Maguire explained.

"Anything useful?"

"Car's registered to Annabelle Birch, 1314 Chipmunk Drive, Ithiel Falls, Vermont," Hutch said, as he read the registration document.

"Chipmunk Drive?" Antonucci asked. "Who the heck names these streets?"

"A bored government employee, apparently," Hutch said, as he continued to scan the document. "Car is a 2012 Volvo S60, copper in color. She's the only owner on file."

"Anything else?" Maguire asked.

"Checking her license now," Hutch replied, as he selected the other attached document.

"Jesus H. Christ," he said softly, as he leaned back in the seat. "We have a big problem."

"What's wrong?" Maguire asked.

Hutch turned the computer around so that the two men could see the screen. To Maguire and Antonucci the image on the license showed the smiling face of an attractive young girl with brown hair.

"That's Susan Waltham," he said. "She's Penobscot's very own serial killer."

Maguire glanced back down at the image, staring into the woman's eyes and suddenly felt a cold chill run through him.

CHAPTER THIRTY-SEVEN

It had taken awhile for Alex to carefully reposition the glass shard in her hand. Despite the urgency of the situation, carelessness was not an option. She knew that she would never get a second chance at this; so she made sure that she had a good hold of it at all times.

Fortunately for her, Susan hadn't been paying close attention when she had retied her to the bed. As a result, the length of rope, which held her right hand in place, went directly over the palm of her hand and not behind it, providing her much easier access.

Alex couldn't actually see where she was cutting, thanks to the hood, so she kept her eyes closed and did it by *feeling*; holding the glass shard tightly between her thumb and her index finger, as she imagined the strands of rope in her mind. The process itself was painstakingly slow to the point that she could literally hear each individual strand as it was being severed.

Several times she'd had to pause, as her hand cramped up from holding the glass so tightly. When that happened she would transfer the shard back into her palm and cover it protectively with her fingers. Once the soreness had abated she would begin the whole process over again.

It had not been without incident. On her second attempt, as she tried to negotiate the glass from fingers to her palm, the glass slipped from her grasp.

Alex felt her heart sink, as she saw her hopes for escape immediately dashed, but then realized that she hadn't heard it hit the floor. Then she felt a sharp pinch against her skin and knew that it had gotten caught between the rope and her wrist. With judicious concentration she managed to stretch her fingers far enough so that, with a little bit of wrist contortion, she was able to slip the shard back into her palm.

Now, as she methodically slid the glass against the taut rope, she heard another strand break away.

How fucking thick is this rope? she wondered.

That thought was interrupted by the sound of the front door opening and closing.

Oh shit, she thought, as if she needed another reminder that time was not on her side.

Alex knew that this was something that she could not rush. She took a deep breath, as she recalled an old quote, *"Fast is fine, but accuracy is final. You must learn to be slow in a hurry."* Then she closed her eyes and went back to work.

CHAPTER THIRTY-EIGHT

"What do you have for me, Vee?" Hutch asked.

"Just heard back from the guys over in Waterbury," she said. "The address is an open field."

"That's great," he replied dejectedly.

"One of the investigators had a *plat* book and they were able to identify the owner. They took a ride over to his place and showed him the photo, but he had no idea who she was."

"I appreciate the effort, Vee."

"We got the BOLO you put out," she replied. "I know it's a long shot, but I have my people checking all the local motels and rest stops. If anything should pop up I'll let you know."

"Thanks."

"Hey, if you want any extra help, I get off at four. I can head over that way."

"I appreciate the offer, but right now we are just grasping at straws. I'd rather have you there if I need something local done quickly."

"I understand," she said. "Call me if anything pops up."

"I will, hon," Hutch replied. "Talk to you later."

He ended the call and then walked out into the squad room.

Now that they knew Susan Waltham was in town they were openly pursuing this as an abduction case. That meant there was no need to hide what was going on. Anyone who wasn't working a shift had been brought in to help. In addition the state police and sheriff's department were also providing additional manpower to scour the surrounding roads. Because of the amount of time that had passed a BOLO had been issued throughout the entire New England region as well as New York State.

"I just got off the phone with the Vermont State Police," Hutch said to Maguire.

"I take it they have nothing," Maguire replied.

"Good address, but it's an empty field," Hutch said, as he poured himself a cup of coffee. "They tracked down the property owner, but he's never seen her before."

"She's smart," Maguire said.

"She's a fucking psychopath is what she is."

"Yeah, I'm familiar with the type. How many bodies does she have?"

"That we are sure of? Six," Hutch replied. "That we suspect her of? Possibly a seventh, but we can't prove it yet."

"All local?"

"The majority of them were. A few were from outside the area, but all were in New Hampshire."

"When was the last one?"

"Confirmed? November of 2012, but we also got notified of a possible sighting back in February of last year."

"Where?" Maguire asked.

"Some place in Georgia, a run-off from a gas station, but it never amounted to anything. They sent us some video, but the photo was too grainy to say it was her with any level of certainty."

"Where the hell does a young kid like that get money to go long distance sightseeing?"

"Alex had a theory that the sex ring her mother had been running was a cash operation and that Susan had found it," Hutch replied.

"That would certainly help, but it's kind of difficult to believe that she has managed to stay off the radar for as long as she has without help."

"You think that whoever was in the car is an accomplice?"

"It wouldn't shock me," Maguire said, "and it would make a whole lot more sense. You can cover a whole lot more ground with two people. What gets me is that if they made it as far as Georgia why would she come back here?"

"Oh, I can tell you why," Hutch replied. "She has a longer list of targets."

"What do you mean?"

"Alex had found a note pad, during the original investigation, that had what she believed was a hit list."

"Hit list?"

"Yeah, There were a total of nine names on the page," Hutch replied. "I guess they were the ones that Susan believed had screwed her over. By the time we found it she had already killed one of them. So we notified the remainder of our concerns. Most didn't take it all too seriously until the second death in November.

After that about half of the remaining folks on the list left Penobscot."

"So you think that's why she came back, to find the others?"

"It would make sense."

"But then why go after Alex?" Maguire asked. "I get that the others were personal, but going after a cop is a whole different level of crazy."

"Hey, wait a minute," Hutch said, and headed back into the office.

A moment later he returned with a manila case folder and began leafing through the reports.

"What are you looking for?" Maguire asked.

"This is the case folder from the convenience store shooting," Hutch replied, as he flipped the pages. "Yeah, here it is."

"What?"

"There was supposedly a blonde haired girl in the store prior to the shooting. One of the witnesses is a teacher, a Mrs. Booker; she thought it could have been one of her students."

"You think it was Susan?" Maguire asked.

"Maybe she was back for someone else and then got scared that Alex might be able to identify her," Hutch said. "If she got rid of her quickly, then she could still carry out her original plans."

"How'd the others die?"

"Well, let's see, Hannah Kurtz was drowned, Lou Jenkins and Paige Wilson had their throats slit and the rest were all poisoned."

"Poisoned? Did you see anything unusual when you went over to Alex's house?"

"No, not really," Hutch said. "Everything looked pretty much normal. Wait, there was an empty bottle of whiskey next to the note, you don't think she was poisoned, do you?"

"No, worse than that," Maguire replied. "If they just wanted to kill her, they'd have left the body. I think she was drugged and then abducted, the only question is why. Have someone go over to her house and secure that bottle. I wanted it tested so that we at least know what we are dealing."

Hutch turned around and waved Abby over.

"What do you need, Hutch?"

"I need you to go out to Alex's place and get that whiskey bottle," he said. "Treat it as evidence."

"Sure thing," she replied.

"Captain Blackshear is on his way here now," Hutch said. "I'll see if he can get someone to run it over to the lab."

"I'll call the colonel," Maguire said. "I'll see if he can get his lab ready to run it when it arrives."

"Then what?" Hutch asked.

"Then we pray like hell to catch a break."

CHAPTER THIRTY-NINE

Tatiana knew something was wrong the minute she walked through the front door. Susan was sitting on the couch staring at the television, but it was the young woman's posture that set off the alarm bells.

Her feet were propped up on the edge of the couch, with her arms crossed tightly in front of her, and Tatiana could see that the muscles of her jaw were clenched tightly.

"Is everything alright?"

"*Fine*," Susan replied, without looking up at her.

There are few words in the English language that will cause someone to immediately cringe and seek out the nearest manner of emergency egress, but the word *fine*, spoken by an angry woman, is at the top of the list. In this particular case things were most certainly *not* fine.

Tatiana walked over to the kitchenette and poured herself a cup of coffee, as she contemplated her next course of action. Unfortunately, none of the scenarios that played out in her head ended well, so she just decided to take her coffee out on the deck and steer a wide berth around Susan until the storm had passed.

Like that's gonna happen, she thought, as she stepped outside.

They'd been together a little over a year now and, for the most part, that time had been filled with an intoxicating blend of lust and mayhem. Tatiana had been truly enamored with the young woman, both in and out of the bedroom. They had fed off of each other's vibrant energy; each trying to outdo the other, but lately things had begun to cool off just a bit. It was as if they had finally moved past the honeymoon phase and things weren't as rosy as they had initially seemed.

In a way Tatiana was jealous of her. They each had an extensive list of victims, but Susan's was just a bit longer. It was also true that her youth and girl-next-door good looks went a long way toward luring in more victims. People were naturally drawn to her and let down their guard down a lot quicker. It was exciting to watch Susan, but it also served to remind Tatiana how much more work she had to put into achieving the same results.

Tatiana took a sip of coffee, as she stared off across the stream. She watched as an unseen fish caused a ripple on the water's surface. The tight, concentric rings slowly spread out, growing wider with each moment, until they final disappeared.

Was that us? she wondered. *Have we finally spread so far apart that we are about to disappear?*

It was an interesting metaphor, but the real world consequences for them were truly frightening. Serial killers didn't just break up.

Stop over thinking shit, she chided herself. *This is just a rough patch; every couple goes through them.*

As much as she wanted to pretend this was just a normal part of the relational process, she also knew that her desire for Alex had caused the schism between her and Susan to grow. She wanted to say that this was all about revenge, but she knew that it wasn't. There was just something about the woman that she couldn't let go of, even if that meant that it came between her and Susan.

But will she break? she wondered.

In a way her fantasy had coming crashing down to earth after her first *chat* with Alex. With Susan she had freedom. The two of them were partners in crime, literally. They were like two wild lionesses, roaming the savannah. They did as they pleased, where they pleased, when they pleased and that was very fulfilling, but now her personal desires had them anchored here, like caged animals at the zoo.

She knew she had a choice to make, but it was like asking her to choose her own poison. Did she roll the dice and take the chance that she could have something magical with Alex or did she trade in her fantasy for the familiar and try to repair the fractured relationship she currently had with Susan.

"Fuck me," Tatiana said softly, as she fished the pack of cigarettes out of her pocket and pondered her choices.

CHAPTER FORTY

"Hey, Momma," Melody said, as she walked into the salon. "Welcome home."

Gen jumped up from the couch and ran toward Melody.

"Oh, I've missed you," she squealed, as she wrapped her arms around Melody.

"How was the trip?"

"Oh, it was so much fun," she replied, as the two women sat down on the couch to catch up. "Gregor's family is so sweet."

"I can't wait to hear all about it," Melody replied. "Speaking of which, where are Gregor and Wolfie?"

"Wolfie's still asleep," she replied, "and Gregor is over at the office catching up on what's been happening."

"God he never stops, does he?"

"Nope," Gen said with a laugh. "He's my little Terminator-Energizer Bunny."

"So how was Germany?" Melody asked.

"Amazing! The scenery was incredible. I don't think I've walked as much in my entire life as I did in the last week, which was a good thing because the food was out of this world and fattening as fuck."

Melody laughed at her friend's enthusiasm.

"I hope you took plenty of pictures," she said.

"Ton's" Gen replied, as she took a sip of coffee. "I felt like a Japanese tourist, plus I wanted to make sure that I got a lot of Wolfie with Gregor's family."

"Awesome, I can't wait to see them."

"So, what's been going on here?"

"Well, you got my email about Alex being missing."

"Yeah, that whole situation is insane," Gen said. "Has there been anything new?"

"James called me and said that they think she was abducted."

"Abducted? How? Why?"

"They think it's a suspect in a prior murder case that she'd investigated."

"Oh my God, that's crazy," Gen replied. "Do they have any leads?"

"Not really. They have a photo of the suspect and a description of the car she is in, but that's about it."

"The world is going insane."

"Yeah, sometimes I miss the little bubble I once lived in," Melody replied. "Where the only dramatic things took place in the board room."

"Ain't that the truth," Gen replied.

"I need some coffee," Melody said. "Want a refill?"

"Yeah, but I'll get it."

"No, you just sit there and relax," Melody said, as she got up from the couch. "Hand me your cup."

Gen handed the cup to her friend. "*Danke schoen*, darling, *danke schoen*."

"I will say that it has been a very interesting two years," Melody said, as she walked over to the serving table that held the coffee carafe.

"That's the understatement of the year, chicky," her friend said with a laugh. "I think we could all use a healthy dose of monotony for a change."

"Yes, but then what would we have to complain about?"

"Oh, I don't know. Acquisitions, contracts, profits, price to earnings ratio,…… You know; normal stuff."

"Who would have ever thought that those things would end up being boring?"

"Speaking of not boring, how did things go with your meeting in D.C.?"

Melody handed the coffee cup back to Gen and sat down.

"*Interesting*," she replied.

"Oh really? How so?"

"Well, let's just say that I got the feeling Eliza Cook was auditioning me."

"Are you shitting me?" Gen said, sitting up straight. "For what?"

"That's the question I'm wondering about," Melody replied. "I ran into Peter Constantine and after the usual D.C. foreplay he told me that she wants to meet with me in May."

"Dear Lord, Melody, this is so *not* boring."

"I don't know. Perhaps I'm reading too much into it. Maybe it's all just a lot of nothing and she only wants me to write a big donation check to her campaign."

"Eliza Cook has a bigger war chest than the GDP of some countries," Gen said with a laugh. "I don't think she wants nor needs your money."

"Maybe that's what scares me," Melody said, raising her coffee cup to her lips.

"Nothing scares you."

"Damnit!" Melody exclaimed, as the cup toppled from her hand and fell to the floor, shattering into pieces as it hit the tiled floor.

"Holy shit, Mel, are you alright?" Gen exclaimed.

"Yes, yes, I'm fine," she said, as she stood up.

"Don't worry, I'll get it."

"No, I got this," Melody said, as she went back to the serving table where she retrieved some napkins and a small bowl.

"What happened?"

"Oh, it's nothing. I was working out this week and I think I pinched a nerve in my wrist."

"I told you that gym is a death trap," Gen said with a laugh, as she helped pick up the broken mug and put the pieces in the bowl, "but did you listen to me? Nooooo!"

"Okay, Miss Smart Ass, we'll see how funny you think it is when gravity takes hold of that perfect little body of yours."

"Hey, redheads are naturally immune to such mortal issues."

"Uh huh, whatever helps you sleep at night," Melody said sarcastically, as she walked over and dumped the remnants of the broken mug into the trash. "Just don't come crying to me when you're wearing those spandex mom jeans."

"You know you can be so hateful," Gen said with a smirk. "I hope Eliza Cook never sees this side of you."

"Honestly, I think they patterned more than a few Hollywood bad girls after that woman," Melody said, as she finished pouring herself a refill.

"She has the look, that's for sure, but you haven't answered the question. What are you going to do if it isn't a check she's after?"

"I honestly don't know," Melody replied. "It's a weird feeling for me. There was a time when I thought I would love to get into politics, but after seeing it close-up I realized how ugly the creatures were that lived in that swamp. Now I'm coming to terms with the fact that I just might be asked to join them."

"Well, the truth is that most of those people weren't ugly when they first got there. They allowed that to happen to them; usually through greed and lust for power. The reality is that you already have both wealth and power. Some could rightly argue that government work might even be seen as a step down for you."

"The question is can I keep from being corrupted?"

"Hey, don't worry," Gen replied. "That's what you have me for."

"Now I really am scared."

CHAPTER FORTY-ONE

The chill in the living room had not dissipated by the time Tatiana had come back in; nor had the expression on Susan's face changed.

If anything, that meant that the situation was even more serious than she had previously thought. She cautiously made her way into the kitchen area to get a refill, but the pot was now empty.

"Hey, I'm going to make a fresh pot, do you want some?"

"I don't care," came Susan's frosty reply.

Tatiana gripped the edge of the countertop tightly and stared at the wall in front of her.

Fuck you, you goddamn fucking little cunt, she screamed inwardly and then slowly counted to ten.

When the moment had passed, she reached up and removed the coffee basket then dumped the old grounds into the trash; hearing the familiar clinking noise, as it landed against the broken glass.

Tatiana glanced down at the trash can.

"What happened to the glass?" she asked.

"It broke," Susan replied.

"*Goddamnit*, Susan," Tatiana snapped, as she turned around to face her. "I can see that it's broke. I'm asking you *how* it broke."

As she watched, Susan turned around slowly and stared up at her. Her normally warm and vibrant brown eyes were gone, replaced by something cold and decidedly darker.

"Watch your tone with me, Tee," Susan said softly.

There was something very menacing in the woman's measured voice which immediately caused Tatiana to take pause.

"I was just wondering what happened, hon," she replied warily.

"You want to know what happened? I'll tell you what happened, *she* happened," Susan said, pointing at the locked door.

"I know you don't like it, but I have a plan, you know that."

Susan laughed sardonically, as she crossed her arms, "Oh I bet you do, Tee."

"What's that supposed to mean?"

"Oh I think you know exactly what that means."

"If you're accusing me of something, at least have the balls to say it to my face," Tatiana chafed, "and not talk in fucking riddles."

"Hmmmm, I'd have thought that balls would be the last thing on your mind," Susan said with a smirk.

Tatiana threw up her hands, an exasperated look forming on her face.

"You know what, I'm done," she said. "All I wanted to know was how the glass got broken, but screw it; it's not worth fighting over."

"You want to know how it got broken, Tee? I'll tell you how. It got broken when that little bitch you have locked up in there tried to escape."

Tatiana, who had been heading back outside to find some peace and quiet, spun around suddenly. "What did you say?"

"You heard me," Susan replied.

"How did she try to escape? Why the hell were you even in there?"

"Oh, gee, thanks for your concern," Susan said dryly. "No need to worry about little old me, I'm fine."

"Damn it, Susan, this isn't a joke," Tatiana replied. "Why were you in there alone? You know better than to do that."

"To get answers," Susan exploded.

"You talked to her?"

"Yes, I did."

"Jesus Christ," Tatiana said, as she collapsed into the chair across from her. "Why did you go and do that?"

"Instead of answering that question maybe I should be the one asking why it is that you pretended like you didn't know her."

An uneasy silence gripped the atmosphere, as the two women stared at each other, but only one of them was wrestling with what to say next.

What the fuck did you think was going to happen? she wondered.

It was a good question, but the truth was she hadn't thought that far in advance. Tatiana had been caught up in the moment, living out a fantasy, ever since she had first laid eyes on Alex that cold winter's night a few months back. Up until that point she had always planned things methodically, like a chess grandmaster, considering every possible move and counter-move, but the sight of the woman had caused her to throw all caution to the wind and she realized that she was about to pay the price for that mistake. The only question that remained was just how high a price it would be.

"I just didn't think you'd understand...."

"*Sonofabitch*," Susan said angrily, as she slammed her hand down onto the end table next to her.

She'd been sitting on the fence, wavering, torn between what Alex had told her and what she wanted to believe. Tatiana's admission had toppled her from her perch and brought her plummeting to the ground below.

Susan leaned forward, elbows resting on her knees, as her hands held her head. Deep within her, anger and hurt battled for control over her heart, as well as her mind.

"How could you do this to me?" she demanded. "How could you do this to us?"

The visceral pain that that Susan was feeling emanated in her words.

"I didn't know how to explain it to you," Tatiana replied. "I didn't know how you would take it."

"Bullshit, Tee," Susan said angrily. "I know you better than that. I've shared everything with you, the good, the bad and the ugly, but you haven't. You've only shared what you wanted to with me and compartmentalized the rest. I don't even know what is real anymore."

Tatiana got up and walked over to the couch, sitting down next to Susan. She tried to put her arm around the woman's shoulder, but Susan shrugged it off.

"Don't," she said angrily. "You can't make this better."

"I love you," Tatiana said. "You know that."

"Do I?" Susan asked. "Exactly what part of this screams 'I love you' to you, Tee? The part where you lied to me or the part where you drug me so that you can sneak into her room to get off?"

"What did she tell you?"

"She told me enough."

The anger raged inside Tatiana, but she did her best to repress it. Exploding was the worst thing she could do at this point. She knew she needed to dial things back a bit; to get hold of the situation before it went nuclear.

"I'm sorry," she said. "I never meant to hurt you, hon. When I first saw her I was completely dumbfounded; it was like a gut punch and I didn't know how to process it."

"You should have just told me!"

"I know I should have now, but I just didn't know how to process it then. Hell I didn't even know if it was really her."

"Well, you obviously did at some point; so that's a piss poor reason."

"You're right and I have no excuse."

"Seriously, what the fuck where you thinking, Tee?" Susan asked, as she turned to face her lover. "That you could have your cake and eat it too?"

"No," Tatiana bristled. "It was nothing like that. It's just that I was caught off guard and didn't have time to process everything.

When I did I realized that I was already wrong and was afraid you'd get mad."

"Well that worked out pretty well for you, didn't it?"

Tatiana ignored the dig.

"We both have people we want to make suffer for what they did to us. She's one of those people."

"Oh, so last night was just about making her suffer, huh?"

"No, I was drunk," Tatiana said sheepishly. "I was angry."

"Oh, that makes it so much better," Susan replied sarcastically. "Now every time we have an argument I just have to worry about you getting drunk and doing whatever the fuck you want."

"No, I didn't mean it that way."

"How the hell am I ever supposed to trust you again?"

"I don't know," Tatiana admitted. "It was a mistake. I was wrong."

"You're goddamn right it was wrong, Tee, but it was far from a mistake. You knew exactly what you were doing."

"Things just got carried away,....."

"Oh, please spare me the bullshit sob story," Susan snapped. "Now you sound like one of those pathetic politicians who got caught with their fingers in the kitty and somehow it's not really their fault."

"What do you want me to do?"

"Woman-up and take responsibility for your shit."

"Fine, I'm guilty. There, I said it. Are you happy now?"

"Jesus Christ," Susan said, glaring at Tatiana. "Yes, Tee, I'm friggin' ecstatic; can't you just see the joy and happiness radiating on my face?"

"What do you want me to do? Beg?"

"No!" Susan screamed. "What I want you to do is to fix the goddamn problem that *you* created in the first place."

"I told you I would."

"When?"

"Soon," Tatiana replied.

"Fuck you, Tee," Susan yelled, as she jumped up from the couch. "That's not good enough for me."

"Well what would be good enough for you?"

Susan pointed at the closed door, "For you to just go and take care of your shit, right now."

"I can't," Tatiana replied. "Now's not the right time. It's not part of the plan."

"There is no fucking plan, Tee," Susan screamed, "but if you won't fix this then I will."

Tatiana watched, a look of panic gripping her face, as Susan spun around and headed for the door. She lept from the couch and chased after her, catching her just before she reached the door.

"Stop," she shouted, as she reached out to stop her.

There was no malice intended, but that fact got lost very quickly. As Tatiana's hand reached out to grab the woman's shoulder, Susan turned slightly. The end result was that that she narrowly missed grabbing her by the shoulder and instead grabbed a fistful of her hair.

And then the fight was on.

Susan felt her head jerk back suddenly and then experienced a sharp, burning sensation, as her forward travel was arrested. Almost immediately Tatiana had released the woman's hair, when she realized the mistake, but it was too late.

Despite their size difference, Susan turned on her heels and delivered a devastating right hook to Tatiana's jaw that sent the woman staggering backward into the living room. It was all the opportunity Susan needed and she flung herself into the stunned woman, the two of them collapsing to the floor.

"You fucking bitch," Susan screamed, tears streaming down her face, as she swung her fists at Tatiana.

"Stop it, Susan," Tatiana protested, as she covered up her face. "I didn't mean it."

"Fuck you."

Susan's punches were landing wildly now, caused by her inability to see through her tears. Tatiana took the opportunity and grabbed her by the wrists.

"Susan, stop it," she implored.

"Let go of me!"

"Not until you stop."

Susan's body went limp.

"God, I hate you," she said, as she began to sob uncontrollably.

"No you don't," Tatiana said, as she tried to comfort her.

Unfortunately for Tatiana, Susan's emotions were on a roller coaster ride and it was currently traveling at breakneck speeds. Anger gave way to sadness and then back again to anger in almost the blink of an eye.

"Let go of me."

"Susan...."

"I said *let go of me.*"

Tatiana released her wrists and Susan scrambled to her feet.

"I'm done, Tee. I'm done playing this game."

"Baby, we're just going through a bad time. I promise it will get better."

"No, it won't. I can't live this way. I'd rather be alone."

"You're not serious, Susan. You don't mean that."

"I'm as serious as a heart attack," she replied. "I'm out of here."

"You can't leave."

Tatiana's voice was calm and measured, but Susan understood the thinly veiled threat and it gave her pause.

"Are you going to stop me, Tee?" Susan asked. "Am I going to end up tied to the bed like her?"

"I didn't mean it that way," Tatiana replied.

"What way did you mean it?"

"Look, let's just take a deep breath and relax. Tomorrow things will look a lot better."

A few days earlier and she would have scoffed at anyone who'd suggested that their relationship would be facing such an existential threat; yet here they were, squared off like two gladiators in an arena. To make matter's even worse, Tatiana was now standing directly in front of the door blocking her path.

"Move out of the way, Tee."

"I can't do that, Susan. I won't do that."

"I'm serious, Tee, get out of my way."

"Make me," Tatiana said defiantly.

Susan slid the knife out of her back pocket; the spring assisted blade snapping open with an audible *crack*.

Tatiana eyed the knife, and then looked at Susan, "C'mon, babe, you can't be serious?"

"I asked you twice, I won't ask a third time."

"What? You're going to cut me?"

"I poisoned my parents," Susan said in a cold, monotone voice, as she walked ever closer. "I watched my father die, gasping for air, as his throat closed shut. Then I slit my best friend's throat and watched her bleed out like a pig, all while eating a bag of chips. You know what common denominator they all shared, Tee? They all lied to me."

Tatiana's eyes glanced down at the knife the woman held in her hand. She could see the serrations in the blade, as the sunlight streaming through the living room window reflected off the steel. Knife fights were never pretty.

"You might be bigger than me, Tee, but don't think for one moment that's going to stop me."

For a moment, Tatiana war-gamed the current situation. She knew that she had a slight advantage over Susan, in terms of physical strength, but that only really mattered if she was willing to get physical with her. Despite the fact that the two of them were squared off presently, she still truly loved her.

If it devolves into this will we ever be able to recover from it? she wondered.

Deep inside she knew the answer was no. If she tried to stop Susan in her present state, there was no doubt that it would become a fight. She knew Susan wasn't thinking right and the thought of getting stabbed wasn't very appealing. Tatiana knew that she had to defuse the situation so, grudgingly, she slowly turned and moved away from the door.

For her part, Susan kept a watchful eye on the woman, as the two of them slowly moved in opposite directions. She knew too much about Tatiana than to let her guard down. They had just crossed a line in their relationship from which there was most likely no going back. In her mind she knew that she had just become a liability.

"Please just think this through," Tatiana pleaded.

"I have, Tee," Susan replied, as she reached behind her and grabbed the door knob. "Maybe you should have."

"I'm begging you, Susan. Don't leave."

"You still have your prize," Susan said, as she opened the door and stepped outside. "You'll be fine."

Tatiana watched as Susan closed the door. She wanted to follow after her, to drag her back in if need be, but what was the point in doing that? The confrontation would turn violent and then she would have two captives to contend with. Her only hope now was that Susan just needed a cooling off period and that she would come back when she had really allowed herself to think things through.

Outside the cabin, Susan continued to walk backwards, maintaining a vigilant watch over the door. Part of her anticipated seeing Tatiana come barreling through it at any moment. When she reached the car her calmness finally gave out and her hand fumbled nervously for the handle. She felt her knees weaken a bit, as she took her eyes off the door and got in the driver's seat, shutting the door frantically behind her.

This was how it always happened in the horror movies, isn't it? she thought. *The victim always thinks they are home free and then boom, the monster appears and kills them.*

Susan looked up nervously, a part of her expecting to see the front door mysteriously wide open with no one standing there, only to see Tatiana materialize at the driver's side door a moment later. But the door remained closed and no one appeared. She transitioned the knife to her left hand, as the right one opened the console and grabbed the keys out. Her hand shook, as she jabbed at the ignition switch with the key, missing several times.

"Fuck!" she exclaimed, as she fought to control her nerves.

Finally the key slipped in and she turned it over, listening as the engine roared to life. Her heart was racing wildly, as she dropped it into reverse and sped backward down the private driveway, spraying gravel as she went. A few moments later the car shot out wildly onto the main road and she threw it into drive.

Susan raced along the quiet, rural road, as she tried to put as much distance as she could between her and Tatiana. She didn't understand why, but her heart was still racing and she truly felt terrified. Maybe it was because she knew exactly what the woman was capable of doing.

As the minutes ticked by, and their distance apart grew bigger, Susan finally felt herself begin to relax. The adrenaline rush, which had been fueled by a mix of anger and fear, now began to dissipate. Anger turned to pain and the fear turned to heartache, as she realized what had just happened.

As dysfunctional a relationship as theirs might have been, it was still the most incredible thing she had ever felt before in her young life. Tatiana had been a lover, a teacher, and a maternal figure to her. The short time they had spent together had left her feeling both loved for who she was and protected. Now she had lost it all. Maybe that was why it hurt so badly.

The emotional conflict raged deep within her, as she began to question the decision she had just made.

This was your choice, she thought.

Susan swallowed hard, as she felt the stinging sensation of the tears welling up in her eyes. She fought valiantly to hold them back, but it was futile and she knew it. As soon as she felt the first one hit her cheek she succumbed to her emotions and began to sob uncontrollably.

"God damn you, Tee," she screamed, her voice breaking, as she pounded her fists angrily against the steering wheel.

Susan rubbed at her eyes, blinking hard, as she tried to clear her cloudy vision.

You just need some space, she thought. *Some quite time to figure this all out.*

They had long ago established an alternate mode of communication, a type of dead drop, in the event that they had become separated and needed to re-establish contact with each other surreptitiously. She knew that Tatiana would begin to monitor it, hoping that Susan would get back in contact with her.

Things were bad now, but maybe they could recover. If Tatiana would agree to get rid of that bitch, once and for all, perhaps they could find a way to heal their relationship; to learn from this and grow stronger.

She reached over, opening the glove box, and remove a napkin to dry her eyes. As she did, her left hand turned ever so slightly to the right, causing the car to veer off toward the shoulder. As Susan looked up she saw a large maple tree looming in her immediate path.

"Shit!"

A seasoned driver might have responded differently, gently correcting the car's steering, but Susan was young and inexperienced. She jerked the wheel in the opposite direction, taking her away from the tree but putting herself into the path of an oncoming SUV. She slammed on the brakes; fighting to slow the vehicle down and it was *almost* successful.

The Volvo crossed the double yellow line and clipped the left rear quarter panel of the Explorer ever so slightly, but it was just enough to send the smaller vehicle spinning around, out of control. It completed two full rotations, as it slid through the oncoming lane, before careening down an embankment where it struck a tree.

Miraculously, it somehow managed not to flip over, but the force of the collision had ripped Susan's hands from the steering wheel and she was violently tossed around the car's interior like a rag doll. At some point the side of her head struck the driver's side passenger window.

The last thing she saw, before she passed out, was the image of the SUV's driver running toward her.

CHAPTER FORTY-TWO

"How are things going?" Melody asked.

"Quietly busy," Maguire replied.

"I don't think I have ever heard that term before."

"That's what happens when you have a bunch of cops hanging around, chomping at the bit, with nothing to do."

"So no new news I take it?" Melody asked.

"No, unfortunately."

"Are you going to stay up there?"

"Yeah," Maguire replied. "I called Tony Ameche and filled him in on what's going on. He's going to take the helm for a few days."

"I know this isn't a good time, but maybe now you'll start to think about appointing a new first dep to take your place."

"Yeah, yeah, yeah," Maguire replied sarcastically. "It's on my to-do list."

"It's on your procrastination list," Melody shot back. "And you know I'm right."

Maguire said nothing, which only validated her point.

It wasn't that he didn't want to, but it was something he had just continued to struggle with. His taking over as police commissioner had left a void in the Department hierarchy, but filling the spot had proved to be a lot more difficult for him.

The positon of first deputy commissioner was akin to a second in command. Maguire had accepted the role, when it was offered, because his friend had asked him to. At the time, some in the media had questioned that move, since Maguire's career within the NYPD had ended at detective, but he had brought those questions to a screeching halt as he skillfully guided the Department through some very difficult events. Becoming police commissioner, under the circumstances he been given, had granted him a brief respite, but he also knew that the current media honeymoon he was enjoying would soon end.

Back in his office at 1 Police Plaza he had a stack of folders sitting on his desk for very well qualified candidates. They included numerous members of the NYPD, as well as a host of others from outside the Department, but he still struggled with it all. He reasoned with himself that finding the right person was too important to rush into a choice, but perhaps he was haunted by the fact that, by selecting his own replacement, he was acknowledging the fact that Rich was really gone.

Maguire leaned back in the chair, as he casually surveyed the small office. It was simple, almost quaint, and he couldn't help wonder if this environment appealed to Alex. Compared to the hustle and bustle he dealt with on a daily basis, this seemed so much more appealing.

"Hello?"

Maguire blinked and quickly sat upright.

"Sorry," he said, rubbing his face. "I was just thinking."

"Uh huh," Melody replied. "Maybe you should pick a woman. You could benefit from someone used to making timely decisions."

"Are you available?"

"No," Melody replied smartly, "and you couldn't afford me if I was."

"Hey, don't I get a family discount?"

"You only get that after this engagement ring turns into a wedding ring, cowboy."

"Are you going to tell Eliza Cooke that she can't afford you?"

"I'm not crossing that bridge until I come to it," Melody said. "For now it's all just wild speculation."

"Maybe," Maguire replied, "maybe not, but you'd better break out the road map just in case."

"I will," she replied. "Right after you choose your first dep."

"Touché," he replied.

Just then there was a knock at on the door.

"Yes?" Maguire asked, as he looked up to see Tom Blackshear standing in the doorway.

"Hutch is on the phone with VSP," Blackshear said. "They just finished reviewing the traffic video out of Colton."

"I'll be right there, Tom," Maguire replied, and then returned to the call. "Sorry, angel, just getting an update."

"I heard," Melody said. "Get back to work slacker. Call me if you learn anything new."

"I will," he replied. "I love ya."

"Love ya too."

Maguire heard the line go silent. He put the phone in his pocket and got up from the desk. Hutch was just hanging up the phone when he walked outside.

"What did they say?" Maguire asked hopefully.

It had been a *Hail Mary* play, but it was all they had at this point. The city of Colton sat on the Vermont / New Hampshire border. It was the convergence of three major roadways and was the last big city before the Canadian border. As a result, the U.S. Department of Transportation had issued a grant for the installation of traffic cameras. The official reason given for the grant was just another new federal traffic safety initiative, designed to cut down on road fatalities nationwide, which had been secured through the hard work of the areas congressional representative. The actual reason was to discretely monitor border crossing activity.

The money had been quietly allocated to the Department of Transportation through the Drug Enforcement Administration. The cities selected had all been chosen in advance by the DEA and all the state reps had to do was take credit without doing any work. As far as politics went, it was a perfect win / win scenario.

While America's attention, and by extension its media coverage, had been focused on its neighbor to the south, its northern neighbor had emerged as a key player in international drug shipments. After a period of violence, which saw numerous members of the Canadian drug trade killed in Mexico, relations had *normalized*. Canada had now become a major transshipment point for drugs being shipped into Europe and Australia; so much so that Canada had been ranked second only to Chile in supplying cocaine to Australia. Now, all eyes, including the electronic ones, were focused to the north.

"They went back over the traffic cam videos for the last several days," Hutch replied, "but there were no hits."

"Which means they still might be in the area," Blackshear replied.

"Or they came and went from a completely different direction," Maguire responded.

"So what do we do now?" Blackshear asked. "Put up a map and throw darts?"

"We already have state and local units monitoring a majority of the roads in and out of the area," Hutch said, "but realistically we can't keep that up forever."

"Whatever they might be, these two have certainly proven to be extremely resourceful," Maguire replied, as he walked over toward the coffee pot and poured himself a fresh cup.

"Do you have any other suggestions?" Hutch asked.

"Pray," Maguire said thoughtfully.

Quietness fell over the room of investigators, as each contemplated the remark. Collectively there was over two centuries of law enforcement experience currently assembled in the office of the Penobscot Police Department and yet there only remaining hope was being pinned on a prayer.

The big clock ticking on the wall kept its vigil; it was a constant reminder to them that time was running out.

CHAPTER FORTY-THREE

Tatiana sat on the couch, a vacant stare on her face, as she peered out the window to where the car had previously been parked. The pain she had felt in her heart, as she had watched the Volvo pull away, was gone now; replaced by a numbness that gripped her body, as she struggled with the realization that Susan was not coming back.

Just beyond the window pane the world outside was alive, but here inside the small room it was as if she was in mourning. The tears that had fallen on her cheeks had long ago dried up. Now all that remained were the streaks left behind to mark their passing.

A part of her wanted to ask what had happened, but she had to admit that she already knew the answer. The hardest part of introspection was being brutally honest with ones self. The truth was that she had wanted to have her cake and eat it to.

It seemed so readily apparent to her now that it had been a losing proposition from the start; yet her aroused emotional state had clouded her judgment and prevented her from seeing that.

This time, last week, the two of them were sitting on the small dock together, their feet splashing playfully in the waters below, as they shared a bottle of wine and discussed the future. They had been making plans to head out west for the summer. Susan talked about hitting Vegas and Hollywood, maybe even heading north and settling down in Oregon for a bit. The idea of being able to be seen openly as a couple, instead of pretending to be mother and daughter, appealed to both of them.

One week was all that separated the highest of highs from the lowest of lows.

What I wouldn't give now to go back in time one week, she thought, as she reached down and grabbed the bottle of whiskey off the coffee table.

But would you really make a different choice?

Tatiana took a long drink, feeling the burn, as the whiskey went down her throat. She glanced over at the closed door and felt a wave of anger wash over her.

It bothered her deeply that she knew the answer to that question was an emphatic no. The woman on the other side of that door had done something to her; touched her in a place that she couldn't simply move past emotionally. She truly loved Susan, but she physically lusted after Alex in a way that thrilled her and caused her to make completely irrational choices.

Even now, as she cursed herself for forcing Susan's hand, driving her out of her life, she couldn't shake the desire she felt inside.

The numbness she had previously felt began to slowly dissipate and was replaced by something else, something more primal, which was being fed by a mix of anger and alcohol.

Tatiana's eyes narrowed menacingly, as she took another drink and accepted what she already knew that she needed to do.

CHAPTER FORTY-FOUR

New Hampshire State Trooper, Scott Mendes, pulled his marked Dodge Charger into the *authorized vehicles only* crossing and placed the car into park.

Traffic was particularly slow on this stretch of roadway and it would afford him some time to catch up on some of his electronic paperwork. It had been an unusually busy day thus far and he was happy that the radio had gone quiet for a bit. It was quickly approaching the end of his shift and, with any luck, he would be able to make it home in plenty of time to get ready for his daughter's 11th birthday party.

He reached over, removing the Styrofoam cup of coffee from the cup holder and carefully pried back the plastic lid; a rush of steam rising up from the opening.

"Troop F to 631," his radio chirped, as he raised the cup to his lips.

"Oh for the love of God," he exclaimed, as he sat the cup back down in the holder and picked up the radio mic.

"631, 10-3," he replied.

"631 are you available to respond to a 10-25 with personal injury, eastbound on 26, approximately a quarter mile west of Robichaud?"

"Anyone closer?"

"Negative, sheriff's office is out on a 10-37 and has no units available at this time."

Mendes glanced down at his watch and frowned at the realization that he was probably going to miss yet another family event.

"10-5," he replied, as he put the car in drive and pulled back onto the roadway.

Even running lights and sirens it took nearly twenty minutes to arrive at the scene. A fire engine from the local department had blocked off a portion of the roadway, and an ambulance was already on scene, by the time he arrived. A black SUV was parked on the shoulder and he could see several firemen standing in the ditch were another car had come to a rest.

"Lovely," he said, as he pulled past the accident scene and then looped back around.

Mendes blocked off a portion of the roadway with his vehicle and left his emergency lights on. Then he grabbed his hat and exited the vehicle.

"What do we have?" he asked the fire lieutenant who was walking toward him.

"According to the driver of the Explorer the Volvo in the ditch was heading westbound and veered over into the eastbound lane and struck them."

Mendes glanced over at the ambulance, seeing the EMT's working on a young girl in the back.

"That the driver of the Volvo?"

"Yeah, we had to extricate her from the car, but she doesn't seem to be in that bad of shape," the lieutenant said. "Just a little banged up more than anything else."

"She's lucky to be alive," Mendes replied, as he glanced down at the mangled remains of the car resting against the tree.

"Don't you remember when you were young and invincible?" the lieutenant asked.

"Yes, but I don't discuss it because the statute of limitations hasn't expired on some stuff," Mendes said with a laugh.

"You and me both," the other man said. "Oh, here's the Volvo driver's license. We needed the information for the callout."

Mendes took the license and glanced down at the smiling face of the young driver and then at her date of birth.

God they keep getting younger and younger, he thought.

No, you just keep getting older and older, he corrected.

"Well, we're done here," the lieutenant interrupted, "so if you don't mind we are going to clear out."

"Yeah, no problem," Mendes replied, as he continued to scan the driver's license. "Thanks for the response."

"Anytime," the man replied, as he walked away.

He never saw the color drain from Mendes' face when the trooper finally looked at the driver's name.

CHAPTER FORTY-FIVE

"Thank you very much, Bob," Maguire said into the cell phone. "We're happy that the Bureau is taking an interest in the case and I will let you know personally if there is anything we need."

He swayed lazily in the office chair and gave Hutch, who was sitting across from him, a look of disgust.

"Yes, I'd love to get together over lunch. Have your secretary contact mine the next time you're in town and we'll make it happen."

Maguire closed his eyes and rested his head against the fingers of his left hand.

"Yes, good speaking to you too, Bob. We'll talk soon."

Maguire looked down at the phone, pushing the *end call* button and ensuring that it had disconnected, before he spoke.

"Fucking douche," he exclaimed, tossing the phone onto the desk and taking a sip of his lukewarm coffee.

"What was that all about?" Hutch asked.

"Box ticking," Maguire replied.

"Box ticking?" Hutch asked, taking a sip of his own coffee. "What the hell is that?"

"That's when you have zero intention of doing anything, but you need to look like you are."

"So the FBI isn't going to do anything?"

"Oh no, they are going to *monitor* the situation," Maguire explained.

"Monitor?"

"Yes, they are serial monitors."

"So I've heard," Hutch replied dismissively.

"Honestly, in a way it's better," Maguire replied. "The rank and file investigators are aces, some of the best in the business, but for the most part the higher-ups quickly turn into political animals. They can be more of a hindrance then a help at times."

"Even the FBI Director?"

Maguire motioned toward the door and Hutch leaned over to close it.

"He's the absolute worst," Maguire replied.

"Really?"

"I worked with him on several cases when I was a detective and he was a supervisory special agent back in the New York Field Office. Back then he ran a task force and was generally dismissed as being wholly incompetent."

"Then how did he become the FBI Director?" Hutch asked.

"Politics," Maguire replied. "He's third generation Bureau. His grandfather was one of Hoover's right-hand men. His father served in many of the Bureau's high profile spots and made it all the way up to Assistant Director. Junior rode their coattails. Any time he screwed up badly they simply promoted him and moved him; the whole *out-of-sight, out-of-mind* philosophy."

"So that really does happen?" Hutch asked, taking a bite of his donut.

"More times than you'd believe," Maguire said. "Anyway, rumor has it that a certain someone made something, that was extremely politically incriminating, conveniently *disappear* and was thusly rewarded."

"And they have the nerve to break our balls?"

"It's a cruel, cruel world, my friend," Maguire replied. "Like Orwell said, 'All animals are equal, but some animals are more equal than others.'"

"Yeah, well I'm glad I'm just a small town cop and I don't have to deal with that bullshit."

"Sometimes I wish I was as well," Maguire laughed. "Then I wouldn't have to deal with assholes like that."

"Better you than me," Hutch replied. "I couldn't imagine having lunch with someone like that."

"Oh, Coleman will be long gone before we ever have to share a table."

"How do you know that?"

"There's a general consensus in Washington, which is itself rather rare, that Coleman was illegitimately put in the spot by the President over more qualified people. Coleman's selection rankled a number of people, on both sides of the aisle, so with the elections right around the corner the next President will move to replace him rather quickly. They'll only get a token push back and then it will go from front page news to buried rather quickly."

"I really hate politics."

"So do I."

"So why do you do it?" Hutch asked, before finishing off his coffee. "I may be wrong, but to me, outside of Washington, D.C., New York City is the next big political machine."

Maguire leaned back in the chair, as he contemplated the question.

"It is," Maguire replied, "and I will admit that sometimes I really don't know, Hutch. I guess there is still a part of me that really does want to help people."

"But do they even want our help?"

Maguire frowned. "No one loves the warrior, until the enemy is at the gate."

The conversation was interrupted suddenly by a flurry of commotion coming from just beyond the closed door.

"What the...." Hutch exclaimed, as the door next to him swung open.

"We got a hit," Blackshear shouted, as he rushed inside the office.

"What?" Maguire asked, getting up from the chair. "Where?"

"Annabelle Birch was just involved in a motor vehicle accident on Route 26," Blackshear replied. "About twenty minutes from here."

"I can get us there in ten," Hutch said, as he grabbed his jacket.

"Okay, slow down," Maguire replied. "What's the current situation at the scene?"

"A trooper was dispatched to an accident and when he got there he recognized the name on the license and confirmed the BOLO on the plate."

"Has he spoken to her?" Maguire asked.

"No, not yet," Blackshear replied. "She's being treated for some minor injuries she sustained, but the EMT's are getting antsy. They want to remove her to the hospital."

"Okay, tell him not to talk to her at all," Maguire replied. "Tell him to play it nonchalant. Give the EMT's some BS story that the computer system is down and it should only be a few minutes and he can give her back the paperwork and then they can leave."

"Shouldn't we just collar her?" Hutch asked.

"No," Maguire said. "I gotta believe she's a smart girl and they've planned for the eventuality of something like this. You slap cuffs on her now and she is going to shut up and demand a lawyer. That's something we don't have any time for right now."

"I assume you have another option?" Blackshear asked.

"Yeah," Maguire said coldly. "Fear."

CHAPTER FORTY-SIX

"How much longer is this going to take?" Susan asked the EMT sitting next to her. "I'm starting to feel nauseous."

"I really don't know," he replied, as he reached over to take her pulse.

"I'm starting to feel really bad," Susan said, ushering up a contrived look of pain on her face.

"This is just bullshit," he remarked angrily. "He's intentionally dragging his ass. If I had to guess I'd say he's probably waiting for the sheriff to come so he doesn't have to do the report."

"I'm starting to have this tingling feeling in my legs."

"Hold on for a minute," he said, getting up and moving toward the driver's cab.

Susan quickly surveyed the interior of ambulance. She spied a pair of trauma shears, which the man had left on the seat next to him. She glanced over her shoulder, making sure the man's back was too her, and then grabbed them. She slipped her hand back under the blanket and secreted the shears inside the waistband of her jeans.

She didn't know what was going on, but Tatiana had drilled it into her head that she always needed to have a plan 'B' in place; just in case things took a sudden turn for the worse.

"Do you know who this state cop is, Brenda?" the man asked his partner, who was impatiently sitting in the driver's seat of the ambulance.

"No, but he's about on my last goddamn nerve," she replied angrily.

"Can you go and check how much longer it is going to be," the man replied. "If he tries to give you any shit, just tell him I'm going to call the E.R. and have them file a complaint."

"Fine," the woman replied with a heavy sigh.

She exited the ambulance and made her way back to where the police car was parked.

She could see the trooper sitting behind the wheel and her anger only grew as she realized he wasn't doing anything. She watched as the window slowly rolled down.

"Yes?" Mendes asked.

"Listen, I'm not trying to be a bitch here, but we're leaving."

"No you're not."

The comment didn't come from the trooper, so she turned sharply to look back in the direction of the men who were approaching the car.

"Excuse me?" she asked with a shocked expression.

"I said you're not leaving."

"And who the hell are you?"

"That's on a need to know basis and you don't," Maguire replied.

The man looked vaguely familiar to her, but the suddenness of the encounter left her unable to properly process what was happening. She turned her attention from him to the other two men, one of whom she did recognize.

"Hutch, what's going on here?"

"I need you to come with me for a minute, Brenda," Hutch said. "I'll explain what's happening."

The men watched as Hutch escorted the woman back toward his patrol car and then turned their attention to the trooper.

"Anything change?" Blackshear asked.

"Nope, she's still waiting in the back of the ambulance, sir."

"Thank you for your help, Trooper," Blackshear said. "Just hang back here for a few."

"Yes, sir," Mendes replied.

Maguire and Blackshear made their way toward the back of the Ambulance.

"You sure this is how you want to play it?" Blackshear asked.

"You have a better idea, Tom?"

"No," the man admitted.

"Then we have to go with the only option that we have available to us."

"I can't even begin to count all the ways that this can go wrong."

"Just remember what General Patton said," Maguire replied, as they reached the back of the ambulance, "A good plan executed now is better than a perfect plan executed next week."

"I hope that sounds as uplifting and motivational in court," Blackshear said with a frown, as he opened the back door of the ambulance.

"Who the hell are you?" the EMT asked.

"State police," Blackshear replied. "I need you to step out for a minute."

"Are you for real?" the man asked angrily. "We have a patient that needs to go to the hospital, now!"

"Sir, step out of the ambulance," Blackshear replied.

The man was getting ready to argue, but something in the look of the two men standing there gave him pause.

"Fine," he conceded, getting up and stepping out of the vehicle, "but just so you know I plan on filing a formal complaint about this."

Maguire climbed into the back of the ambulance, sitting down across from the young woman lying on the stretcher, and stared at her. He could see the uncertainty in her eyes. Watching intently as she struggled internally to figure out what was going on. Then he saw the muscles in her jaw ripple, as her teeth clenched tightly. He knew that she'd put enough of it together to know that she was caught.

"Well I guess we can dispose of the Annabelle Birch charade now," he said.

"What do you want?" she asked coolly.

"To give you choices," he replied.

"Choices?" she scoffed. "I know who you are. I know all about you."

"Then I suggest that you listen closely, because I'm only going to say this one time."

"You don't scare me."

"Oh, I'm not trying to scare you, Susan."

"Then what do you want?"

"Just answers," Maguire replied.

"What if I don't want to talk to you?" she asked smugly. "Maybe I just tell you to go fuck yourself and advise you that I want to talk to my lawyer."

"That's one choice," he replied, "but I would caution you strongly against using that."

"Oh please, spare me the melodrama," Susan said.

She watched as Maguire reached inside his jack and removed some papers.

"What's that?"

"This? Oh, this is a list of your greatest hits, Susan." Maguire replied. "Your mother and father, Hannah Kurtz, Lou Jenkins, Paige Wilson...."

Maguire's voice trailed off, as he continued to look through the papers.

"Oooh, I'm busted, Mr. Policeman," she said with a laugh, as she raised her arms up and held her wrists together, waiting to be handcuffed.

"I'm not sure how cheerful I would be if I was looking at that much time," Maguire replied.

"We both know there is a huge difference between being charged with a crime and being convicted of one. I can spout off over a dozen other names, but that doesn't mean you can tie me to any of them."

"How about Alex Taylor?"

Maguire watched as the smirk disappeared from Susan's face.

"Sorry, not doing anything for me."

"Really?" Maguire asked.

"Guess I'm not big on names," Susan replied.

"I would have thought it would ring a bell," he replied, as he handed her one of the papers.

She took it and stared at the black and white photocopy of her car that the security camera had captured.

"Yeah, that's my car, so what?" Susan replied arrogantly.

"It's your car coming from the same direction that Alex Taylor went missing from," Maguire replied. "It was also at the same time that we captured a cellphone signal."

Susan fought hard to maintain her calm appearance, even as the anger inside her threatened to bubble up to the top.

"You don't say," she replied. "Sounds like coincidence to me."

"Oh, I'm sure it does," Maguire replied, "but I highly doubt that theory is going to survive the light of day after the forensic techs get done tearing apart your car."

"Sorry, I've had a lot of folks in my car," she said ominously. "I enjoy giving people a one-way ride."

"Well, where you're going, you'll have plenty of time to contemplate all the ones you've left behind."

"You honestly think I'm afraid of going to Goffstown?" Susan asked, referring to the New Hampshire State Prison for Women.

"No, I don't," Maguire replied softly, "but who said anything about Goffstown?"

"Isn't that where female prisoners go to in New Hampshire?" Susan asked quizzically.

"Yes, state prisoners go there, Susan, but you're not going to be a state prisoner."

"Wait, what do you mean?"

"Did you honestly think your exploits were going unnoticed outside of New Hampshire?"

"I don't understand," Susan replied, as she felt a wave of panic begin to well up inside her.

"What's not to understand, Susan?" Maguire said matter-of-factly. "You're a serial killer,"

For some reason, hearing those words made her inwardly cringe.

"You've made quite a name for yourself, Susan," Maguire continued, "and now we have a paper trail. The Penobscot Police Department has made an official request to have the F.B.I.'s Behavioral Analysis Unit join the investigation. Your abduction of Chief Taylor, along with your crisscrossing of state lines, has taken this investigation to a whole new level, a *federal* one."

"So what does that mean?"

"It means that when they get done with you, Goffstown is going to sound like a five star luxury resort compared to where you're going to end up."

Susan stared at Maguire stoically, but her gaze was met with an equally impassive look. Something in the man's cold, blue eyes told her that he wasn't bluffing and she wasn't going to win this battle.

"You said I had choices," Susan said.

"Tell me what you did with Alex," Maguire replied.

"This wasn't my idea," she replied. "I wasn't the one that wanted to kidnap her."

"You only have one opportunity to tell me what happened, Susan."

"She'll kill me," Susan replied angrily.

It was an unexpected reply, but Maguire had interrogated enough people over the years to know better than to be caught off guard. He took the nugget of information and pushed it to the side for a moment. The young woman's cold façade had cracked and her false bravado was gone. He couldn't let the moment get away from him.

"Let me make this absolutely crystal clear for you, Susan. The window for you telling me what I want to know is closing rapidly. You might have just gone along for the ride, but if anything happens to her I promise you that I will make it my life's mission to ensure that the Attorney General takes this case through federal court and that you end up with the death penalty."

"That doesn't sound like much of a choice."

"Well, that all depends on your outlook," he replied. "If anything happens to her you can be rest assured that you will spend the rest of your days in solitary confinement, in a windowless cell at the Carswell federal penitentiary, without any other human contact. There you will live with each and every one of the ghosts that you have made; ghosts who will haunt you until you make that final trip to the Terra Haute where they'll stick a needle in your arm and send you off to meet your maker. Most folks can do it for a day or two, maybe even a week, but then the walls begin to close in and the noise in your head will become unbearable. You'll become paranoid, maybe even psychotic, as you try and determine what is real and what is imaginary. Some inmates say that they begin to see their victims, so I imagine that little cell of yours will get crowded awfully fast. If you were a lot older you could find some comfort in knowing that you might die soon, but being young you'll have decades of fun to look forward to."

Susan swallowed hard.

"Or maybe you'll take the coward's way out," Maguire continued. I hear that a lot of folks opt for suicide as a way to break their earthly bonds. That becomes a tad bit harder when you are in solitary, but it's not impossible. I heard of one inmate that reached the end of his rope and killed himself by literally gnawing at his own wrist."

Maguire shook his head in revulsion at the image.

"But just remember to make sure you get it right the first time, because ending up in a psychiatric seclusion cell is even worse. Or, you can avoid all of that. Just tell me what I want to know and

338

you can stay here in New Hampshire. At least in Goffstown you will be able to feel the sun on your face every day."

"You talk like I've already been found guilty," Susan replied, as she fought hard to keep her voice from cracking.

Maguire reached back into his pocket and removed another piece of paper. It was a photocopy of the letter she had left behind in her father's apartment.

"I'm not a lawyer, but this unsolicited confession looks like pretty good grounds for premeditation," he replied. "Couple that with the kidnapping and murder of a cop and I'd say that you're pretty much royally screwed. The folks over at the FBI are pretty good at what they do. I bet they can tack on a few interstate murders without too much effort. That being said, if you help us out, with any luck you might get a good appeals lawyer who makes a 'she was not in her right mind' argument and gets you a reduced sentence."

Maguire could almost see the gears in her head spinning, as she tried to figure her next play. It was a scene he'd watch play out hundreds of times. The smiling, laughing faces of perps on the street that inevitably turned to crying and pleading when the cuffs went on. It was easy to be brave when you were surrounded by your peers, but the impudence was short lived when they came face to face with reality.

"I want protection," Susan said softly.

"I can give you that," Maguire replied.

"And no death penalty," she added.

"That I can't promise you, but I will guarantee that your cooperation will be made known to any prosecutors or judges assigned to your case. Likewise, if you hold anything back from me, I will make that clear as well. It's the best I can do."

Susan weighed her dwindling options and reached the only viable conclusion.

"Give me a pen."

CHAPTER FORTY-SEVEN

The whiskey had finally done its job.

Tatiana stared down vacantly at the tumbler she cradled in her hands. The hurt and pain she had first felt with Susan's departure was gone now, replaced by a slow, simmering anger that held her ever-darkening thoughts in a vise-like grip. Any feelings of personal responsibility that she might have felt had been steadily transferred to the woman in the other room. If anything, Tatiana's only fault was not doing something sooner to insulate Susan from the evil machinations of that deceitful little whore.

Susan was young, impressionable, and Tatiana was quite sure that Alex had known exactly what she was doing when the two of them talked. She could envision her filling Susan's head with all manner of lies. Alex may have thought she was being smart, as she drove the wedge of jealousy deep into Susan's mind, but with the young woman out of the picture now all that remained was Alex.

That is who you wanted after all, isn't it? she thought.

A smile slowly began to appear on Tatiana's face, as she recalled the time in the cabin. She closed her eyes, thinking about the way she looked, how she smelled, even the warmth of her lips. Tatiana felt a flash of heat course through her body and she shuddered in anticipation of what was to come.

"Well, I guess it's time the little bitch paid the piper," she said, before lifting the glass up to her lips and taking the final drink.

She sat it down on the table in front of her before getting up from the couch. Her state of arousal, coupled with the alcohol, caused her to feel a sudden rush, and she steadied herself on the arm for a moment.

"Easy there, kiddo," she chided herself. "You need to start pacing yourself."

She walked carefully over to the door, unlocking it, and entered the room.

Her heart began to beat quicker as she entered the room and she paused for a moment to appreciate the site of Alex's body lying on the bed. She knew first hand that after tonight things would be different between the two of them and she wanted to commit this image to her memory.

Was this what went through his mind as well? she wondered.

She recalled every moment of that first time with Banning; the ferocity, the depravity. The first few times she had tried to fight back, to scream for help, but it was pointless and it only seemed to excite him more. He delighted in taking her against her will; his eyes going wild with unbridled lust as he tore and cut the clothing from her body.

There was a cruel barbarity in what he had done to her in the beginning. The more she resisted the more physically abusive he was. So many times she would lay there alone afterwards, her body bruised and battered, the metallic taste of blood on her lips, begging to die.

Death would have been so welcome over what he did to her on a daily basis.

Eventually she stopped fighting back and just let him do as he pleased. He was still callous, but it was over much quicker that way. It was as if her mind had shut down. Whenever he would come in she would just go to her happy place until he was finished. Then one day something changed. Banning had just finished and collapsed on top of her. She could feel the warmth of his skin against hers; felt his heart beating rapidly. All along she had felt as if he was just using her for sex, but now she came to the realization it wasn't about that, it was about her. For one singular moment everything seemed to align perfectly and it changed her world view forever. Banning truly *wanted* her.

The next time they were together she didn't go to her happy place, but instead stayed present in the moment. At first she believed that she was surrendering to his desire, but with each passing moment she realized that she was giving in to her own. As the momentum built, her mind was overcome by the sensory onslaught that was occurring within her. It was all new territory for her. No one, man or woman, had ever brought her to this place before. She felt like a goddess. It was her, not him, who was doing the taking. Banning might not have realized it at the time, but he was serving *her* now, giving her everything that she wanted. Her mind had given in fully to her corporeal desire and it culminated in an orgasm beyond anything that she had ever felt before.

It was after that moment of incredible self-awareness that her life had changed. She had come to the realization that the bonds of captivity were ones she had placed on herself. Sex was only a vehicle, but she could choose the destination.

But she's not there yet, she reminded herself.

Everyone was different. In retrospect, she had given in rather quickly. It probably helped that she'd been used and abused by others in her life, but Alex was different. She was a cop and she would probably do anything and everything to fight back. It would take a while to break her, but the reality was that everyone had their breaking point. In the interim, she would take a cue from Banning and just enjoy each and every glorious moment that was about to come.

Losing Susan may have been emotionally hard, but the truth was that there was only so much she could physically do with her.

With Alex, those limitations were now removed and she could give in to her more depraved desires with reckless abandon.

In the immediate future she would have to make plans to get out of here with her prize. The area was secluded enough that she didn't have to really worry about anyone stumbling across them, but why tempt fate. For the moment she could at least have a little fun, but to truly enjoy Alex, in all the ways that she wanted, she would have to find a more remote playground.

Tatiana walked over and stood beside the bed. Her eyes gravitated toward Alex's chest and she bit her lower lip, as she watched her breasts rise up with every breath.

After allowing herself a moment to enjoy the sensual *calm before the storm*, she reached down and slowly removed the hood. She would not deny herself the pleasure of watching Alex's emotions play out on her face as she raped her.

"Hey there," Tatiana said, watching Alex's eyes squint, as they acclimated to the light, while she removed the gag. "How are you feeling?"

"I'm fine," Alex replied, "but it sounds like you might be having a little trouble in paradise."

"Me? Trouble in paradise? Why would you ever say that?" Tatiana asked, as she sat down in the chair.

"My mouth might be gagged, but my ears work just fine," Alex said sarcastically. "Judging from that obscenity laced tirade I heard coming out of your little *inamorata's* mouth, I'm surprised you're not out buying bulk amounts of roses and chocolates."

"Oh that," Tatiana replied, waving her hand dismissively. "Susan is young. Girls her age have a certain penchant for being melodramatic."

"You can call it melodramatic, I'd call it sleeping with one eye open for a while."

"You flatter her," Tatiana said, as she lit up a cigarette and set the pack down on the table next to the chair.

"Well, you have to admit that she has a respectable resume," Alex replied. "Personally, I'd be a little bit worried that Cupid's arrow might be tipped with poison."

"Mmmmmm," Tatiana murmured, as she took a drag. "Perhaps it might be respectable *numerically*, but overall it is not very impressive when you consider them individually. You see, by and large, Susan's victims all tended to be idiots who had their heads buried in the sand. Confrontation is not her forte, subterfuge is more her style. Look how poorly things almost turned out when the two of you squared off."

"Whatever," Alex replied with a smirk. "She's sharing your bed, not mine."

That remark elicited a genuine laugh.

"It's funny you should say mention that, Alex," Tatiana said.

"What do you mean by that?"

"Well, after your little stunt before I don't think I have to worry about what side of the bed I'll be sleeping on for a while."

"So there *is* trouble in paradise."

"No, no trouble," Tatiana replied. "Let's just say that I merely switched islands."

"I don't get it?"

Tatiana took a drag on the cigarette, and then blew a perfect smoke ring into the air. "I'm sure you thought it would be quite humorous to drive a wedge between Susan and me, but in reality the only thing you actually accomplished was to accelerate my plan."

"Oh, you have a plan," Alex said mockingly. "I can't wait to hear this."

"Susan was an amazing girl," Tatiana replied, "and I would be lying if I said that I didn't have fun with her, but she was still just a girl."

"God, you have issues."

Tatiana let the barb pass unanswered, as she rolled the cigarette between her fingers, a contemplative look on her face. "You know, I guess it is how an older man feels when he has a much younger woman on his arm. They might be great in bed, but they lack the familiarity of life that a peer of equal maturity brings to the equation."

"Happy hunting, bitch."

"Oh, my hunting days are over, Alex," Tatiana replied, taking a final drag on the cigarette and then dropping it to the floor below where she crushed it beneath her shoe.

"Fuck you."

"Mmmmmmmm, those were my thoughts exactly," Tatiana said with a smile, as she stood up from the chair. "I guess great minds think alike."

"Touch me again and I'll fucking kill you," Alex replied menacingly.

"I so understand where you're coming from," Tatiana said, as she hovered above her. "You'll have a change of heart,..... *eventually*, but until then I'm going to enjoy every second of breaking you."

"I'm warning you,....."

Tatiana climbed on top of Alex, straddling her legs, and reached down, grabbing the hem of Alex's shirt roughly. With both hands she began ripping it apart, watching intently as she exposed bare skin beneath. When she was done she stared down at the tattered remnants of the shirt. There was something so incredibly intoxicating with taking what you wanted by force. It established the foundations of the relationship.

She reached down and began caressing Alex's breasts playfully through the bra.

God, they're so much more impressive then Susan's, she thought, as she felt the nipples begin to harden.

"Don't you fucking dare..." Alex said angrily through gritted teeth.

Tatiana pinched the nipples roughly; hard enough to elicit a yelp of pain from the woman.

"Or what?" she sneered, as she slowly released her grip and then began caressing them softly through the bra's material. "Besides, it looks like the only thing saying no right now is your mouth."

"Don't say I didn't warn you," Alex replied.

"I own you now, bitch, just accept it."

Tatiana lowered her face toward Alex's chest, her hands cupping them firmly. The real *fun* would begin shortly, but for the moment she just wanted to enjoy them in their pristine state.

An argument could be made that her alcohol fueled lust, coupled with her sense of self, had made Tatiana oblivious to just how dangerous Alex could be. Her mind was swirling with images of how she was going to brutally ravage the woman's body, so it was understandable that she had missed a number of clues. None of which mattered when Alex's knee rose up and rammed into her with enough force to drive her forward.

Tatiana gasped loudly, her eyes going wide, as pain radiated throughout her lower extremities. Before she had a chance to recover that pain was matched by an equally excruciating one, as Alex brought her left hand down and drove the glass shard into the woman's back.

Alex seized the moment, releasing her hold on the glass and began pummeling Tatiana's head with her left fist. Most of the blows landed harmlessly, as the woman instinctively raised her arms up to ward off the blows. But one devastating shot made it through and Alex's fist landed squarely on her temple, snapping her head sharply. The result was that Tatiana's brain slammed violently against her skull body and her body immediately went limp. Alex thrust her hips up and rolled her upper body toward the left so that Tatiana slid off of her and landed on the floor below with a resounding *thud*.

"I warned you, bitch," Alex said smugly, as she reached over with her left hand and began untying the last rope that held her to the bed.

When she'd freed herself, she sat up and slid her feet over the edge, resting them on the body beneath her.

You're getting way too old for this kinda shit, she thought.

Slowly she got up and made her way out of the room, looking for something to tie the woman up.

There wasn't much to find in the living room or kitchen. She rummaged through the cabinets, but there wasn't even a plastic garbage bag that she could repurpose. She gave up the search and made her way into the adjoining bedroom. She began rummaging through the closet where she located a pair of pantyhose and a long sleeve blouse. It wasn't a pair of handcuffs, but they would make do in a pinch.

Alex turned around and headed toward the backroom, pausing when she got in the doorway, as she realized Tatiana was gone.

"What the.....?" was all she managed to mutter, before she felt Tatiana come crashing into her from the bathroom.

Alex landed on her side, her ribs crashing into the edge of the bedframe and knocking the wind out of her. Tatiana seized the advantage and began punching Alex. Now it was her turn to cover up, as blow after blow rained down upon her. One shot land squarely on Alex's jaw causing blood to spray from her mouth onto the sheet below her.

Oh shit, this isn't good, she thought, as she felt her body begin to go limp.

She raised her right arm over her head protectively, as blow after blow continued to rain down upon her.

"I told you I owned you," Tatiana screamed defiantly.

Alex rammed the palm of her hand into the edge of the bed, moving it forward just enough that her body fell to the floor. This caused Tatiana to lose balance momentarily, which was all the time Alex needed. She turned her body slightly, then exploded backward and drove her elbow viciously into Tatiana's chest. It didn't take the fight out of her, but it drove her back just enough that Alex was able to turn around and get herself on a better footing.

"Own this bitch."

Tatiana might have had the size advantage, but Alex was a scrappy street fighter who had done her fair share of back alley, bare-knuckle brawling. She managed to grab hold of Tatiana's hair, jerking her head backward, as the two women rolled around on the bedroom floor, then proceeded to land several blows to her face. One blow snapped her head back with enough force that it caused it to slam against the ground with a loud *crack*. Immediately the fight went out of her and Tatiana's body went limp.

Alex scrambled backward, breathing heavily, as she put some space between them.

"Fuck me," she muttered, as she wiped the blood away from her lips.

She got to her feet and walked over to Tatiana. Blood was now pooling on the floor beneath the woman's head. She was out of the fight for the moment, but Alex wasn't about to take any more chances.

She looked around, spotting the blouse next to the bed and immediately tied up Tatiana's hands securely. When she was done, she looked around for the pantyhose, but couldn't find them.

The adrenaline that had been coursing through her body just seconds earlier drained from her in a rush. A sense of physical weariness kicked in and then her body began to tremble. Her body felt heavy and she found herself leaning back against the wall for support.

Fuck it, she thought and allowed her body to slide slowly to the ground.

Alex felt incredibly tired and just needed to take a break for a moment. She leaned over, retrieving the nearby pack of cigarettes and lighter off the floor and lit one up, as she kept a wary eye on the unconscious woman.

"You don't mind, do you, *babe*?"

CHAPTER FORTY-EIGHT

Maguire stared out the windshield, drumming his fingers on the center console, as the patrol car barreled down the road. The wail of the car's siren was doing its best to herald the impending arrival of the cavalry, *but would it be too late?*

This was always the hardest time for a cop, the period of time between the initial call for help and arrival on the scene, where you were utterly helpless. While en route to a call most cops would search their brains trying to recall something about the location that would aid them when they arrived.

Had they ever been there before? What type of location was it? Did any of the occupants have a history of weapons or violence?

But New Hampshire was all uncharted territory for Maguire and he was only left with his thoughts of what condition they might find Alex in.

A moment later the car took a severe right turn, sharp enough to cause the back end to slide out, until Hutch spun the wheel around and all four tires gripped the road again.

Maguire had to hand it to him; the kid was a helluva wheelman.

The car left the hard pavement and began racing up a stretch of gravel roadway. Up ahead a small rustic cabin appeared. As they drew closer, time began to slow considerably, as Maguire saw a figure appear in the doorway.

Alex!

Maguire felt the brakes on the car lock-up, spraying gravel, and threw open the door. He rushed toward Alex just as she came limping down from the porch.

"Nice of you to show up, rookie," she said. "It's about friggin' time."

"Jesus Christ, you look like shit," he exclaimed, as he drew closer.

"Well if you think I look that bad, you should get a look at your psycho-bitch ex-girlfriend."

Maguire looked at Alex with a quizzical expression. "What?"

"Bat shit crazy Patty," Alex replied. "You remember her, don't you?"

"She's still here?"

"Oh yeah," Alex said, "but she's gonna have a massive headache when she wakes up."

"I'm so sorry, Alex," Maguire said.

The thought that someone he had once loved could have caused so much pain and suffering still troubled him deeply, even more since it was directed at someone else he loved.

"Yeah, well that's another one you owe me," she said dryly.

"We can talk about who owes who what later," he said, "but right now we need to get you to the hospital."

"No, what you need to do is get me a damn drink," she replied.

"We can talk about that on the way to the hospital," he said, as he reached out to take her by the hand.

Alex began to protest, but it was cut short by a sudden, searing pain she felt in her hand.

She'd known Maguire for almost two decades and never in that time had he ever been physically rough to her. Yet the pain she now felt coursing through her right arm was entirely all too real. Alex looked toward him in shock, but his eyes were no longer looking at hers.

What the…..?

Midway through the thought it was suddenly cut-off, as Maguire cocked his arm back and pulled her body toward him. The force caused her legs to partially give way and she found herself stumbling forward, moving past him, and in the direction of the others cops, who also seemed to be in some state of urgency.

Bang! Bang! Bang!

The rapid shots reverberated off the nearby mountains, further adding to her confusion as she fell to the ground. Her body slid several feet along the rough gravel roadway, tearing at her exposed skin, before she came to a halt. She pushed past the pain and immediately scrambled to her feet, trying to put as much distance as she could to whatever threat was behind her.

The other cops had their guns out now, leveled at the unseen threat, but only silence gripped the air. A moment later she careened into the waiting arms of Abby Simpson.

"I got you," Abby exclaimed.

Alex felt the woman's strong arms, wrap around her tightly, arresting her momentum and bringing her to a complete stop.

"What the fuck?" Alex said, giving word to her thoughts.

"It's okay; it's over," Abby said.

Alex turned around and saw the crumbled body of Tatiana lying on the ground a few feet from the porch.

"Jesus Christ, doesn't that bitch ever give up?" she asked.

CHAPTER FORTY-NINE

Maguire cautiously walked forward; the green front sight of the Smith & Wesson lining up perfectly on the body sprawled out in front of him.

With each advancing step the realization of who it was before him was driven home. A million thoughts and images wrestled for control of his mind, but he chased them all away. In this line of work familiarity killed and no one was more familiar to him than she was.

A few steps later he reached the woman and kicked away the silver revolver lying by her side. Strands of her long brown hair lay matted across her face and blood had begun to stain the shirt from the entry wounds in her upper torso.

Maguire knelt down and placed his fingers on the woman's wrist. She still had a heartbeat, but the reality was that the woman, whom he had known as Patricia Ann Browning, was most likely dying in front of him.

The entire scene seemed so surreal.

As Maguire watched, her eyes opened slowly and she smiled with recognition.

"You took the shot after all," she said softly.

"Don't talk," he replied. "The ambulance is on the way."

"They won't make it in time, James," she replied knowingly.

"You don't know that, Tricia."

"But I do."

"Why?" Maguire asked.

Browning just nodded her head dismissively.

"You at least owe me an answer to that question," he said angrily.

"People change," she replied. "Just look at you."

"I changed because of the circumstances I was put through," Maguire replied. "I didn't ask for it to happen."

"Did you ever ask me?"

"Don't do that, Tricia, don't push it back on me," he said. "I spoke to Lena. She told me what happened, but it should have been you telling me."

"You left me," Browning replied. "You made your choice."

"*Goddamnit*, that's not fair, Tricia," he said. "I loved you and you know that. You were the one who pushed me away."

Hearing the words took away the fight. For years she had blamed him because he had left her. Left her in that town, left her with Browning, left her with Lena and somewhere along the line she had re-invented the story, but that wouldn't work with him. The truth was always the truth, no matter how hard you tried to spin it.

"I'm sorry," she said, as the tears began to stream down her face. "I'm sorry for everything, sorry for the monster that I have become."

"It's over," he said, as he wiped a strand of hair from her face.

"I didn't mean to," she replied. "I just wanted to hurt you. I wanted you to feel pain the same pain I did."

"I understand, but Alex is going to be fine."

"Alex?" the woman replied. "I wasn't taking about her."

"What do you mean?" Maguire asked. "Who were you talking about?"

"Your friend, Rich," Tricia said. "I killed him."

Maguire's eyes went wide in shock.

Rich Stargold, the former New York City Police Commissioner and Maguire's best friend, had died at the hands of Gerald F. Spangler, Jr., a psychotic killer who had left behind a trail of NYPD bodies in his short but bloody killing spree. At least that was the working theory.

There hadn't been any concrete evidence linking Stargold's killing to the previous ones, but the caliber used, coupled with the hit list they had found, had pointed to the obvious. There was no way to ask him, since Spangler had already been dispatched to the afterlife, but the killings had all come to an abrupt halt following his demise.

"You killed him?" Maguire asked incredulously. "That's impossible."

"No, James, that was me," Browning said with a smile. "I sweet talked my way into that elderly couple's apartment and then I shot them. The rest was just a waiting game."

"Why Rich?" Maguire asked.

"To be honest, when I saw you in the scope, I toyed with the idea of just killing you, but that seemed way too impersonal for me. The idea of you having to suffer the guilt over not being able to protect your friend was so much more appealing to me."

"He didn't do anything," Maguire lamented.

"People die, James," she replied. "That's just life. Sometimes they die for other people's amusement."

Off in the distance, the faint wail of a siren could be heard drawing closer.

"Hey," Browning said, with a weak smile. "Maybe I'll make it after all."

Maguire stared down into the woman's brown eyes. Almost immediately his mind was brought back to that summer's day, on the cliffs overlooking Corlaer Bay, when he had first shared his feelings for her, but, try as he might, the warmth he had once seen in her eyes was gone. With great reluctance, he finally accepted the fact that woman he had loved was truly lost forever.

"No, Tricia," he said, as his hand reached up and came to rest on the curve of her neck. "You won't."

She looked up into his cold, blue eyes and smiled softly. "I guess it's better this way."

CHAPTER FIFTY

Alex aimed the controller at the T.V. that was hung on the wall across from her hospital bed and angrily pressed the channel select button. The image of several women appeared, sitting around the discussion table, flashed onto the screen and raucous cackling began to come from the small speaker attached to the bed.

"Three hundred fucking stations and all they play is bullshit," she remarked angrily, as she turned off the set.

She'd been vehemently opposed to staying for observation, but Maguire had strongly *insisted* she stay and she knew that it was futile to argue with him when he got like that.

"Knock, Knock."

Alex looked over at the doorway and saw Maguire standing in the threshold.

"You'd better have booze," she said with a dirty look.

"No booze, partner," he replied, "but I did come bearing gifts."

Alex watched as he held up a paper bag emblazoned with the Dunkin' Donuts emblem.

"It's a start," she replied. "Come on in."

"How are you feeling?"

"Like I just went ten rounds with Iron Mike," Alex replied.

"That's understandable," he replied, setting the bag and cup on the bed table before leaning down and kissing her forehead.

Alex closed her eyes for the briefest of moments, as she felt the warmth of his lips on her skin. Any lingering pain that she might have felt was pushed out of her mind and she felt her whole body tingle.

"I'm just glad you're alright."

"Oh, I'm just great," she replied without thinking.

"What?" Maguire asked, as he reached into the bag and removed two Styrofoam containers of coffee.

"Huh?" Alex replied sheepishly, as she fought to regain her composure. "I just meant all things considered, I'm doing great."

"Oh," he replied, sitting down in the chair next to the bed. "For a moment I thought you were being sarcastic."

"Nah, not any more than I usually am," she replied, "but what about your ex-girlfriend? She didn't rise up from the slab when the moon came out last night, did she?"

"No," Maguire replied, shaking his head. "I think she used up the last of her nine lives."

"Can't say I'm sorry about that, but, all gallows humor aside, it has to be tough as hell on you."

"It wasn't exactly how I envisioned things coming to an end, but I guess in retrospect it was the best outcome."

"Still, it wasn't some unknown," Alex said. "I can't imagine what I would have done in your position."

"I don't know if any thought went into it," he confessed. "It was more like I just responded. I saw the threat and acted."

"I have to admit it was rather weird. You damn near pulled my arm out of my socket."

"Better than taking a shot to the back," he replied.

"True," Alex said, as she peeled back the lid on the coffee and took a sip. "It's also nice to know that I was right and I wasn't hallucinating about seeing the gun. So did she say anything to you? Did you get any closure?"

Maguire took a sip of his coffee, as he contemplated the answer.

He hadn't gotten closure, but he had gotten answers. Answers he didn't necessarily want or need to share.

"No," he lied. "She was just rambling incoherently."

"That sucks," Alex replied, as she reached into the bag and removed the toasted coconut donut. "What about her sidekick? I heard she tried to make a run for it."

"Yeah, she did," he replied. "I guess her age and looks made her seem less threatening than she truly was."

"What the heck happened?"

"Apparently she'd been able to hide one of the EMT's shears inside her waistband," Maguire replied. "Guess she played the old sex card during the initial frisk. The state cop got nervous that he was going to be accused of sexual assault and decided to have a female do a more thorough search at in-take. As he was taking her out of the car she pulled the shears and sliced him."

"Is he okay?" she asked.

"Yeah, he'll be fine, but he's incredibly lucky," Maguire replied. "Another inch over and he would have probably bled out before helped arrived."

"Unreal."

"He managed to get a shot off as she was running away. He hit her in the lower back. Last I heard she'd made it out of surgery, but they doubt she'll ever walk again."

"It's kind of hard to feel any empathy for her," Alex replied. "Knowing what she has done."

"I agree, but still, that's a tough way to spend the rest of your life."

"Guess it's sort of karmic."

"It is that," he replied. "But enough of that shit, what have the doctors said about you?"

"Apparently I have *normal* readings, which is probably a first for me," she replied. "Rumor is they are jettisoning me late this afternoon, which means I get the unparalleled joy of yet another amazing hospital meal before I go."

"Say it isn't so?" he asked, patting his chest in mock surprise.

"Tis' true," she replied. "I get the choice of grey or green mystery meat and apple juice."

"So how are you really doing? Honestly."

"I'm okay,… I guess," she said, shrugging her shoulders.

"That's not very convincing."

"I mean if you're asking if I'm nuts or anything, the answer is no," Alex replied. "Well, not any more than I already was."

"Than what are you feeling?"

"It's gonna sound weird, but this whole kidnapping thing has been actually quite cathartic."

"How so?" Maguire asked, more than a bit intrigued by her reply.

"I don't know how to put it, but being tied up like that, unable to move, caused me to do a lot of self-introspection," she explained. "Admittedly, I wasn't exactly sure I was going to make it out, if you know what I mean."

"Trust me, I understand completely," Maguire replied.

Something in the way he said it led her to believe that he was being sincere.

"I had a lot of time to examine my life and I've come to realize that not only have I screwed up a lot, but I've also let down a lot of people, like you."

"That's not true," he objected. "You haven't let me down."

"Don't argue with me, rookie," she said sternly. "This is the new Alex Taylor."

"Yes ma'am," he said, hoisting up his coffee cup. "Please, continue."

"Well, I came to the realization that I have spent the majority of my life running from one problem after the other, but I've never really addressed any of them. So I promised God that if, by some miraculous intervention, I survived, I would change all that. Clearly, the good Lord has a sense of humor because here I am."

"Clearly," Maguire said with a smirk.

"Anyway,......." Alex replied curtly. "I'm not exactly sure how I go about it, but I know that I need to come to terms with my life and the people in it."

For a moment they just stared at each other. Then Maguire nodded solemnly. He knew her better than anyone else and he knew she was right.

"So what are you going to do?" he asked.

"Start acting like an adult, I guess," she replied. "I think I have a lot of heart to heart chats in my future."

"Oh yeah? Where does that line form?"

Alex took a sip of coffee and thought about the question.

"Here, I guess," she replied, setting the cup back down on the table. "Close the door."

Maguire got up and closed the door over, then returned back to his seat. "I'm all ears."

"I wanted to say that I'm sorry about last Christmas."

"You don't need too....."

"Yes, I do," she replied. "So shut up and listen. I'm not saying that I'm sorry about what I said, James, I'm just sorry that I waited as long as I did to say it."

"Why did you?"

"Scared more than anything," she replied. "I don't think I ever told you, but deep inside I always believed that you were the best thing that ever happened to me. The day you got transferred was the worst day of my life. It felt as if I had lost everything."

"You didn't lose me, Alex," he replied.

"Maybe to you, but to me it was as if my life came to a screeching halt, James. It wasn't your fault, but my inability to cope. My life had always seemed to be one catastrophe after another. That was until your green-horn ass came strolling into the seven-three. I was hooked on you from the first moment I met you."

"You didn't act it," Maguire replied. "I actually thought you hated me."

"Well, maybe I did a little bit, but you grew on me," she said. "Anyway, the reality is I used you as an excuse, both for why I did better while you were around as well as why I crashed after you left."

"I'm sorry, Alex."

"Don't be, this isn't about you, it's about me and my lack of personal responsibility. I've had some pretty shitty stuff happen to me, but how I responded was always my choice to make and I didn't always choose correctly. I've used everyone, even my dip-shit mother, as an excuse for why I succeeded or why I failed and now it is time for me to make amends."

"There are no amends you have to make with me."

"Yes, there are," she replied. "If only to say that I am sorry I didn't tell you how I felt before. Now I feel that we've lost our moment and, while I am not happy about it, I have to let you go."

"Do I get a say?" he asked.

"No," she replied with a sad smile. "The reality is that I will always have feelings for you, but I am not what you need. I have no filter and I have zero fucks to give. Bottom line is that I will never be her and I'm okay with that."

"How do you just turn your feelings off?"

"I find that two parts whiskey and one part porn do the trick nicely," she replied with a wink.

Maguire frowned, clenching his jaw firmly.

"Don't you dare," she scolded him. "You have the world by the balls right now. I'm not going to let you screw things up because of me and my alcohol fueled idiocy. Besides, I can barely live with myself, let alone another human being. I think I'm just gonna start out with a dog and see how well that progresses."

"Well, if you can't live with me how about working with me?" he asked.

"What?"

"I have an opening for you," he replied.

"What you need a chief dog-catcher?"

"No, I need a right hand. You've done your penance up here, how about you come to work for me?"

Alex stared at him, waiting for the punchline to drop, but it never came.

"Jesus H. Christ, you're actually serious?"

"I am," he replied. "I need a new first dep. The pays a lot better and you'd get an office with an amazing view."

"Dear God in Heaven," she said, leaning back in the bed and staring up at the ceiling. "Do you have any idea how well that would go over?"

"I'd imagine that a few folks will choke on their morning bagels when they hear the news," he replied.

"A few?" she asked. "I'm thinking you'll lose a shit load just to the *Heart Bill* alone."

"You'd be doing me a favor," Maguire said. "It might be the only way to move some of the dead weight."

Alex looked over at him and smiled. "Thank you, but I'm going to have to say no."

"Seriously? Maguire said, as he crossed his arms over one another and stared at her quizzically.

"Seriously," she replied.

"So you're telling me that *purgatory with a pine scent* is growing on you?"

"For all the bitching and moaning I've done, the reality is that I have actually grown to like this place."

"I'm at a loss for words."

"Good," she said. "Besides, for some unfathomable reason, the folks here seem to actually like me."

"I've noticed."

"I don't think I've ever seen Hutch as happy as when he got *demoted* back to officer."

"I'm genuinely happy for you, Alex," Maguire said.

"Thank you," she said, stifling a yawn. "God all this honesty shit is emotionally draining. No wonder I have avoided it."

Maguire got up and walked over to the bed.

Alex leaned back in the bed. "You're not gonna hit me are you?"

"No," he said, then leaned down and kissed her softly on the lips. "Love ya, partner."

Alex swallowed hard.

"I hate you," she said softly, staring up into his eyes.

"It'll pass," he replied.

The intimate moment was interrupted by a sudden knock at the door.

The two of them looked over to see Peter Bates standing in the door way holding a vase with flowers.

"I hope I'm not intruding," he said.

"No, not at all," Maguire replied. "I was just saying goodbye."

"Oh, please don't leave on my account," the man said. "I just stopped in to see how Alex was."

"No, I really do have to go. It's only Monday morning and already my phone has started to melt. I'll be lucky if the city isn't in flames by the time I get back."

"Well it was good to see you again, James," Bates said.

"Likewise, Peter," he replied, shaking the man's hand. "You too have fun. She's in a *very* chatty mood."

"Don't forget to give my love to, *Mel*," Alex said sarcastically.

"Oh, I will, I promise."

"Yeah, I bet you will."

Maguire paused in the doorway and looked back at her.

"How about Deputy Commissioner, Strategic Communications?" he asked.

Alex slowly raised up her right hand and flipped him the bird. "Is that strategic enough for you?"

Maguire laughed as he walked out into the hallway and made his way toward the elevator.

He didn't know how the conversation between Alex and Peter was about to play out, but he did know that for the very first time that he felt his old partner was going to truly be alright and that was all that really mattered to him; at least for now.

ABOUT THE AUTHOR

Andrew Nelson spent twenty-two years in law enforcement, including twenty years with the New York City Police Department. During his tenure with the NYPD he served as a detective in the elite Intelligence Division, conducting investigations and providing dignitary protection to numerous world leaders. He achieved the rank of sergeant before retiring in 2005. He is also a graduate of the State University of New York. He and his wife have four children and reside in central Illinois with their Irish Wolfhound.

He is the author of both the James Maguire and Alex Taylor mystery series. He has also written two books which chronicle the insignia of the New York City Police Department's Emergency Service Unit.

For more information please visit us at:

www.andrewgnelson.org

ANDREW G.
NELSON

49357286R00212